LOVE THE one YOU HATE

USA TODAY BESTSELLING AUTHOR
R.S. GREY

LOVE THE ONE YOU HATE
Copyright © 2020 R.S. Grey
All rights reserved. No part of this book may be reproduced or transmitted in any form, including electronic or mechanical, without written permission from the publisher, except in the case of brief quotations embodied in critical articles or reviews.

This book is a piece of fiction. Names, characters, places, and incidents are the product of the author's imagination or are used fictitiously. Any resemblance to actual events, locales, or persons, living or dead, is coincidental.

This book is licensed for your personal enjoyment only. This book may not be re-sold or given away to other people. If you are reading this book and did not purchase it, or it was not purchased for your use only, then you should return it to the seller and purchase your own copy. Thank you for respecting the author's work.

Published: R.S. Grey 2020
authorrsgrey@gmail.com
Editing: Editing by C. Marie
Proofreading: Red Leaf Proofing, Julia Griffis
Cover Design: R.S. Grey
ISBN: 9798635675403

PROLOGUE

He stands across the ballroom, a devil in black. His tailored tuxedo glides over his tall figure. His half-mask conceals most of his face, but the parts I can see hint that the unveiled image would stop me in my tracks. He has a strong jaw, dark thick hair, and unsmiling lips.

Just a brief glance from him makes the hairs on the back of my neck stand on end. I don't know him, but he's staring like he knows me. Like he *hates me*, rather. He tilts his head as he continues to study me and my heart is a hummingbird, racing in my chest. I have the urge to get away even before he starts to cut through the crowd to get to me. A hunted animal knows when it's time to run, so I do. I slip through the double doors that lead out to the empty garden.

But the devil follows.

NICHOLAS

"Money beyond what most of us can imagine. Lineages dating back to the founding fathers. Connections that ensure barriers to entry don't exist for them. We've all wondered what life is like for America's wealthiest families, and today we're going to take you behind the gilded doors for an exclusive look inside the private lives of the Cromwells."

The producers cut to a montage of footage they've captured of my family over the years: my mother and father at the New York Opera, my grandmother's annual Easter egg hunt, me leaving a bar back in college, annoyance evident on my face when I spot the cameras.

Even though I'm tempted, I don't sling my remote at the TV; instead, I use it to turn off the salacious news story. I can't watch it, and I don't have to. Across town, a team of lawyers sit huddled in front of the broadcast, taking dutiful notes and preparing a written statement we'll release to the press before noon.

The phone on my desk rings and I grab it hastily, immediately recognizing the number on the caller ID.

"Are you watching?" Rhett asks.

"Just turned it off."

I lean back in my chair, turning to look out the window. My office is housed in a redone brownstone on the Upper East Side, three levels packed to the gills. Outside my door, interns and young associates toil away. I'll join them soon, but not until I get my head wrapped around this catastrophe.

"It's really not that bad," Rhett assures me as I watch an old woman walk down the sidewalk with a dog no bigger than a teacup biting at her heels. "Oh, there you are again, scowling at the camera as you leave The Polo Bar. Hey! That's me! Dammit, they cut away."

I nearly smile, but I don't. "You're not helping."

"Ah, c'mon. I'm just trying to lighten the mood. It's not that bad."

He's right, of course. This isn't *that* bad in the grand scheme of things, but there's a reason my family values privacy above all else. Our goal is to keep our name out of the press. We're not usually splashed across magazine covers or billed as the top story on America's most-watched morning show. We're discrete and quiet and largely go unnoticed—until a story like this hits, and then suddenly we're thrust back into the limelight. The effects of this latest story are already visible. The woman with the dog stops to let him pee, and behind her, barely concealed, is a photographer poised across the street, hoping I'll show my face.

"Why wasn't this story killed?" Rhett asks.

We employ a team of people whose sole job is to make sure we're kept out of the headlines. Lawsuits, coercion, bribery—I have no doubt they employ every tactic necessary, and yet, still, sometimes stories slip through. Like this one. I'm sure the show and its parent company weighed their options thoroughly. They knew we'd come after them with everything we had if they ran the story, and they still did it, because it's worth that much to them.

Rhett knows that. I don't have to explain it to him.

"Loyalty is dead," he says with a disgusted grunt.

Through the phone, I can hear his TV, and I know they've switched to the live interview with Michael Lewis, the man I'd love to strangle.

My grandmother's old driver.

He was only with us for a year after coming highly recommended through an organization that connects families like ours with well-trained staff. We paid him well in exchange for his discretion and trust, and we would have continued to do so if I hadn't caught him stealing from my grandmother.

I keep track of her accounts myself, and it was obvious the moment he got his hands on her checkbook. Three checks made out to an unregistered S corp, all signed by my grandmother, all cashed by him.

I fired The Talented Mr. Ripley right away.

He claimed innocence. *"How could I possibly have written those checks? They had your grandmother's signature on them!"*

He should have been thanking his lucky stars I wasn't pursuing legal action. It wasn't out of empathy for him, but out of hope that the small scandal would die down swiftly. I didn't want my grandmother to be the subject of scrutiny and drama. I didn't want her title as the matriarch of our family tainted by accusations of senile naivety.

I thought he'd leave well enough alone, but it appears Mr. Lewis has found another way to make a quick buck off my grandmother. Murmurs started last week, a potential article exposing the secrets and scandal of our family. What secrets and scandals he claims to have? Who knows. I'm sure he felt that after driving my grandmother around for a year, he had more than enough information to run to the press with. I hope it was worth it for him.

The non-disclosure agreement he signed before starting employment with us was ironclad. I almost pity him.

Another call interrupts Rhett's rambling diatribe about how we all need to be more careful about the people we let into our lives. It's my lawyers; I'm sure they want me to read the statement they've prepared.

I have real work on the docket for today, items on my agenda that matter more than this petty bullshit. I'm angry with Michael Lewis all over again. Angry that he took advantage of my grandmother. Angry that he stole from her and, when caught, didn't have the decency to slink off somewhere to rot. Now, he's sucking up even more of my time, which could be better used elsewhere. I cut Rhett off, tell him I'll see him in Newport soon, and then switch over to line two.

I don't let my attorney get the first word in.

I make it perfectly clear that I want Michael Lewis obliterated.

No one hurts my family and gets away with it.

MAREN

"Hold up! Got one more for you!"

I turn to see a guy sporting a hairnet and a white apron thoroughly stained with food. He's running toward me carrying a black garbage bag, and it's near bursting. He's straining under its weight.

"There's no more ro—" I don't get the full protest out before he lugs the bag up and over the lid of the cart I'm pushing, piling it on top of all the other trash bags. "—om."

He gives me two thumbs up. "You got it, right?"

I don't *got* it, but his question is clearly rhetorical seeing as he's already turning on his heels to dash back down the hallway.

"This isn't my job!" I shout in protest. "Food prep needs to take out their own garbage!"

There's no reply from him. He's already turning the corner, leaving me with an overflowing cart filled with refuse. It smells. I'm surprised there aren't cartoonish squiggly green lines shooting out of it in every direction. I try not to gag as I push it forward.

The dumpsters are outside the nursing home, all the way at the back of the parking lot.

I push the door open and warm air rushes in to greet me. Some kind of sludge seeps out of the side of the cart, and I accidentally step in it. My sensible black shoes—the kind all the orderlies wear—now make a lovely squelching sound with every step I take. I curse that food prep guy to hell and heave in a deep breath as I push the bulky cart over uneven pavement.

Up front, near the entrance of Holly Home, it's all rose bushes and neatly trimmed hedges. Out back, it's tired cooks smoking against the wall and blinking flood lights failing to illuminate the curb I smack directly into. Trash spills over the sides of the cart, and for one second, I think this is it. This is the last day I work this job. I'm going to hand in my resignation, yank off this white uniform, and walk out of this place in the buff with my head held high.

The glorious thought dies a swift death once I remember my reality: how long it took me to find this job in the first place and the unlikelihood that I'd find anything better.

This is my lot in life, I remind myself as I make it to the dumpster and start to toss bags up and over the side.

When I'm done, I push the cart back to its spot in the maintenance department, under the opening beneath the trash shoot. Leroy is there, sitting at his desk. He shoots me a hesitant smile.

"Sorry about that, Maren."

He glances down to his ankle, the one he twisted pretty bad yesterday, making his job here all but impossible. He hasn't told our boss about it—worried she'll cut him loose—so I volunteered to step up where

I could. My shift is over anyway. I was about to clock out.

I give him a little salute and a smile.

"Hey, it wasn't so bad," I say with a wink. "Now I don't even need to worry about getting in a workout today."

It's a blatant joke. Working out is for privileged people who have calories to spare.

Leroy doesn't laugh. Instead, he holds up half a sandwich wrapped in waxy brown paper.

"Benita brought it down for me from the kitchen. I left half for you."

I step forward and take it without any preamble about how "I couldn't possibly." I *could* possibly. I'm starving.

I hold it up in thanks and head back out into the hallway toward my locker. Freedom beckons. I have the next hour mapped out in my head like a luxurious dream. I'm going to get out of here in time to catch the 9:05 bus back to the group home. I'll eat my sandwich on the way and finish it in three, maybe four bites. Once there, I'll take a quick shower—because no one should be hogging the bathroom at this time—and make it to my bed in the bunkroom with enough energy to read for a little while before promptly passing out. I nearly shiver with delight thinking of how good it will feel right before my boss, Mrs. Buchanan, appears from around the corner. She's a tall woman with a deep voice and wears clothes that look like they've been run through the wash so many times they've lost all their color: muted brown, gray, dull blacks.

"Oh good, Maren—I was hoping to catch you before you leave. Would you mind coming into my office for a moment?"

I've learned over the years that people look at you differently if you're a foster kid, like you've got nothing to lose and everything to gain. I switched schools a lot after my parents died, moved around often. Everywhere I went, I felt watchful eyes on me. *Wonder how she got those shoes. Hey, that watch Maren's wearing looks a lot like the one I lost last week.*

So when Mrs. Buchanan calls me into her office, I know by her inability to meet my eyes and the tightness to her smile that I'm not going to like what I hear.

"I'm just covering all my bases," is how she phrases it. "I'm not singling you out by any means." No, it's just that I'm the first and only person she's going to interview about a piece of jewelry that was stolen from Mrs. Dyer's room during my last shift.

"I'm not suggesting you took the ring. I'm just wondering if you happened to see anything suspicious. I'd rather not have to call the authorities if we can put this matter to rest on our own. Do you see what I mean?"

Accusations have shaved my heart down to a wilting limp thing over the years. I'm surprised it still beats.

"No, Mrs. Buchanan," I say, voice monotone. Flat. Dead. "I didn't see anything and I didn't take anything."

She purses her lips, upset by my refusal to give her the version of the truth she's so desperately seeking. It's my fault this is all happening even though I had nothing to do with the theft. That's how I feel as she excuses me and tells me I'm free to go. This isn't over, of course.

Next, I'll have to sit down with the police and somehow try to prove to them that I'm a decent person, just like everyone else. It's surprising how few people believe that. Prejudice is a pervasive disease.

I have an overwhelming fear that I will always be painted by a stained brush, that no matter how I dress or talk or smile or spritz on perfume to cover the scent of the mold in the group home, there's no denying that I'm Maren Mitchell—less than.

The next day when I arrive for another shift at Holly Home, it's clear that Mrs. Buchanan has spread the word about my alleged theft. Coworkers who didn't pay me much attention before now give me a wide berth, afraid of becoming tainted by association. Fortunately, the residents haven't been made aware of the accusations.

Most of them are as excited to see me as usual. As an orderly, my duties are vague enough that any department is free to use me as an extra set of hands. That means, oftentimes, I pick up the slack for other people, especially when it comes to residents I really like.

Take Mrs. Archer, for instance. She's placed all the way at the end of the hall on the second floor, which means more often than not, she's the last on the list to get breakfast and fresh linens and assistance outside on days when she's up for taking a walk. I hate that. So, I volunteer to take her breakfast up, and I know where housekeeping stores the sheets and such, so I change hers out whenever I think she needs it.

She's quiet. I don't think she's said more than a handful of words to me in the months I've been here, but still, I know she likes me. She smiles when I come in and nods for me to continue talking if I get carried away with a story. I tell her about the toddler I sat next to on the bus as I help lead her down the hall toward the rec room.

In the doorway, she nods toward the back corner, to the chair that sits beside a fading grand piano. It's her favorite spot, and I don't mind what it implies. She wants me to play for her.

"I can't right now. I have to get back to work, but I go on break in thirty minutes. I can come back then?"

She smiles and pats my hand. "I would like that very much."

I glance up to the clock on the wall to make sure I don't leave her waiting for one minute longer than I have to.

I'm not surprised to find her right where I left her when I return. Except, she's not alone. Her friend sits beside her.

Mrs. Archer has more visitors than other residents. Her grandchildren and friends come to Holly Home often, but this particular visitor is my favorite. In my head, I refer to her as the queen because she reminds me so much of the old monarchs I've read about in novels. Stately and beautiful, but sharp too, like a finely cut gem. She wears her white hair in a short pixie cut that frames a pair of glacier blue eyes, which hold me captive any time she aims a question my way.

She looks almost frigid sitting there in a simple, perfectly starched button-down tunic with the cuffs rolled to her elbows. It's layered over navy pants and paired with cream flats. Her collar stands up around a heavy beaded necklace, and her wrists are covered in thin bracelets. Her emerald wedding band glitters in the light.

With her perfect posture and watchful gaze, she looks like she's holding court. Hence why I call her the queen even though I know her name is Cornelia. She introduced herself to me a few weeks ago, and I fumbled in shaking her hand because she held it out to me as if expecting me to kiss it.

"Ah, there's the child now," she says when she sees me walk in.

At twenty-three, I wouldn't say I'm a child, but I don't dare correct her. She intimidates me into near silence, something not so easily done anymore.

"Come and play for us, won't you? Annette said you could take a few minutes off, and I've traveled a long way to visit my friend," she says, patting Mrs. Archer's hand. "Though I'll admit, I had another selfish motive for visiting Holly Home today, and it was so I could hear you play."

I blush and nod. "Of course. Yes, I can play for a few minutes."

There's no sheet music for me to reference. When I first started working here and inquired about the piano, Mrs. Buchanan told me no one ever bothered to play it. She wanted to get rid of it to make room for more seating, but it was too heavy and too expensive to deal with, so here it sits, slightly out of tune, collecting dust, and completely untouched except by my hands. Mrs. Archer was the person who first encouraged me to play it. We were out in the hall on a short walk, and she was leaning on my arm, asking me about myself. I mentioned that I could play piano—or at least used to be able to—and she demanded we turn and head toward the rec room. That day, I sat down on the wobbly bench with its one leg slightly shorter than the rest so that I'm perpetually rocking back and forth, and I played for the first time in years.

No sheet music means I'm forced to play everything by memory. Even with the practice I've had over the last few months, there are only a few songs to draw from, the old melodies that live in my bones.

I choose a piece my dad used to play for me when I was young, something I would never play for near strangers unless I truly believed they would feel it like I do.

Rêverie.

The piece resonates so quickly with a familiar audience that Cornelia sighs.

"Ah, Debussy. What wonderful taste you have."

I smile as I continue to play, concentrating on the succeeding notes so intently that Mrs. Buchanan has to walk over to the piano and wave her hand in front of my face before I realize she's been trying to get my attention for the last few moments.

I immediately stop playing.

"I've been standing at the door calling your name," she chides.

"She was playing for us," Cornelia says, coming to my defense.

Unfortunately, Mrs. Buchanan's annoyance isn't lessened by Cornelia's explanation. She's made it clear on multiple occasions that the nursing home isn't paying me to sit on my butt, even if I am playing at the request of one of the residents.

I open my mouth to defend myself. I'm on break; I wasn't slacking off. I could go sit in the locker room like everyone else does, but I see there's no point in speaking up. She's not here to get onto me for playing the piano.

She nods her head toward the door.

"We need to have another chat."

I've been interrogated by police officers before, and my second meeting with Mrs. Buchanan feels a lot like that.

Her words read right out of a bad cop film. Is there anything new I'd like to tell her? Have I told her the whole truth? She wants to help me. She's on my side.

When I hold my ground and insist on my innocence, she sighs and presents new "evidence".

Apparently, since last night, two eye witnesses have come forward and claimed to have seen Mrs. Dyer's ring in my possession.

"I didn't steal her ring," I say for what feels like the hundredth time.

And if I did, why would I be so stupid as to keep it in plain sight after the fact?

"So you're accusing these two individuals of *lying*?" She emphasizes that crime as if it's worse than the theft itself.

I shrug. I don't know what their motive is for implicating me. Maybe they *think* they saw me with the ring. Maybe they're covering up for someone else. I should tell her point-blank that they're lying, but I don't want to get on anyone's bad side. I know better.

In response to my silence, she rearranges some papers on her desk then straightens her glasses on the bridge of her thin nose. When she glances back to me, her eyes are narrowed.

"I didn't want to have to do this, Maren. I know how important this job is to you, but I went out on a limb hiring you…"

I tune out the rest of her spiel, having heard it plenty of times before. Mrs. Buchanan enjoys rearranging the narrative to cast herself as the hero and me as the serf, but I know for a fact Holly Home gets a tax credit from the state for employing me.

Her next words do catch my attention though. In fact, they pierce straight through me.

"I'm afraid I'll have to contact your group home. They'll be calling me in a few days anyway for your monthly check-in," she says, dropping the threat like a grenade and hoping it'll do the trick.

I come close to giving her what she wants: an emotional response. My lower lip trembles and my stomach clenches tight. I didn't think I had any hope left in me for people like her, but I was wrong. After all this time, I'm still somehow wounded.

She knows she's backed me into a corner. My group home is for young adults with criminal records who've aged out of the foster care system and need a safe place to go. We have to adhere to certain rules in exchange for the low rent. One of those rules is not breaking any laws.

"But if you confess…" She lets the suggestion hang for a moment before she continues. "Well, I'd be willing to come to some kind of arrangement with you."

So she's offering me a plea bargain: confess to a crime I didn't commit in exchange for a lenient sentence. It's bullshit, and instead of saying that to her face, I jerk to my feet and walk right out of her office.

I don't have a moment to spare either. Tears are personal. My pain is my own, and I'm grateful that I make it out into the hall before I start to cry. I give in to one or two moments of soul-crushing anger, and then I inhale deeply, wipe my cheeks, and throw back my shoulders, unwillingly to succumb to the self-pity knocking at my door. I'll figure out who's trying to pin this on me. I'll get an alibi. I'll ask Mrs. Archer to vouch for my good character. I'll hunt down Mrs. Dyer's ring and get it back to her myself! Anything but admit to a crime I didn't commit. I won't do it—consequences be damned.

"Oh good, I was hoping to find you before I left."

I jump when a voice speaks from down the hall, and I realize to my shame that Mrs. Archer's visitor, Cornelia, has just witnessed my embarrassing breakdown.

Oh god. I wipe aggressively at my face as if trying to force the tears back to where they came from.

If she notices my state, she doesn't let on. She strolls toward me on quiet feet with a brown leather bag swishing back and forth on her forearm. I recognize the bag. I don't know the name, but I've seen it on the covers of magazines and know it's worth more money than I'll ever have in this life or the next.

I'm still staring at her bag, so it takes me a second to realize she's holding something out for me to take.

"I wanted to give you this before I left."

I accept the card, holding it in my hand like it's a delicate photograph I don't want to smudge with my dirty fingerprints. It's thick and yet still, somehow, delicate. Gold rimmed and simple. Cornelia Cromwell is printed across the top. Below that, a phone number.

"Wh-what is this?"

She laughs. "It's a calling card, dear."

I stare up at her with my brows furrowed in disbelief. "And why are you giving it to me?"

She smiles then, the first I've seen from her, and I immediately feel bad for thinking she looked frigid earlier. She's not. I see that now.

"Because I have a proposition for you."

3
MAREN

I turn that card over and over in my hand like it's one of Willy Wonka's golden tickets. I study it on the bus after my shift while squashed against the window because my seatmate has enough meat on his bones to warrant having an entire row to himself. I study it as I wait in line to use the bathroom back at the group home and after, while I heat up a can of soup in the communal kitchen. My wet hair accidentally leaves a drop of water on the edge of Cornelia's name and I have to hurry to grab a paper towel and wipe it off.

I don't work up the courage to call her until I suffer through another shift at Holly Home. The stares in the locker room and the whispered defamations in the break room make it clear that everyone on staff, including Mrs. Buchanan, really thinks I took that ring. They're all so sure of my guilt that I have one brain-bending moment in which I actually ask myself, *Did I steal it? Do they know something I don't?*

I barely consider it before sanity sets in. During my break, I head to Mrs. Archer's room, hoping to borrow her phone. She's not there when I arrive; the schedule printed on her door says she's currently in a physical therapy session. Still, I have to go in. This is the last break I have on my shift and there's not another phone I can use. I wish I had one of my own, but I had to cut off service a few months back so I could use the money to purchase my work uniform and shoes.

I go into rooms when the residents aren't in them all the time to help clean and replace bed linens, but this feels different. I hesitate for a moment at her door, telling myself I don't have another option. Whose phone am I going to borrow if I don't use Mrs. Archer's? Mrs. Buchanan's? *Ha.* I'd ask Leroy—I think he still believes I'm innocent—but he's not here today.

I turn the handle and hurry inside, my heart racing like I'm doing something wrong. Maybe I am, but there's no going back now.

I pull Cornelia's card out of my pocket and hurry to the phone on the bedside table. I dial the number and wait while it rings. Mrs. Archer has the volume turned all the way up so when the call connects and someone speaks, I wince and jerk the phone away from my ear, no doubt having gone completely deaf.

"Cromwell residence. Collins speaking."

When he repeats the introduction a second time, I scramble to reply.

"Oh, uh…is Mrs. Cornelia there? Er, Mrs. Cromwell, that is."

He clears his throat like I've already annoyed him and then says in a polished tone, "And who might I tell her is calling?"

"Right. Um, you can tell her this is Maren Mitchell. From the nursing home."

"Maren Mitchell from the nursing home," he repeats back to me, as if in disbelief, and I turn red from my hair to my toes. "Please give me a moment. I'll see if Mrs. Cromwell is available to take your call."

I'm left on hold, staring at the door, willing it to stay shut. If Mrs. Archer's physical therapy session finishes early or if someone from housekeeping needs to access her room, they'll find me in here talking on the phone. The tableau would be difficult to explain away. *I was just cleaning her receiver!*

"Maren Mitchell."

Cornelia's voice is a welcome relief a few moments later.

"Hi!" I say the word and then realize I don't have a single thing to follow it up with. *How are you?* might be an appropriate question, but I don't have all day, so instead of sprinkling in niceties, I cut right to the chase. "I'm calling you because I'm curious to hear about your proposition."

"Direct—good, I like that. Yes, 'proposition'…is that what I said yesterday? Sounds very ominous, that word."

I wrap the phone cord around my finger, shifting my weight between my feet, anxious to get to the end of this call, to the part where she tells me she needs me to take extra care of Mrs. Archer or something. Maybe she'd even be willing to pay me a little more on the side.

"I'd like to hire you, Maren, and bring you out to Rosethorn."

Words.

They mean nothing because I'm pretty sure I've heard them wrong.

"I have a job," is the first lame thing I say. Followed swiftly by, "What's Rosethorn?"

I can hear her amusement in her reply. "It's where I live."

"And what would I do there?"

She chuckles. "It's difficult to explain over the phone. I think it might be better if you come to me and we can discuss everything over tea. Do you take tea?"

I've never had tea a day in my life. My nose scrunches and I almost give in to the impulse to lie. *Tea? Love it! All kinds. Black...and...green?*

"Um, I'm not sure," I say instead, opting for the sad truth.

She tuts. "A travesty. I'll send a car for you tomorrow. Around, say, noon? How's that? I've got to run. I'm having lunch at the club, but I'll put Collins back on and you can direct him as to where he should send my driver."

And then before I can confirm whether or not I'm free at that time and willing to take her up on her odd offer, she's gone, replaced by the prim and proper Collins, who asks for my address.

I give it to him because he has an air of authority that makes it clear he doesn't like to be questioned. Then he tells me the driver will be there promptly at noon, delivers a curt "Good day," and hangs up.

I stare down at the phone, not quite sure I understand what just happened.

A job? At Rosethorn?

I've come to expect unfortunate events to derail my life like it's a universal law as irrefutable as gravity. I view any turn of luck through a lens of skepticism. There's always a catch. Always. A coworker offers me a ride home from work? It's because he's hoping I'll be an easy score. A girl sits next to me in class, offering friendship? It's because she wants to cheat off my test. I've lived and I've learned. Some would call it being jaded. I just call it being smart.

Cornelia's offer is too good to be true; I know that for a fact. Why would she want to hire me? What skills could I possibly possess that she would be seeking? Is she looking for someone who knows how to perfectly heat a Hot Pocket? Watch ten episodes of *Friends* in one sitting? Read for an entire day? Not likely.

I have a high school diploma and one semester's worth of community college credit hours. My resume consists of a string of bad jobs with titles like "deli technician" and "retail consultant". In reality, I made soggy paninis and folded t-shirts that teenagers left tossed around the Old Navy dressing rooms.

She can't want me for my exceptional skillset, and she can't want me for my glowing personality either because I'm not all that personable. At least that's what people have told me in the past.

"Lighten up, Maren!"

"We're at a party—have fun!"

My friend Ariana used to constantly call me a bore, and the nickname still stings.

The few encounters I've had with Cornelia don't help me pinpoint her motive either. I've only seen her at Holly Home a few times. We've never had a long conversation or a meaningful moment. I know she enjoys when I play the piano, but I've only done that on occasion, and probably not all that well. In my defense, that beast of an instrument they keep there would make Beethoven sound like an amateur.

So as I stand out on the curb in front of the group home the following day, I waver between feeling hopeful that this might be the first day of a new and exciting path in my life and berating myself for thinking it'll be anything different than what I've experienced in the decade since my parents' car accident.

Don't get your hopes up, I tell myself as a black Range Rover turns the corner and slows to a stop in front of me.

The driver, an older gentleman, puts the SUV in park and opens his door so he can round the hood and walk toward me.

"Maren Mitchell?" he asks, all business.

I nod, taking in his black suit and tie and white gloves. Trimmed salt and pepper hair peeks out from beneath his driver's cap. He's dressed fancier than I ever have in my whole life, and all he's doing is sitting behind the wheel of a car. I'm a little stunned.

He misreads my reaction.

"Is something wrong?"

I shake my head quickly. "No."

He scans the curb around my feet, frowning when he finds it empty. "Do you have anything you'd like me to load into the trunk?"

I glance down at my red pleather crossbody purse, a bag I scored at a resale shop and that has survived quite a bit of wear and tear. Inside, I have my wallet, an apple, and a book—the essentials.

"Nope, I'm all set."

He issues a curt nod and then reaches back to open the passenger door for me. I slide onto the seat, immediately aware of the rich leather smell as he shuts the door behind me.

The cupholders hold an unopened bottle of water and a little bag filled with an array of snacks: English biscuits I don't recognize, a granola bar that looks like it would taste like bark, and some toffee. I don't touch any of it. I don't touch anything, in fact, outside of buckling my seatbelt. When that's done, I place my hands on my thighs and leave them there.

When the driver retakes his seat, he straightens his rearview mirror then glances back at me.

"My name is Frank. I'm one of the drivers employed by the Cromwell family. If you need anything during the drive, I'd be happy to assist you."

"Okay. Thank you."

"We should arrive in about an hour."

"An hour!?"

"Yes. Occasionally, I can get to Newport in less time, but not with this traffic."

Newport.

It occurs to me now that I should have asked where Rosethorn is located, but then I don't even know what Rosethorn *is*. Another nursing home? *Please god no.*

I had just assumed the driver would be taking me somewhere in Providence, but now that I know I'm wrong, it feels too late to pump the brakes—literally. Frank has already pulled away from the curb, and I'd look like a crazy person if I asked him to pull back over so I could leap out of the car. So instead, I sit quietly. We don't say a word to each other for the entire drive.

He keeps the radio dialed in to classical music, and I love every minute of it. I can't remember the last time I listened to music like this, uninterrupted, with Rhode Island's early summer landscape whipping past the windows.

The farther from Providence we travel, the more water splashes across the scene. Small pockets turn into expansive bays that stretch to the horizon. Once we're on Aquidneck Island, we continue south until Memorial Boulevard takes us to the very tip of the world. I look out onto a sandy beach hosting a few brave souls as we climb a steep hill that eventually deposits us onto a road lined with shops that look straight out of a theme park. They're all perfectly matching, a long line of two-story Tudor-style townhomes with green scalloped-edged awnings announcing cafes and art galleries, tennis shops and boutiques. We pass them by and then continue on into a neighborhood—at least that's the only word I can think of to describe this place. Each house we pass is slightly bigger than the last. Properties expand. Gates grow toward the sky until it's impossible to make out what's concealed behind them.

I've heard of Newport; everyone in Rhode Island has. I'm pretty sure the rumors are only half true, but the story goes that there's no world more exclusive, no property values more expensive. The difference between the Hamptons and Newport, as I've heard it, is that the Hamptons are where people move when they have a few million to spare. Newport, on the other hand, doesn't have a price tag. The mansions here aren't sold; they're inherited.

I think of what it would be like to see one of them, almost working up the nerve to ask Frank if we can stop just to take a quick peek behind one of the gates, but then he clicks his blinker on and pulls off the road to the left, onto a long drive.

My first thought is that he's headed in the wrong direction and needs to make a U-turn, but then he pulls up to a soaring limestone-framed gate with a pair of heavy copper gas lanterns, and he presses a button on the remote mounted on his sun visor.

The huge iron doors swing open and we pass through. At the last moment, before the gate disappears from view, I turn back to glance over my shoulder and notice the delicate word formed by scrolling ironwork at the very top.

Rosethorn.

4
MAREN

I'm standing in a room waiting for Cornelia to join me. Just like when I was inside the Range Rover, I'm scared to touch anything. The housekeeper who brought me in here told me to make myself at home, but I don't dare. I hover near the door, off the carpet. I feel compelled to take off my shoes, but I don't. I'm not sure my socks are any cleaner, and besides, I'm not sure what the etiquette is when you're a guest at a palace.

Yes, *palace*.

One so grand I wouldn't be surprised to find it was originally built for some long-deceased French king, one of the Louis, probably. From the front gate, I witnessed Rosethorn come into view through a dense forest of trees, nearly unbelieving as I took in its proud two-story marble facade. It boasted thick columns and arched windows accompanied by carefully trimmed boxwoods and soaring cypress trees. A pair of lions ushered me into the front entry with its glistening floors and hanging portraits.

Even now, in this "drawing room", as the housekeeper called it before she left me here, ornate statues stare at me from atop the fireplace mantel. I wonder with a silent laugh if they're on loan from some fancy museum.

The furniture is traditional and old, all of it coordinated to blend into a combination of blues. I get the feeling it's supposed to be an intimate space meant to put visitors at ease, and it is "quaint" compared to what I've seen of the rest of the house. However, I don't think a room with four separate seating areas, a large marble fireplace, and a grand piano can ever truly be called *intimate*.

I glance over at the piano again, nearly salivating.

It's more beautiful than any I've seen, black lacquered and in pristine condition from what I can tell at a distance. The tufted bench is angled invitingly. My stomach squeezes tight with longing, and then the door to the drawing room opens and Cornelia strolls in right past me.

She takes three more confident steps in, stops on a dime, and glances around, confused until she finds me back near the door.

She laughs. "What in the world are you doing over there?"

"Waiting for you."

"Didn't Diane tell you to sit down?"

I nod. "She did. She just didn't tell me *where*."

Cornelia smiles. "Of course. Right. This room does have a lot of options. I find that the couches are the most comfortable. Why don't we sit over there?"

I do as she suggests, letting her take a seat first before I perch on the edge of the couch across from her. A flower arrangement with four white orchids cuts off our view of one another until she leans forward and pushes it a smidge to the side.

Then, with no preamble, she says, "Tell me about yourself."

I jerk my gaze up to her. What does she want to know? My favorite movies? How I take my coffee?

"That's so open-ended. Don't you have something more specific you'd like to know about me?"

"Yes, of course. Let's start with your childhood. Annette told me you lost your parents when you were quite young?"

I don't really mind that Mrs. Archer divulged this information. I don't get the sense that Cornelia is trying to use it against me. She just seems curious, so I answer her openly.

"When I was thirteen."

She hums sadly. "Very young indeed. Were you close with them?"

I shrug. "I was a young teenager with strong opinions. We fought a lot and had grown apart. But when I was younger, yes, I was close with them. Especially my dad."

I get the feeling she's poised to ask me another probing question, so I speak quickly, before she can.

"Mrs. Cromwell—"

"Cornelia."

"Cornelia, you mentioned on the phone that you had a job for me, and I'd like to know what it is."

"Of course. You've come a long way, and I'm sure you're exhausted."

She leans over to a side table where a thin silver phone sits on a dock. She picks it up, presses a button, and then gives instructions to the person on the other end of the line.

"Rita, would you please have tea brought in? Yes, that would be lovely, and add a few of those little sandwiches you know I like—the same ones Chef made last week with the creamed salmon."

Sounds disgusting, but I smile when she sets the phone back on the dock and glances back to me.

"Patricia will be right in with tea."

Patricia? I thought she just said Rita.

"How many people work here?"

Maybe I'm not supposed to ask blunt questions like that, but I might be one of these people soon enough and I'm curious to know how many coworkers I'll have.

"At present?" She waves her hand in the air like it's a frivolous thing. "There's a staff of fifteen, but that includes the groundkeepers and drivers and kitchen staff. In housekeeping, there's Patricia, Diane, and Rita. Collins is the butler, and Bruce is the footman."

Footman, right. Because apparently Frank didn't just drive me to Newport—he also drove me back to the 1800s.

I smile nervously. "I don't mean to sound ungrateful for the opportunity, it's just that it sounds like you have everyone you might need."

What could she possibly need me to do, wipe her butt? *Yeah right!* I'm sure she already has a team of servants doing that.

She narrows her eyes, studying me gently with a tilt of her head. "I'll admit the role I have in mind for you is a little unorthodox. In fact, I'm not sure what to call it except to say you'd be my companion."

"Companion," I repeat.

I've heard that euphemism before, but only from seedy old men looking to get laid.

I try to clarify. "Do you mean I'd be your assistant?"

She weighs the idea in her head. "Occasionally you'd help me remember my appointments and that sort of thing, yes. My memory isn't what it once was."

The drawing room doors open, cutting off our conversation, and in walks a middle-aged woman with chestnut brown hair similar to mine, except hers isn't hanging loose down her back. It's wrapped in a tight bun, pulled up and off her face. She's wearing dark blue pants and a pale blue sweater. In the corner, just above her heart, a pink rose is embroidered with an overlapping monogram. I saw it on the front of Frank's hat as well, and I see now that it's made of two interlocking Cs, no doubt for Cornelia Cromwell.

I wonder if I'll be wearing a similar uniform soon.

In the woman's hands is a silver tray topped with a tiered tower of cookies, an ornate teapot, two cups and saucers, and a few plates of sandwiches. It's enough food to feed ten people. I almost expect her to leave a few of the items and take the rest somewhere else, but she sets the entire thing down on the coffee table between us and then straightens, smiling at Cornelia.

"This looks wonderful, Patricia. Thank you."

Patricia bows her head, casting me a quick smile before exiting the room on silent steps.

I wait for Cornelia to make the first move and watch as she pours us each a cup of tea with steady hands. I notice the way she keeps one of her hands carefully placed on the lid so it doesn't fall off.

"Do you take milk and sugar?" she asks, gesturing to both.

"Um, yes. I think so."

"Oh, that's right. This is your first cup of tea, isn't it? Well, if I were you, I'd go heavy on both. It can't hurt you one bit anyway. You're tiny, dear—liable to disappear into thin air. Here, have some cookies too. And a sandwich. Do you like salmon?"

I must make a disgusted face before I catch myself, but she doesn't take offense.

"You'll try it. That's the polite thing to do when someone offers you food. One bite, that's all."

She fills a small china plate with a heaping mound of food and then holds it out for me to take.

There's no need to urge me twice; I eat my way through the delicate finger foods—salmon sandwich and all—until I uncover the same gold monogram and its accompanying rose etched in the center of the plate.

When I'm done, I find Cornelia studying me. I reach forward to take a cotton napkin from the tea tray and dab it against my mouth. I realize now I probably should have slowed down instead of doing my best impression of a vacuum.

"I can't help but notice you didn't bring any of your things with you today," she says, holding my gaze. "Did Frank already take your bags?"

"Bags?"

"Yes, with your clothes and toiletries."

"I didn't know I was supposed to bring any of that with me."

I'm still wearing my red purse. It's all I thought I needed.

"Yes, well, no need. I would have likely had Collins toss most everything into the furnace anyway. What are those things you have on your legs?"

I look down in confusion.

"*Jeans?*"

Surely she's seen denim before.

She furrows her brow. "They have so many holes in them. Is that because you've had them for so long they're threadbare?"

I smile. "No, it's the style."

"*Style.*" She bats away the suggestion like it offends her. "No, dear, I'm afraid that's not quite the right word."

I can't help but laugh. She's clearly not much for subtlety. Maybe in some people that would rub me the wrong way, but with her I find it refreshing.

She reaches back to pick up her phone and dials out again. "Rita, can you come to the blue drawing room, please? I'd like you to show Maren to her suite."

My mouth opens to correct her, but I wait until she's hung up.

"I don't need a suite."

I've already put her out enough as it is.

That seems to upset her. "So you aren't taking the job?"

"We haven't even talked about a job," I push. "Not really. You've fed me tea and cookies and mentioned I'd be your companion, but we haven't talked about references or past job experience or…" I look away, slightly ashamed to bring it up. "Pay."

"Of course. How rude of me not to mention that earlier. I think we'll start with an allowance of one hundred a year and work up from there. Though if you think you'd need more, I'm sure we could figure something out."

My jaw is gaping open so wide I'm surprised there's no rug burn on my chin. "One hundred *thousand*?"

"Yes, dear."

I blink rapidly as dollar signs swirl in my head. That's more money than I'd earn in three years working at Holly Home. She can't be serious.

"And as far as references, Annette had nothing but wonderful things to say about you, and I've witnessed your work ethic firsthand. I'm convinced you'll make a splendid fit."

A moment later, another maid appears in the doorway, and Cornelia turns to address her. "Rita, would you mind installing Maren in the rose garden suite?"

Rita is an older woman with bright red hair streaked with gray. Her round rosy cheeks become more pronounced when she smiles wide. "Of course. We prepared it for her arrival this morning as requested."

None of this sounds right.

"Where does the rest of your staff stay?" I ask. They can't all have their own suites here…*can they?*

"Women are up on the third floor. Men are down below," Cornelia replies, as if it's a completely commonplace explanation.

"Then I'd like a room on the third floor, please."

I have no idea what I'm saying. I don't need a room. I haven't agreed to stay—I'm *not* staying. It's just that if I were *going* to stay, I'd want to be with all the other staff members.

My request isn't granted.

"I admire your tact. As a guest, it's unseemly to overburden one's host. That's a lesson you'd do well to remember. But the rose garden suite is already made up, so it will do. Rita? Would you mind finishing Maren's tour before you show her to her room? I'd like her to get the lay of the land so she isn't reluctant to explore on her own if she should feel the urge."

"Of course, ma'am."

Then Cornelia stands and tosses one end of her lightweight sage green scarf over her shoulder. "I'd do it myself, but I'm late for the club. Lydia is expecting me. You'll meet her soon, and her granddaughter is about your age. I think you two will get along famously. Dinner tonight is at eight PM in the formal dining room. I'll expect you to look nice. Rita will instruct you."

Then she's gone, sauntering out of the drawing room with regal confidence, and I'm left wondering if any of this is real. The house, the conversation, the amazingly delicious finger sandwiches—the sheer decadence of it all has cast such a dreamlike quality over the day that I wouldn't be surprised to wake up and find myself right back on my bunk at the group home, late for a shift at Holly Home.

Outside the drawing room, I follow Rita through the marbled hall, past busts resting on ornate pedestals and underneath excessively large chandeliers, each more detailed than the last. In the front hall, where I originally entered the house, Rita leads me up a carpeted grand staircase that branches off in two directions.

She's explaining the origins of one of the tapestries on the walls, and my mind can't keep up.

"Would it be okay if we skipped the tour?" I ask tentatively. "I'm a little tired."

She gives me an emphatic nod. "Of course. Your bed is made, so you can lie down on the settee in your room if you'd like. Or if you prefer, I can turn down the bed and you can rest there."

I don't even know what a settee is, but I still say, "The settee will be fine, I'm sure. Thank you though."

She takes me down one of the long hallways that runs parallel to the cliffs outside. It's the first time I've seen the back yard, and I realize now why all the wealthy families must have decided to build their houses here all those years ago. We're right on the ocean. The manicured lawn sprawls forever until suddenly, it drops off to the cliffs below, the bright green grass giving way to blue ocean tinged with teal. Above it, a pale blue cloudless sky. It's like stepping into an oil painting.

"Your room has a similar view," Rita assures me, urging me along.

I follow after her, but my attention stays outside as I wonder how it's possible that some people get so lucky. *Cornelia wakes up to this view every day.* I shake my head in wonder before hurrying my steps to catch up to Rita.

As promised, the windows in my room face the ocean, but they also provide a sweeping view of the rose gardens below, hence the name of my suite, I suppose. In early summer, the roses are in full bloom, but that's only one of the things drawing my curiosity.

The room itself matches the ornateness of the rest of the house, and somehow, that's shocking to me. The furniture in here looks old and *breakable*. Carved antique chairs sit beside a large armoire that could easily house everything I own.

The decor is not exactly my taste. It's extremely girly and decadent with floral wallpaper covering all four walls. The pink striped drapes over the windows coordinate perfectly, as do the linens on the four-poster canopied bed. It's a room fit for a princess.

"What do you think?" Rita asks, standing near the door as I turn in a slow circle inside the room.

"It's really pretty, but so…fancy."

She laughs lightly. "Most of the furniture are heirlooms, yes. That writing desk belonged to Cornelia's mother. It was brought over from France."

I make a mental note to stay far away from it.

"To the left is your ensuite bathroom. Feel free to use it to freshen up. I'll be back at six o'clock to help you get ready for dinner."

I frown.

"I don't think I need help."

My rebuff doesn't seem to sit well with her, so I quickly amend my words. "That is, I can probably get ready for dinner on my own."

The tension between her brows lessens. "I think you'll find it easier if I help with your hair and dress. Besides, I enjoy doing it."

Not wanting to hurt her feelings, I nod.

"Right, okay. Maybe it'll be beneficial to see how it's done. I'll be working here soon…I think."

Rita smiles. "Yes. Cornelia told us you'd be arriving today."

Oh really?

"Can I ask what she said about me?"

Enlighten me, *please*.

"Oh, she didn't go into too much detail. She mentioned that she was expecting a young guest, said you would be her new charge."

Charge?

"But that's not right. I'm not a guest—I'm working here."

She smiles, humoring me. "I'm sure you two will hammer out the details soon enough. For now, you'll have to excuse me for treating you as she instructed. Cornelia is formal and likes things done a certain way, so I'll be back promptly at six to help you get ready."

5
NICHOLAS

I have four young associates and two interns in my office. It's six PM and none of us could leave even if we wanted to. There's no clear path to the door. Papers litter every available surface. Empty coffee cups and food wrappers haven't quite made it into the trash can, and I stand at a whiteboard writing down a potential lead for our defendant, Antonio Owens.

This is just another day in the office for me. In law school, I thought I'd go into public defense and dabble in some pro bono work here and there. In reality, it's all I do. I founded the Innocence Group upon graduating five years ago, heavily influenced by one of my professors at Yale. He lectured us time and time again on the number of wrongly convicted innocent people who remain incarcerated with no representation, and rather than lamenting the injustice, I decided to do something about it.

"Has anyone found the cell records for July 8, 2014 yet?" I ask, turning to look at the group scattered behind me.

"I'm at June 2014," one of the interns says, whipping through papers. "I'm getting there."

The phone rings on my desk, and someone leaps to answer it.

"Innocence Group. Alex speaking." There's a pause, and then Alex looks up at me. "Yes, he's right here."

I reach for my phone over the tangled mess of people, the cord barely reaching where I stand. Alex has to hold the base up and over someone's head so I don't rip the thing out of the wall.

"Nicholas," I say, wedging the phone between my head and shoulder so I can continue to write on the whiteboard.

"What a wonderful greeting from my grandson."

I smile. "You should know better than to call me at the office. What'd you expect?"

"Oh, yes yes. I know you're busy. I was just bragging about your work at the club today, in fact."

"Is that why you called?"

"No, though I can see you're trying to rush me off the phone, so I'll be brief. I just wanted to inform you that I have a new employee. I know you like to know about these things, so here I am, telling you."

I immediately stop writing and wave my hand to shoo everyone out of the room. They all jump to their feet, leaping and hopping over tiny mountains of paper. Trash crunches under their feet as someone trips and nearly goes down. In a few seconds, the door shuts behind them and I'm alone.

"Employee?" I ask. "I thought you already hired a new driver. Is Frank not working out?"

"Frank is wonderful. No, I hired someone else."

"To do what exactly?"

"Handle my personal affairs. Nothing you'd be interested in."

I pinch my eyes shut. "I prefer conducting your employee interviews myself. Especially after what happened last week, I think it'd be prudent to vet anyone you invite into our lives."

"This was a unique case."

"Did you check references? Ask for a resume?"

"I don't think I quite like your tone right now."

I send a silent groan skyward. "At least tell me where you met the person?"

"At Holly Home. You know that's where Annette is staying, and I go to visit her from time to time."

"Is your new employee a resident there?"

My grandmother laughs at the suggestion. "No. She worked there. She's quite young actually."

"What's her name?"

"Maren Mitchell."

"The moment we hang up the phone, I'm looking into her. Background check, references, the works. We haven't even surfaced from the news articles that were published last week—you realize that, don't you?"

"Michael was an outlier. I knew something was off with him from the start, and I should have followed my instincts. I assure you that's not the case here."

"You understand I'm still going to have an investigator look into her, right? Tell me you've had her sign an NDA."

"Not yet. The lawyers are drafting it now. As I said, this is a unique situation. She only arrived today."

I sigh and glance down at the literal mounds of work waiting for me.

"I'm just trying to look out for you," I say softly.

"Yes, and your mother would be proud."

She says she needs to run, and once we hang up, I dial a number I know by heart.

"Derek, I need you to look into someone for me. No, it's not for a case. It's personal."

6
MAREN

I'm too scared to leave my room before Rita comes back at six on the dot. I spend the early moments of the afternoon going over various scenarios in my mind and weighing the pros and cons of staying here versus asking Frank to drive me home. Leaving my old life behind isn't simple. In the event that this job at Rosethorn proves to be too good to be true, it's not like I can just pick up right where I left off. It took six months before the group home had a vacant bed available for me, not to mention how long it took for me to secure the job at Holly Home. Granted, it might not even currently be waiting for me anyway if Mrs. Buchanan insists on pinning that stupid theft on me.

The safe bet would be to return to Providence as soon as possible and beg Mrs. Buchanan to believe in my innocence and keep me on at Holly Home. I should go down and find Frank immediately; chances are I could still make it back in time for my shift tonight.

I look down at my feet as if willing them to move me in the right direction.

Go, dammit!

They stay put on the plush rug.

This is reckless! I shout to myself. *Too good to be true!*

Nothing in my life has ever come this easy. There has to be a catch to this arrangement, some fine print I'm missing.

My internal warnings fall on completely deaf ears. It's as if my brain and my body are on two different wavelengths. My body wants a break. My body sees this fancy room and that wonderfully large bed with all its fluffy pillows and it *wants* it, fine print be damned.

My brain decides one night can't hurt. I'll just give myself a little more time to think it over. I walk over to the desk and pick up the phone so I can call Mrs. Buchanan to tell her I won't be there for my shift later, but it's not as easy as it sounds. I punch in the telephone number to the nursing home but am met with a heavy dial tone no matter how many times I try it. Eventually, with a frustrated growl, I set down the receiver and give up, walking over to the pair of windows that overlook the back half of the property.

Cornelia's rose garden is the largest I've ever seen. It's situated on the left side, encompassing a good portion of the yard. It's symmetrically laid out along a long gravel path, trimmed with tiny boxwoods that delineate one variety of rose from another. There must be more than thirty different kinds, ranging from vibrant orange to deep red to pale pink. A gardener is out there now, tending them with gloved hands.

I stand there watching him for a good while—paralyzed by indecision—before I give in, take the apple and the book out of my purse, and sit down on the settee to read.

As promised, Rita returns to help me get dressed. The poofy pink gown she has hanging over her arm catches my attention right away.

"Is that for me?"

She smiles. "If it fits."

"Can't I just wear what I already have on?"

Her smile fades, and it's obvious she's horrified by the suggestion. "Cornelia has requested dinner in the formal dining room, and guests are expected to dress appropriately."

I don't argue. I take a seat in front of the vanity at Rita's suggestion and let her treat me like a doll. I never got my hair or makeup done for special occasions when I was growing up, so I'm not sure what to expect as she pulls out a curling iron, heats it up, and starts to brush out my long hair.

Then she opens the drawers of the vanity to reveal an array of makeup, all of which is brand new.

I stare at my reflection in the mirror as it slowly transforms. Green eyes, which I always thought were my best feature, are made to appear even bigger and brighter with the right shades of eyeshadow. Blush sweeps across my high cheekbones. A dusky red stain paints my lips. She leaves my hair down but pins it back on one side, pushing most of the long curls over the other shoulder.

"You're so good at this," I tell her, in awe. I don't usually bother doing anything with my hair. It's so long and thick, most days I just throw it up into a ponytail.

"I've done Cornelia's hair for years, and when Judith was young, I styled her hair as well."

"Judith?" I ask, trying to recall if I met a Judith today.

"Mrs. Cromwell's late daughter."

"Oh."

I didn't realize her daughter had passed away.

She meets my eyes in the mirror and smiles gently. "I think she'll be very pleased by your appearance tonight. You're a beautiful young woman."

Beautiful.

What a word.

She's right though; the person in the mirror does look beautiful. Oh, sure, I've thought I looked pretty before, but always in a thrown together sort of way. Never as beautiful as this, never quite so delicate and soft. I wonder what my parents would say if they could see me now.

"Now let's get you dressed and hope that gown fits."

Fortunately, it does, though it's a little snug in the chest and long at the hemline. Rita doesn't have any shoes for me to wear, so I'm forced to put my tennis shoes back on. Fortunately, the bottom of the dress conceals them most of the time. I think it looks totally ridiculous even still, but Rita assures me it's fine as she ushers me out of the room.

"I'll take you down to the dining room so you aren't late."

I follow after her, aware that we're heading down a wing of the house I didn't see earlier. More doors and hallways branch off on either side. Paintings, sculptures, floral arrangements—there isn't a single wasted space in the whole house.

We turn down another hall, one with paintings in gilded frames all arranged at the same height on the wall. Most paintings I've seen in the house look like scenes from history or mythology. These are different.

"This is the Cromwell family portrait gallery," Rita says, slowing her pace to match mine.

I pass women in huge vintage gowns posed in front of fireplaces, men wearing three-piece suits while dogs lie submissively at their feet. The portrait at the end of the row catches my eye more than the others, and I stop, curious.

The painting is of a young teenage boy standing at the front of a large sailboat with his chin raised and his eyes focused off into the distance. My first thought is that he looks like some great leader or conqueror, which is silly because he can't be older than thirteen or fourteen in the image. At that age, I looked dweeby, I'm sure. Nothing like this.

"That's Mr. Hunt, Cornelia's grandson," Rita says, circling back to stand behind me.

Ah, that explains the confidence. He was born into this world. He doesn't need to conquer it; it's already his.

"He wouldn't sit for the image," she continues, "so Cornelia had to send off a photo of him to the artist in Italy. Still, I think he captured his likeness well enough. Isn't he handsome?"

No. He's not. And it's not just because I'm not attracted to boys barely starting puberty; it's his entire demeanor. The haughty look in his eyes. The sharp cut of his jaw.

"He looks cruel."

"Ah, it's the hair. Jet black, just like his father's."

"Does he visit Cornelia often?"

"Oh yes. He's a lawyer in New York City, but during the summer he's here off and on. You'll meet him soon enough."

For some inane reason, a shiver runs down my spine.

"Right this way." Rita prods me along, away from the portrait. "We don't want to keep Cornelia waiting."

In the formal dining room, Cornelia sits at the head of the table in a simple square-cut dark green dress with the same sage green scarf from earlier draped over her shoulders. She's speaking to an older, well-dressed servant with a thin frame and stark white hair who's standing beside her chair. Rita deposits me on the threshold and then excuses herself.

Cornelia gazes up at me from beneath her brows, and then my appearance forces her to lift her head and take me in fully.

She unfurls a wide smile. "Beautiful. Rita did such a wonderful job with you, but of course, you were marvelous to begin with. Come. Come sit."

The man at her right pulls out the chair beside her and I rush over to take the seat, not wanting to keep him waiting. Once I sit, he pushes me toward the table, and Cornelia prompts him to bring the first course. I catch that his name is Collins—the man from the phone.

His footsteps carry him out of the room, and Cornelia smiles at me.

"That dress looks lovely on you. You have such a nice warm complexion. You can get away with wearing any color you want, though I still think you'd do well to stay away from yellow. I'd like to see you in green next, I think—something that matches your eyes."

"Do you do this with all of your employees?" I ask, sweeping my hand around the room and down to the fancy pink gown I'm wearing. "Dress them up and sit them at your table?"

She laughs. "No, of course not."

"But I am your employee, right? Rita mentioned that I was your guest, and now I'm confused. Was she mistaken, or am I?"

She hums in thought. "Well let's fix that then. I'm afraid you might not fit perfectly into one single category. I've told you I'd like you to be my companion. During the summer season, I have various functions I need to attend, and I'd like you to come along with me to those. I'll expect you to dine with me in the evenings as well—"

"That doesn't sound like work."

She laughs. "Doesn't it? My grandson would disagree with you. Okay, how about this? In addition to those duties, if I have any errands or pressing matters I don't think my staff can handle, I'll bring them to you. This is all new for me as well. I'm afraid we'll have to learn together. Now, tell me, do you plan on staying?"

"I was still undecided this afternoon, but now I can't see any other option. I think the telephone in my room is broken so I couldn't call my manager at Holly Home to tell her I won't be back for my shift tonight. There's no way I still have a job there."

She frowns. "You should have asked someone for help. The phone system here is set up for dialing in-house. You simply press the extension for the department you're trying to reach. 0 for housekeeping, 1 for the kitchen, and so on. You have to press 9 before you place an outgoing call."

Right. I figured it was something like that and I should have asked someone for help, but I didn't. And maybe that was on purpose, a subconscious way to force the decision in one direction rather than the other.

"I can put in a call to your boss and put her mind at ease if you insist on going back to work there."

The idea depresses me more than I care to admit.

"Or you can stay on here," she adds, her words taking on an uplifting tone.

I peer at her skeptically and press my earlier question. "As your employee or your guest?"

"How about for the time being, we just say both," she replies as Collins returns, carefully holding two bowls of soup. They're filled nearly to the brim and liable to overflow so I shoot to my feet to help him, but Cornelia tuts.

"Maren, sit down. Collins is serving the first course."

And so begins my "work" at Rosethorn.

Any time I try to lift a finger during dinner, I'm told it's not my place. I try to make my bed in the morning—after the most blissful night of sleep I've ever had—and Patricia tells me it'd be best if I let her do it. Then she proceeds to *re*make my bed before freshening up the rest of the room while I sit awkwardly on the settee. I go down into the kitchen to attempt to make my own breakfast and the chef uses a rolling pin to shoo me out. I'm not allowed to help clean up. I can't set the table or take out the trash.

It completely boggles my mind.

Why does Cornelia *actually* want me here? I haven't been the least bit helpful. In fact, I've been a burden. These people have to wait on me hand and foot even when I insist it's not necessary. Rita dotes on me constantly, helping me dress for dinner the next day and curling my hair again. Patricia launders my clothes and keeps my room impeccably clean.

They're all extremely kind, but also reverent, as if I'm not one of them, even though Cornelia promises me I am. It's slightly unsettling. I'm not meant to be the person being waited on. I'm used to doing the waiting.

During tea on Thursday, Cornelia slides a packet of paper in front of me.

"Just a bit of pesky business. Our lawyers insist that all of our employees sign a non-disclosure agreement," she explains, and I don't hesitate to sign.

There's also an I-9 form and a W-4 form. *Or was it a W-2?* I don't know the difference. I sign my name where she tells me to on a dozen different documents then sigh with relief when Rita enters the drawing room carrying the tea tray. I want to stand and help her, but Cornelia's reproachful stare makes it clear I should stay right where I am and let her do her job.

"Tell me about where you lived before you came here," Cornelia says after Rita leaves us, adding a cube of sugar to her cup before swirling it around with her small spoon, never once touching the sides. Meanwhile, when I stir my tea, I bang my spoon so many times even *I* wince. "I know it was a group home."

"Yes, for at-risk young adults."

"And are you 'at-risk', do you think?"

I look down, slightly embarrassed by the subject. "No, but the state seems to think I am. I have made some mistakes—though not in the way you might think," I add quickly, not wanting her to get the wrong idea. "I just put my faith in the wrong people at times, and I'm still suffering the consequences. It's made it really difficult to find good jobs and decent places to live. The group home was a good fit for me because the rent was really low and they didn't care about my past."

"And you liked it there?"

I think of the cold concrete floors and the hard twin mattress I slept on every night. I think of the other girls I never quite got along with and the loneliness I tried hard to ignore. It's funny that until this moment I'd never considered if I liked it or not. It simply was my only option. Beggars can't be choosers.

"It served its purpose," I say matter-of-factly. "Gave me a place to sleep at night, a consistency I've found hard to replicate since my parents' deaths."

I look up to find she doesn't look too pleased. Her deep frown doesn't sit well with me.

"It sounds worse than it is," I assure her.

Her lips purse. "Somehow I doubt that."

"I really should give them another call. I let them know I'd be gone for a few days, but space is pretty limited there and I feel bad taking a spot away from someone who really needs it. That is…if I am really going to stay on here with you."

She nods quickly as if there's no doubt in her mind. "I'll have Frank drive down this Saturday and pick up your things. He can alert the staff about your new address and have your mail forwarded here. That should cover everything."

Oh good. One more person running around doing my bidding.

"He doesn't have to do that. I can go myself," I protest.

"No, actually, you can't. You and I have an appointment on Saturday."

I sip my tea—a drink I'm quickly starting to love—and let Cornelia lead the conversation wherever she might like. It's interesting how easily I've given in to her will to keep me here. It's not exactly worth it for me to fight with her about it. I want to stay here—*who wouldn't?*—and besides, I'm starting to discover that my being here isn't purely for my own benefit. As the days stretch from one to the next and I spend more time with her, I think I start to understand Cornelia's motives for bringing me to Rosethorn. She doesn't need another person polishing silver; that's clear. I think she truly meant what she said when she described me as her companion. Even though she's surrounded by servants and has more "lunch dates at the club" than any one person might need, I think she still might be a little lonely. After all, I can't help but wonder if I weren't here, would she sit in that big dining room all by herself every night? The thought makes me sad.

On top of her suspected loneliness, I get the sense that she feels sorry for me. It comes up on Friday when I prod her, again, about my room situation. I still feel guilty staying in the large suite when everyone else lives in the servants' quarters. Rita let it slip earlier that day, while she was styling my hair, that I'm staying in the room Cornelia's daughter used when she was a young girl.

"Surely I don't deserve to be in there," I tell Cornelia at dinner.

"And why not?" she demands, suddenly annoyed. "Why *don't* you deserve to live in a room as beautiful as that one? Keep up the complaining and I'll have Patricia switch you over to an even *bigger* suite."

I can't help but laugh at her threat.

But I don't take her generosity lying down. Even though I'm not allowed to do traditional tasks, I do carve out little things to do here and there that make me feel useful. One morning, Cornelia takes me into her overflowing rose garden and hands me a set of shears so she can instruct me on where to cut them. Then she helps me arrange a little bouquet. Every other day after that, I make sure to go out and snip a few roses so I can arrange them in a vase and set them in the blue drawing room, where she and I meet for tea in the afternoons.

I make sure to read the newspaper Collins includes with my breakfast tray so I have plenty to discuss with Cornelia at dinner.

When she needs to go into town for shopping or to place an order at a gallery or boutique, I accompany her.

Even still, all these tasks don't amount to much, and they definitely can't be considered work in the least. I feel niggling guilt eating away at me, especially on Saturday, one week since my arrival, when Cornelia brings a fashion designer to the house and insists on having me sit in for the appointment.

I assume, at first, that Vivien is there for Cornelia. We sit at a small oak table in the yellow drawing room, flipping through fabric swatches. I pick out colors and patterns I think would look nice on Cornelia, only to find out once they have a handful of swatches set aside that they've been choosing colors they think *I* should wear. It's an honest mistake. Vivien only speaks French and Cornelia's fluent as well, so I can't understand a single word they're saying to each other. It isn't until Vivien stands me up and starts to take my measurements that I realize something is off.

"What does it matter what my measurements are?" I ask as Cornelia sits back in her chair, completely unbothered as she watches Vivien turn me this way and that like I'm nothing more than a marionette.

"Because you need new clothes. I can't stand to see you wear those jeans with the ripped holes yet another time. I'll throw them into an open flame, I swear it."

I open my mouth to protest—*I have clothes!* Rita has been bringing new outfits for me to wear every morning—but Cornelia holds up her hand to shush me. "Don't bother to refute me. This is one battle I have no plans on losing. I assure you, you will be getting new clothes whether you like them or not. I'm the one who has to look at you. These clothes are for me, *really*. Besides, you don't understand how wonderful it is that Vivien could come see us on such short notice. She's very in demand. She had a modest atelier in the 2nd arrondissement, where I used to visit her when I went to Paris in spring, and she'd design my entire wardrobe for the season. Everyone knew of her, but *I* was the one who succeeded in luring her to our little island. Now, she spends half her time in Paris and half her time in Newport, dressing anyone who's anyone."

So then why the hell is she dressing me, I say in my head, biting back the urge to continue arguing.

"*Restez tranquille!*" Vivien says, poking me with a pin.

That delights Cornelia. "She says to hold still, and I'd do it if I were you. She can get rather testy."

I scrunch my nose at her in a silent tease and then she rings for Patricia to bring in tea for us. I'm allowed a five-minute break before Vivien starts layering fabric all over me, checking colors against my complexion and pinning designs in place.

It feels like we've been at it for hours when Rita strolls in carrying a delicate white dress outstretched in front of her.

Cornelia sits up straight and beckons for her to bring it closer.

"Oh good, Rita. Thank you so much. Would you mind laying it on that chair until Vivien is ready for it?"

"What's that?"

"A gown for you to wear next Saturday."

My brows arch. I've seen gowns—Rita has stuffed me in a new one every evening since my arrival—and *that* is not a gown. It's a piece of art. Delicate white lace drapes to the floor below a corseted off-the-shoulder top.

"What's next Saturday?" I ask, not taking my eyes off the dress. I sound a little awestruck even to my own ears.

"My annual White Ball. It's one of my favorite traditions, and it kicks off the entire social season here in Newport. My mother started it in 1904 and I've continued it in her stead. It's meant to be a recreation of a night in Louis XIV's court. The men are all expected to come in masks. Women wear white." She tosses her hands up. "Oh, sure, it reeks of the puritanical bonds holding women back, as if a woman's value lies only in her ability to be demure. She's meant to be a delicate flower with all her petals intact—nonsense! But still, tradition is tradition, and I do think you'll look lovely in white. We don't have time for Vivien to create something custom, so she'll alter this. I have a feeling you'll wear it as beautifully as its original owner did."

The look in her eye makes me think this is one of her old gowns, and something like pride blossoms in my chest.

I don't bother telling her how much I'd love to wear it. The stars in my eyes are visible to anyone standing in that room.

7

MAREN

I dial my friend Ariana's number, hoping she'll answer. I've tried her three times since my arrival at Rosethorn, but she hasn't picked up once. This time, when the call doesn't connect, I leave a message.

"Ariana, it's Maren. Why aren't you answering your phone? I've been trying to reach you to let you know I moved. I'm actually in Newport..." I let the sentence dwindle, unsure of how many details I want to give her. "It's a long story, but I think I might be here for a while. I got a new job. Kind of." I shake my head. "Anyway, I'll leave the address for you just in case. I hope you're doing okay. I miss you."

When I set the phone back down and look around the rose garden suite, I'm made aware of the sharp contrast between where Ariana likely is right now and where I am. I stare down at the cream and white striped sweater I'm wearing paired with designer jeans and navy flats. My hair and makeup are perfectly applied. My nails are painted a soft pink. I want to ridicule all of it. How ridiculous that Cornelia thinks she can just put me up in this room and dress me up like a doll, but it's actually…nice. I like this nail color, and these jeans *are* better than my old ones.

I want to find Cornelia's entire world utterly absurd. I try to pick out the frivolity and concentrate on it, but it's hard. Yes, on the surface, her every wish is granted. Every meal is decadent. Every outfit costs more than I dare to find out. Her world is filled with carnival attractions around every corner, and I doubt everything is as pearly white as it's made out to be.

And yet, I think there's more to discover.

One morning, when Collins brings in my breakfast, I ask him if he likes his job here. To me, it seems like an off-the-cuff question, but he stops in his tracks and turns to me with his thick white brows pinched together above his eyes.

"Of course. Why do you ask?"

"I'm just curious. I… Cornelia asks so much of you all, and I—"

"And if she didn't ask, what then? I'd be out of a job."

I blink rapidly, taking in his words.

"I didn't mean to offend you."

His expression softens and he nods. "My parents both worked at Rosethorn before me. My father was Edward Cromwell's butler, my mother Cornelia's lady's maid. They were both rewarded handsomely for their servitude and loyalty, and I've found the same home for myself here. Cornelia might be traditional and formal in her home, but she's also one of the most generous humans I've ever known."

As if the universe isn't done proving that point, Collins' words are hammered home over the next few days.

On Monday, Cornelia opens her doors to the children of St. Michael's Day School so they can use her blue drawing room for music lessons. All morning the sound of children singing fills the house. Tuesday, Cornelia welcomes the Historical Society of Newport for a luncheon and lecture about preserving the Gilded Age mansions along Bellevue Avenue, Rosethorn being among them. I sit in for the meeting and take notes. On Thursday, during tea, Cornelia sits down with a slightly hysterical woman. She's stressed about the fact that the venue has fallen through for the Breast Cancer Research Foundation annual luncheon, and without missing a beat, Cornelia offers up Rosethorn's gardens.

"We'll host it here. Have your planners coordinate with Diane."

"I can help too," I volunteer.

The woman turns to me with tears in her eyes, and Cornelia nods. "Yes, perfect. Maren will sit in during our planning meetings and help me remember the details. She's very good at taking notes."

I can't be sure, but I think she's making fun of me for that historical society meeting. Then her wink confirms it.

"You two are absolute angels. You have no idea how much this means to me and to the organization."

Later that day, I'm helping Cornelia organize her closet so we can pull a few items for Dress for Success, or at least that's how it started. We did stack up a large pile of blazers and slacks and sensible heels, but now we're just playing dress-up, putting on the most ridiculous accessories we can find.

"You look like a movie star in those," she assures me as I tip a pair of cat eye sunglasses down the bridge of my nose and give her a teasing wink over the top of them. "You have to keep them."

"No way. They're Chanel," I say. "Even I know that brand."

"Yes, and I haven't worn them in years. Better that you take them."

I slide the glasses off and put them right back where I found them, pointing to a small box in the corner of the room as a way to distract her from the topic.

"What are those?"

The box I'm referring to is overflowing with plaques and awards. Two or three have actually tumbled out and are leaning against the side of the cardboard container. When I step closer, I see they're from all different organizations: the Audubon Society of Newport, the Leukemia and Lymphoma Society, the Bill and Melinda Gates Foundation. Words like *Top Donor* and *Woman of the Year* stand out along with Cornelia's name.

She shrugs like it's nothing. "People love doling out accolades."

"Maybe you deserved them."

"Perhaps, or maybe it's just one's duty to give back and contribute to the world. I don't think I necessarily need a pat on the back for doing so."

"Cleary," I say, dusting one of them off. "I can't believe you have these stuffed in here like this."

"And what should I do with them? Hang them around my neck?" She snorts, and it's the most unladylike thing I've ever seen her do.

I can't help but laugh.

She shoos me away from the box. "Now, go down and ask Collins for a bag for all these clothes. You and

I can drop them at the donation center on our way into town."

Later, when I return to my room to read before dinner, I find a small envelope sitting on my bedside table. I frown, at first thinking it might be a letter from Ariana—not that she's ever written to me—but there's no address printed on the front, only my name in swooping cursive.

Ms. Maren Mitchell.

Inside is a paycheck made out to me. The amount makes my heart drop: more than three thousand dollars for two weeks of work. Work—*ha*.

My hand trembles as I look at the dollar amount again. I think of how far the money could get me. I dream of all the things I could spend it on. And then the moment passes, my stomach squeezes tight, and I open my bedside drawer, depositing the paycheck and the envelope inside.

8
NICHOLAS

When I arrive at Rosethorn on Saturday afternoon, the grounds have already been taken over by delivery trucks and auxiliary staff, preparing the house for my grandmother's ball. I was meant to arrive last night, but I couldn't get away from work until this morning. I park on the gravel drive to the right of the house and step outside, breathing deep. I'm reluctant to leave the ocean breeze, but I'm hungry, and the first item on my agenda is to go down into the kitchen and see what Chef is whipping up for tonight. Surely he needs a taste tester.

I'm stopped by every member of the staff I cross paths with, hugging them and telling them I'm glad to be back. I stay away from Newport in the winters, like a bear going into hibernation, except instead of sleeping, I'm working.

I'm striding down the back hall, which is usually reserved for employees, headed toward the kitchen when I notice music drifting out from the blue drawing room. I stop and listen, finding the sound comforting after so many months away. It's not uncommon for Rosethorn to be filled with music, and my grandmother has always had a soft spot for the piano. She forced me into lessons as a child, but I had no patience for reading music and sitting still. I'd clonk and clank my way through a thirty-minute lesson, always watching the clock and missing keys as my teacher chided me. The moment the hour hand announced the end of our time together, I'd escape to the gardens, running like a fugitive from the law.

When I make it to the kitchen, I spot Collins conferring with Chef, no doubt going over all the food they'll have for the ball. There are a dozen more people in here than usual, staff they've brought in for today to assist in the preparations.

When Collins sees me, he smiles and heads over to greet me. We shake hands and pat each other's backs—nothing overly sentimental, but I know it's his way of letting me know he's happy to see me.

"You look well," he says, inspecting me from every angle. "Though that hair could use a good trim."

I laugh. "Don't worry, I plan on getting it cut before tonight. Has my grandmother started to allow St. Michael's here on the weekends as well?" I ask, nodding in the direction of the music.

Collins beams. "No. That's—"

"Nicky! We didn't expect you until this evening."

I glance over in time to see my grandmother coming in through the back door of the kitchen, the one that leads straight out to the gardens so Chef has easy access to fresh vegetables. She's wearing a loose kaftan and a large sunhat with yellow ribbons dangling down off each side, and her basket is filled with freshly cut roses. She drops them on the prep table nearest me and comes close, kissing both of my cheeks before stepping back and giving me an approving once-over.

"That hair needs a trim."

Collins clears his throat, and I roll my eyes.

"Yes, I'm aware. Have no fear, I'll make it to the barber before tonight."

"Stay for tea?" she asks, already motioning for it to be made up.

"They're expecting me at the yacht club."

She frowns. "But you've only just arrived."

"I haven't sailed in months. Don't make me choose between you and Carina."

"So does that mean we'll miss you at lunch as well?"

"Don't pout. I've made it in time for your ball. You should be grateful."

"*Grateful!* To see my own grandson?"

She looks to Collins for help, but he pretends to inspect the menu in his hand.

"Hurry off then," she says, swatting me with one of her gardening gloves. "Go. The sooner you leave, the sooner you'll return. I expect you to be on time tonight. No carousing with Rhett at the club."

I smirk before leaning in and giving her a kiss on the cheek in farewell. "No promises."

She throws up her hands in despair, but we both know I'll be there, with my hair cut and dressed to the nines, just as she's asked. I've always had a soft spot for my grandmother, and she takes advantage of it every chance she gets.

The marina at the yacht club is filled with sailboats coming out of shipyard storage for the summer. I called yesterday morning and let the staff know of my arrival, so I'm not surprised to see Carina's red and blue striped hull glistening in the sunlight out on the water. I've brought extra gear with me—a jacket and hat—knowing once I'm out on the water, the wind will pick up even more. Though we're creeping into May, the summer heat hasn't completely taken over. The sun is shining overhead, though, and that's enough to tempt me out onto the water.

Rhett is waiting for me on the dock. He spots me as I walk down the hill toward him, waving his hand up and over his head in a goofy gesture. As if I can't spot his ridiculous orange jacket from a mile away. He's worn it since college.

"You're late!" he shouts.

"I had to stop and grab a sandwich at Harvest Market."

"Chef kick you out of the kitchen?" He laughs.

"They're in full swing for tonight. Apparently, they couldn't spare a thing."

He rubs his hands together, creating friction. "Good—that'll mean more for me later. You know I haven't eaten for two days leading up to tonight? I've missed the food at your grandmother's house."

I laugh and toss him a disbelieving glare.

The moment I reach him on the dock, we both get to work preparing Carina for a trip through Brenton Cove and down to Pirate Cave. It's a short journey by our standards, but I promised my grandmother I'd be on time tonight, and it'll take us a while to rig the boat.

We talk as we work. He and I have been sailing together since middle school, for fun and for sport, so at this point, we're two minds working together as one.

I ask him about his work in Boston, knowing full well he's as busy as I am, though he's in finance, not law.

He's considering striking out on his own, starting his own hedge fund.

"You'll help me set it up, won't you?"

I laugh. "You and I both know that's not my specialty."

"Aw c'mon, all that legalese…" He groans. "You know I'm only good with numbers."

I also know he has more than enough money in his trust fund to hire a good team of lawyers, so no, I don't let his moaning persuade me.

"How did everything shake out with Michael Lewis, by the way? Last time we talked, it had started to blow over."

"It has, largely, though my main focus is the new employee my grandmother hired."

"The girl?"

I pause mid-knot and glance up at him. "What do you mean 'the girl'?"

"The girl your grandmother has been parading around town—everyone's confused about who she is. My mom swears she's one of your grandmother's employees, but there are rumors she's some long-lost relative too. I was going to ask you about it."

I curse under my breath.

"I heard she's going tonight. My mom mentioned it."

"Going tonight? To the ball? Why on earth would she do that?"

He shrugs. "Hell if I know. I'm just the messenger—don't shoot me."

What a mess.

I'd hoped my grandmother would use common sense. I'd hoped Maren would be long gone by now. I did exactly as I promised. As soon as I got off the phone with my grandmother two weeks ago, I checked into Maren like my grandmother should have done before hiring her. First, I called her last employer, Holly Home, for a reference.

Her manager there had quite a lot to say about her.

"I hate to bring it up. Sure, she was a nice enough girl, but I think you should know…one of our residents had their wedding ring stolen recently. I had two employees confirm that they saw Maren with the ring, though Maren denies taking it. Police were involved. An investigation was being prepared, but then our resident insisted on dropping the case. I think she was worried she'd get Maren in trouble, but if you ask me, she deserves to face the consequences of her actions. Can you imagine someone cruel enough to target the elderly?"

Then she continued, "Not to mention the fact that she just up and left us high and dry. No two-week notice, nothing. We're still short-staffed because of her, and if you ask me, her quick departure solidifies her guilt in my book."

I thanked her for her time and hung up, staring at my phone, sick to my stomach.

As if that wasn't bad enough, my investigator dug into Maren's past and found that she has a criminal record for possession of a controlled substance. Her felony sentence means it was a Schedule I or II drug, something like ecstasy, cocaine, or oxycodone.

Worse, I can't be certain that's all she's done. If she's smart, she had her juvenile record expunged when she turned eighteen, but other charges or not, it doesn't matter. I don't need there to be more damning evidence against her—it's clear that she shouldn't be at Rosethorn. My grandmother has always had a weakness for wounded birds, and maybe I'd be willing to give her a chance too if not for the recent theft suspicions and the fact that we're still dealing with the ramifications of Michael Lewis. He was able to steal from my grandmother without her even noticing, and my grandmother barely tolerated him. From what I've heard, my grandmother really likes Maren, and that's why I'm even more concerned. This won't end well for her.

I talked to my grandmother this week about Maren. *Again.* I told her all about the theft accusations and her criminal record over the phone, and I demanded that she act accordingly in firing Maren. I thought she had, but apparently I was wrong.

I guess that responsibility falls at my feet.

9
MAREN

I know I should be slightly offended by Cornelia's motive for inviting me to tonight's ball. I know, despite the fact that I'm beginning to establish a role for myself at Rosethorn, I'm still first and foremost a charity case to her. I just can't seem to let that stop me from feeling like a princess as I stand in front of a full-length mirror, twisting this way and that so I can see the overall effect of my gown.

Vivien knows what she's doing.

When I tried this dress on a week ago, it seemed all wrong, too long and too tight in the chest yet gaping at the waist. Now, it's a glove, wrapped around me so well I might never take it off.

The lace is even prettier than I remember, and the corset bodice shows off my figure in a way that makes me want to blush. The heart-shaped neckline dips down almost *too* low, revealing more than a hint of cleavage, but Rita assured me while she was zipping me into it that it's expected. I'll have to take her word for it because I have nothing else to wear.

The dress is off the shoulder and styled so that straps of ruched fabric drape loosely around each of my upper arms. They don't actually hold the dress up at all, but they give it a romantic effect.

My hair is parted to the side and hanging down in soft waves. My makeup is heavier around the eyes and darker on my lips, accentuating every feature I have to offer. I smile at myself as I hear footsteps approaching out in the hall. Sure, I might be a charity case, but for tonight at least, I don't look like one.

Cornelia has spared no expense for the ball. As I walk down the central staircase with my arm looped through hers, I look down at the party in amazement. The entry foyer is already overflowing with guests. As requested, all the women are wearing white, but I'm surprised to find so many varying shades, ranging all the way from blinding snow to dark creams. The men are in black tie, all of them masked.

Cornelia looks beautiful tonight in a satin dress beneath a coordinating floor-length satin jacket. The shades of white are off by a hair—the jacket darker than the dress—so that each contrasts perfectly against the other. Around her neck, she's wearing an ornate diamond necklace with a large round pendant at its center. It matches the smaller-scale version around my neck, on loan for the night.

Cornelia lays her hand over mine and leads me forward into the crush of people. Immediately, guests vie for her attention so they can thank her for their invitations. She introduces me to them all as Maren Mitchell, her ward, and people immediately take interest.

"Wonderful!" one man says with an exuberant handshake. "Are you from the New York Mitchells? Or the Washington arm of the family?"

"Oh, um, neither," I reply, smiling.

"Maren, come along," Cornelia says, pulling me along after her. "George, it was good to see you!"

No one gets more than a few moments with her, which means no one gets more than a few moments with me either. They try their best to use their time wisely, though, asking me a slew of personal questions: my age, alma mater, genetic makeup (I wish I were kidding). "It's just that you have such wonderful cheekbones," one woman says, actually touching my face.

But Cornelia never lets me stand there long enough to answer any of their probing questions. *I don't have an alma mater because I barely graduated high school! Good talking to you though!*

Eventually, we make our way to the ballroom, where a string quartet is stationed in the corner, playing music for all the guests. No one is dancing yet, though it looks like it might take place later. Why else would they have set up the tables only on the perimeter of the room?

Collins is standing at the threshold of the grand space. When he sees us, Cornelia nods, and suddenly he's announcing our entry to everyone there.

"Mrs. Cornelia Cromwell and her guest, Ms. Maren Mitchell."

I feel flustered by the amount of attention aimed at us. Curious stares follow us as we walk through the center of the room. I glance over to Cornelia and see her chin lifted in confidence, so I try to mimic the same posture, hoping it'll have the same effect on my appearance. Doubtful.

We reach a small table in the back corner of the ballroom and Bruce rushes forward to pull Cornelia's seat out for her.

"Maren, I'm parched. Would you mind grabbing us some refreshments from the table over there? Bring something sweet with you as well. I skipped dinner."

She points me in the direction of a table marked by a tower constructed out of hundreds of champagne glasses rising toward the ceiling. It has to be at least six feet tall. I study it as I approach, confused about how it will stay standing through the night if guests retrieve glasses to drink. It's a catastrophe waiting to happen, but the mystery is solved when I spot another batch of pre-filled glasses sitting around an ice sculpture and realize the tower is just for show.

I grab two then slowly peruse the selection of food surrounding the champagne tower. There are layers upon layers of options served in small bite-size portions, each with little placards perched in front bearing the names of the dishes: pork rillettes, Provençal vegetable tarts, tartes flambées, cheddar gougères, zucchini-tomato verrines, and chicken liver pâté. I have no idea what Cornelia would want, so when I see another guest pick up one of the trays off the table and walk off with it, I do the same, adding the glasses of champagne on top so I don't drop them. It's not until I'm halfway across the ballroom and drawing not just curious stares but obvious laughter as well that I realize I might not have done the right thing.

Cornelia's eyes widen when she sees me approaching.

"Bruce, take that from Maren, would you, please?"

He rushes forward and takes the tray, handing it off to a man who dashes over, apologizing for the misunderstanding. He's dressed just like the guest I saw back at the table and I now realize, with reddening cheeks, that they're dressed in uniform. They're working the event, hence why they're carrying the trays.

My blush deepens when I see Cornelia is now sitting with two guests who've had front-row seats to my mistake.

The woman on Cornelia's left is older and impeccably dressed, and the girl sitting beside her is closer to my age, tilting her head and studying me like I'm an animal in a zoo.

"I admire your method, child," the older woman says. "There've been plenty of times I've been at parties like this, practically starved because no one has made it around to my table with some tasty morsel for me to eat. Maybe next time I'll take a tray for myself too."

I try to force a smile. She's being nice, after all, trying to make me feel better, but I can still hear the people laughing behind me and I have the sudden urge to walk right out the door to my right and never return.

"Don't worry about that silliness, Maren. I've seen people do far worse at parties like this," Cornelia assures me. "And anyway, I have introductions to make. This is Lydia Pruitt, my dearest friend, and her granddaughter, Victoria."

Lydia extends her hand for me, palm down, and I know now, from Cornelia's instruction, that I'm supposed to delicately shake it without gripping it too hard. Her granddaughter, Victoria, bows her head in greeting without extending her hand then pats the chair beside her.

"Sit down by me?"

I do, instantly, if only to escape the stares at my back.

Victoria smiles and leans closer. "You have nothing to worry about. At my coming out ball, I tripped going down the stairs after my introduction. My mother was so horrified, she stormed out of the room crying. It was a sight to behold, and *much* worse than what you just did, I promise."

I force a smile, more than a little bit intimidated by her.

Victoria belongs in this ballroom. Everything about her is refined and cultivated. She has the fine bone features of a bird. Even sitting down, I can tell she's tall and impossibly thin, with dark brown hair and brows that stand out against pale ivory skin. Her loose-fitting beaded gown looks vintage, and so does her hairstyle.

She smiles wider, and I realize I've been studying her too closely.

I look away.

"You can call me Tori. All my friends do."

I realize I haven't contributed much to the conversation yet, so I turn back to her. "Did you grow up here in Newport?"

She shrugs, reaching for her champagne glass. "Here and there. My family spent the summers here and the winters in the Caribbean. My boarding school was in Connecticut and my father lived mainly in Tokyo, for business, so I'd visit him there every so often as well. What about you?"

I close my mouth, which dropped open midway through her answer. "I grew up in Providence mainly."

"So then you aren't far from home."

"No, not at all."

Silence fills the gap between us and then she leans in close. "I feel like I should tell you that Cornelia has told me a bit about you." I jerk my attention back to her in alarm, and she holds her hand out to touch my shoulder. "Nothing too personal, just that you might have had a difficult time recently, and well, I just wanted to say I can be a good friend. I'm told I'm a good listener."

I have no reply to this, mostly because it's not what I was expecting her to say.

This woman with her gentle features and luxurious upbringing has every right to be a snooty asshole, and yet she's offering me friendship. Our eyes meet, and I see something complicated lurking behind the surface. Something...sad, I think. Her eyes seem to implore me to take her up on her offer.

"I'd really like that."

She grins. "Good. Do you play tennis?"

"Not at all."

"I'm not so good. My mother didn't want me playing as a child because she was worried it would interfere with my posture. I have no idea where she got that notion, but now I'm taking lessons at the club, and you could join me if you'd like. This Tuesday?"

I look to Cornelia for permission, and she simply nods, obviously approving.

I grin. "It's a date."

Tori and I sit there talking while more guests are introduced at the entrance of the ballroom. The volume increases and bodies press in. Eventually, the quartet starts playing louder, and the dancing begins. I watch from the sidelines, smiling as couples sweep across the dance floor, arm in arm, waltzing to some of my favorite pieces of music.

I hear Cornelia ask Tori if she's heard from Nicholas, and I wonder if Tori has a boyfriend and if I'll get to meet him tonight. Suddenly, I'm hungry to know more people in this world, to find out if they're all as nice as Tori.

My wish is granted a few minutes later when a guy about my age comes over to our table to introduce himself to me with a slight bow, and I'm immediately struck by how handsome he is. Barrett Knox has expertly styled light brown hair and a tailored black tuxedo that accentuates his broad shoulders. Underneath his mask, he has a charming cleft in the center of his chin and a winning smile he aims at me as we're introduced.

"It's good to see a new face in Newport," he says, holding my gaze.

"Barrett is actually my cousin," Tori tells me, leaning in as she throws him a cheeky grin. "He's a few years younger than me and my friends, and he always hated that we didn't include him in our games when we were growing up."

He presses a hand to his heart as if the wound still stings.

"Do we have to dredge up the past?"

"How old are you, Maren?" Tori continues, ignoring him.

"Twenty-three."

She beams. "There, Barrett—now you finally have someone to play with who's your same age."

The look in his eyes makes me think he would enjoy playing with me, though not as children do.

"I'm looking forward to it," he says before excusing himself to make the rounds.

I sag in my chair as he walks away, buzzing from the encounter.

"I'd be careful where he's concerned," Tori says, following my gaze.

"Why?"

She laughs. "Because Barrett only loves Barrett. Sure, he might look pretty on the outside, but I gave up hope a long time ago that he knows what it means to be decent."

He seemed nice enough to me, but then what do I know?

"I'll try to keep my distance," I tell her, though I'm not sure the promise will be kept. It's been so long since I've been interested in a guy, even longer since anything actually came from it. My life hasn't allowed for much romance in between work and bus routes, overdue bills and worry for my future.

I stand to excuse myself so I can go get another glass of champagne, and I take my time strolling around the perimeter of the party. I have the advantage since I know so few people here. I slip by groups undetected in the crowd and can observe everyone from a distance. Jewels sparkle. Champagne fizzes. Dresses swirl in heaps of fabric on the dance floor and I stand apart from it all, sipping a glass of champagne near the doors that lead out to the back terrace and the gardens beyond.

I feel a chill run down my spine, an awareness that seeps in slowly as I bring my glass to my lips and take a shallow sip.

I scan the perimeter of the dance floor with narrowed eyes, halting suddenly when I spot a man staring at me.

He stands across the ballroom, a devil in black. His tailored tuxedo glides over his tall figure. His half-mask conceals most of his face, but the parts I can see hint that the unveiled image would stop me in my tracks. He has a strong jaw, dark thick hair, and unsmiling lips.

Just a brief glance from him makes the hairs on the back of my neck stand on end. I don't know him, but he's staring like he knows me. Like he *hates me*, rather. He tilts his head as he continues to study me and my heart is a hummingbird, racing in my chest. I have the urge to get away even before he starts to cut through the crowd to get to me. A hunted animal knows when it's time to run, so I do. I slip through the double doors that lead out to the empty garden.

But the devil follows.

10
NICHOLAS

I knew Maren would be here and yet I'm shocked to see her. To find her still in my grandmother's employ, as a guest at her ball, draped in jewelry and clad in a very familiar white gown has fury unfurling in my stomach.

She's here, a physical embodiment of Michael Lewis and all the other leeches who've come before him. They see my grandmother as an easy target. They mistake her generosity for a weakness, and they feed off of it.

Maren glides around the room on air, and for a moment, at first glance, I'm struck by her looks, but then I remind myself that her beauty shouldn't be surprising at all. It all fits. It's just another weapon I'm sure she's quick to use to her advantage.

My jaw locks tight as she continues to turn heads. Everyone she passes takes notice. She sweeps past in white lace and leaves necks bending in her wake. She could have anyone here eating out of the palm of her hand with one wag of her finger, as I'm sure she's well aware.

When she picks up a champagne glass and brings it to her lips, I assume it's for show. She has to know how many of us are watching her right now, studying her every move. My eyes narrow and then, suddenly, she glances up and her gaze meets mine. It feels like a solid punch to the gut. Surprised green eyes take me in cautiously, and I'm glad she found me staring so angrily at her. It means the pretense is over.

She frowns, confused by my expression, but I don't soften it. I stare, willing her to see that the jig is up. She's been found out.

Leave, my expression demands, and she listens, just not in the way I would have wanted.

She slips out of the ballroom and walks out into the garden. I follow instinctively, reaching up and untying the ribbon holding my mask in place then stuffing it into the pocket of my tuxedo pants.

The tension inside me only builds with each step I take. Endorphins rush in, anticipating my encounter with her as I step outside.

The ball extends out into my grandmother's rose garden, which has been lit up for guests with twinkle lights that droop heavily from the trees. It's early though, and no one has made it out here yet, except for me and Maren. It's easy to spot her as she walks farther away from the house toward the cliffs at the back edge of the property.

I wonder if she knows I'm following her. I wonder if she wants me to. After all, she's walking slowly, and it doesn't take me long to catch her. If her intent was to slink away unnoticed, she could have tried a little harder.

When my pace matches hers, she stops in the grass and wraps her arms around her waist. I can't tell whether it's from the slight chill in the air or fear of what's about to happen.

I stop too, turning to face her so the lights in the trees shine behind her. She takes on such an ethereal form that I find myself unable to speak.

Who is this person and why is she here? With *us*?

"I was hoping you wouldn't follow me," she says, affecting a neutral, almost bored tone. "You seem upset with me, though I have no idea why." She tips her head, studying me. "Do we know each other?"

"No. We've never met."

She looks down, as if expecting me to extend my hand and issue a formal introduction, but I don't.

Her eyes narrow.

"Are you a guest of Cornelia's?" she asks, turning back toward the house briefly as if suddenly nervous to find herself alone out here with a complete stranger.

"Yes. Are you?"

She nods, but then amends her reply. "Well, tonight at least…I am."

"And tomorrow? What happens then?" I ask, tilting my head.

"Oh…I'm…" She shakes her head and glances down self-consciously. "I'll go back to what I was before."

"Her employee?"

She looks back up at me, shocked by my question. "What? How did you know that? *Who are you?* You seem familiar now that I think about it."

"I'm just someone seeking the truth. And who are you?"

"Oh, are we answering in riddles?" The corners of her full lips rise into a smirk. "Compared to everyone else here? I'm no one."

"Is it your intention to *become* someone then?"

Her arms tighten around her. "I doubt that's possible."

A gust of wind blows off the ocean, sending her hair into disarray. The mess only makes her more beautiful. *No*, I think. She's wrong; with a face like that, it's definitely possible.

"So then why are you here?"

To continue taking advantage of my grandmother?

"Like I said…I'm Cornelia's guest," she says, regaining the ground she lost between us, stepping closer to me as if trying to prove she's not afraid.

I have quite a few inches on her, so she has to tilt her head back to meet my eyes. When she does, I'm surprised by how scared she looks, surprised she can feign the emotion so well.

"You're her *employee*."

Her eyebrows furrow in annoyance.

"So what?"

I ignore the question and get on to matters I'm much more curious about.

"Did Cornelia put you in that dress? And what about that necklace? Was it a gift too?"

She reaches up to touch the diamond draped around her slender neck. "Who says this isn't mine?" she challenges with a cool tone.

I huff out a cruel laugh and step closer, wanting to be sure every word is heard over the howling wind. "*I* say so. That necklace once belonged to my mother."

Her jaw drops and she looks down as if seeing her outfit in a different light now. "I didn't know…" she whispers.

As if that makes it any better.

"I think you should leave."

"The party?"

"Newport," I say, my unyielding tone leaving no room for opposition.

"But I'm Cornelia's—"

"Employee. Yes, we're clear on that. And I'm her grandson."

My blunt words slice through the air and she whispers my name under her breath, anger evident as she gives me a once-over. It's like she's trying to memorize what I look like so she can avoid crossing paths with me ever again.

"What a wonderful introduction we've had. I don't think I'll ever forget it. Now, if you're done trying to intimidate me, I think I'd like to go back to the party. As I am Cornelia's *guest*, she's probably wondering where I've gone. I wouldn't want her to think I've stumbled into harm's way."

She picks up the skirt of her gown and puts her back to me, walking quickly up to the house so that I'm left out there alone, stewing in anger as the remnants of her floral scent still linger in the air.

It's one thing for Cornelia to keep her here, quite another for Maren to insist on staying even after I've asked her to leave.

She must really like the gig she's set up for herself—invitations to exclusive parties, decadent jewelry, designer clothes. I wonder how deeply she plans on embedding herself in my grandmother's life and how long she's willing to put up with me.

II
MAREN

When my parents died in a car accident, I was at home alone, reading. It was their anniversary, and my dad had surprised my mom with tickets to a local play. They were due home before my bedtime. Sometime after dinner, police officers came and banged on the front door of our apartment loud enough to wake the dead. When I unlatched the deadbolt and creaked the door open a smidge, a gruff man peered over the top of my head and asked me if there were any adults present in the house.

I told him the truth, but I should have lied.

There was no one to take me in after their accident, no aunts or uncles or well-meaning neighbors. I was placed in the foster care system almost immediately, shunted around from place to place for the next few years.

I think about what it would have been like if Cornelia was my grandmother, how different my life would have been if she'd swooped in and brought me home to Rosethorn after the accident. What a privilege to have a place to feel safe and at peace, never having to worry where I'd live or how to scrounge for my next meal.

I think about this as I go to sleep that night, replaying Nicholas' words in my head.

"I think you should leave."

And go where, exactly? I should have asked him.

It was Cornelia who uprooted my life. She plucked me from Holly Home like I was one of her roses in need of pruning.

I wake up the next morning, surprised that I'm still in a sour mood. Last night was not at all what I was hoping it'd be. After Nicholas and I argued out on the lawn, I found Cornelia, feigned a headache, and ran straight up to my room, locking the door behind me for good measure.

Nicholas' reaction to me was so strong. The way he looked at me across the ballroom—it's like he hated me upon sight. Is that a thing? People drone on about love at first sight, but what about the opposite? Can someone lay eyes on a stranger one time and decide on a whim to hate them forever after?

I'm not saying he doesn't have his reasons for being *slightly* annoyed.

I understand it was probably a shock to see me in his mother's necklace, but I am going to give it back to Cornelia! And what does it matter anyway? Is *he* going to wear the damn thing? I doubt anyone's even laid eyes on it in years. It was probably collecting dust in some forgotten jewelry box inside this palatial house.

And sure, maybe he was also surprised to find me in attendance at the ball instead of working it like all of Cornelia's other employees, but she's the one who invited me, so if he has an issue, he needs to take it up with her.

Even viewing the events of last night through his eyes, there was no reason for him to be so rude. The way he spoke to me, the look of contempt in his gaze—he would have ground me into dust if he had the chance.

Ordering me to leave like that?

Who does he think he is!?

My hands turn into fists at my sides and my molars clench. If he were in front of me right now, I swear I'd throw something at him, the first thing within reach—my pillow, I guess. Shame. Too bad I don't sleep with an anvil handy.

I stay up in my room all morning, telling anyone who comes by that I still have a headache when, in fact, I'm being a coward.

I can't face him again so soon. I still feel caught off guard by last night. So, I stay in my room and shuffle around, cleaning up anything that looks even remotely untidy. When I'm done, I finish a book I borrowed from Cornelia's library and then reach for another. I brought in a new stack two days ago and plopped it down on my bedside table. I thought it'd take me longer to work through it. At this rate, I'll be done by dinner.

Cornelia comes to check on me, worried that I haven't come down from my room yet.

Fortunately, she finds me back in bed reading. Five minutes earlier and she would have stumbled in on me doing push-ups to cure my boredom.

She feels my forehead then lets her hand gently cup my cheek. "Should I send for a doctor? You're flushed."

Yeah, well…I don't work out a lot.

"No!" My response is too emphatic, so I shift gears. "I'm not that sick. It's just a headache, maybe a mild cold. I bet I'll be better by morning." And if Nicholas is still here, well then maybe this cold will linger for another day or two.

"All right. I'll have Patricia bring up something small for you to nibble on."

I almost ask her about Nicholas before she leaves, but I bite my tongue. He's her grandson, and nothing I say against him could possibly go over well. There's no way she'd take my side over his.

In the early evening, I find the courage to quietly roam the halls, mostly owing to the cabin fever that was starting to set in. It's aimless at first, just a way to get myself out of my room, but when I find myself standing in front of Nicholas' portrait, I realize I was in search of it all along.

I stand back and study it, comparing young Nicholas to the man I met last night. It seems impossible that he could have grown more severe and cold, more confident and haughty, but I have the living proof in my memory.

I think of the way he looked out on the lawn, lit by the warm light spilling out of Rosethorn's ballroom. There are details about him I wish I could smudge out with an eraser. His coal black hair set against his tan skin. His clean-shaven jaw locked tight in annoyance. His piercing brown eyes narrowed down at me. His lips forming cruel words. I doubt his mouth has ever felt the joy of a smile. I doubt he knows what it feels like to be kind.

Ha.

After that one brief encounter with him, I know for a fact he's someone I'd like to never see again. And yet, I stand in front of his portrait until Rita finds me and asks what I'm doing.

I jump out of my skin then turn away, ashamed. "Nothing—wandering. Is Nicholas still here?"

"He had lunch with friends and then he had to leave to go back to New York."

I pretend to study a nearby bust. I have no idea who it is, some old guy in a wig. Meanwhile, relief floods my system.

She frowns and glances back and forth between me and the painting of Nicholas. I know she wants to ask me more, but instead she nods down the hall. "Well, come along. I've been looking for you everywhere. Someone sent you flowers."

There's an overflowing bouquet of pink and white peonies waiting for me on the circular table in the front entry. I've never received flowers from anyone, and if you'd asked my thoughts on them before this moment, I would have groaned about it being a silly gesture perpetuated by the Hallmark Channel. That said, now that I'm looking down on two dozen heavy blooms, all meant for me, I can't help but feel a little flutter of joy deep down inside.

Who in the world sent them? I wonder as I pull out the small white envelope nestled in the blooms.

Sorry we didn't get to spend more time together last night. I hope you feel better. - Barrett

I'm smiling even before I realize I'm happy they're from him.

I can't believe it, really.

I read the note again then hold it up for Cornelia to see when she flutters over, curious about the sender.

"Handsome boy. He was sad you'd left the party, and I'm not surprised he sent these." She touches a bloom and twists it so it catches the light. "They're very pretty."

"I'm sorry. It's probably inappropriate that he sent me flowers."

"Why on earth would it be inappropriate?"

"It's just...I don't know the rules. I'm your employee."

"Please stop saying that."

"But it's the truth."

"Well so what? If Barrett wants to send you flowers or take you out, good for you! I hope you have a wonderful time. You might even see him on Wednesday. We have lunch plans at the club with Lydia and Victoria."

Oh good. I feel bad that I left Tori high and dry. I hope her offer of friendship still stands.

"That is if you're feeling up to it," she adds gently.

"Oh, yes. I'm feeling much better, so you can put me to work now. Do you need me to do anything? Help clean up after the party?"

"It's already been done."

"What about dinner?"

"Chef is taking care of it."

"Has the table been set?"

"By Patricia."

"And what about—"

"You know what? If you're so intent on *doing* something, come play a song for me. I haven't heard you on the piano in days."

On Monday, I try to make myself as useful as possible for Cornelia without getting in anyone's way. I offer to walk into town to pick up her dry cleaning, and Collins actually agrees to let me go because he's so busy with other tasks he had to put off to prepare for the ball. When I get back, I unwrap all the clothing and hang everything up in the designated sections of her very organized closet. Once that's done, I cut fresh roses and replenish the vases in the blue drawing room. Then, I join Cornelia for tea, and when she asks me to read a book aloud to her, I happily oblige. We stay there until the early afternoon reading *Pride and Prejudice* together.

At dinner, we discuss whether or not Elizabeth Bennet should have accepted Darcy's first proposal.

"Absolutely not!" I say, slamming my fist down on the table for added effect. "She thinks Darcy is proud and selfish and assumes, at the time, that marriage to him would be absolutely miserable."

"What if it would save her family from poverty?" she prods.

"No. The sacrifice is still too great."

"So then you'll only marry for love?"

"We aren't talking about me," I say, frowning in consternation.

She smiles then. "No, perhaps not."

After dinner, I play her a few songs on the piano and then go to bed that night feeling less guilty than days prior. I like feeling useful, and I think I could make a real place for myself here if I try hard enough.

On Tuesday, Tori calls the house while I'm out on a walk around the property with Cornelia. Apparently, she was serious about the invitation to play tennis.

"I can't go," I say, looking to Cornelia. "I need to help you prepare for the kids from St. Michael's."

"Nonsense. There's nothing left to do. Now hurry and change or you'll keep Tori waiting."

"Change? Into what?"

"Tennis whites, dear. They're in your closet."

Of course they are, because why wouldn't they be?

An hour later, Frank drops me at the entrance to the yacht club, and I rush to the tennis courts near the edge of the property. Tori's already there with our instructor, a giant of a man with a heavy Russian accent who takes his job very seriously. It's a shame considering the fact that Tori and I barely get to chat as he leads us through a round of Olympic-level tennis training. I'm sweating bullets by the time we're done, and Tori sends me an apologetic smile.

"He wasn't like this last time, I swear."

I can't even catch my breath enough to answer her, so I just wave like, *No worries! Unrelatedly, do you happen to know where they keep those paddles to kickstart a heart just in case mine decides to give out?*

"Maybe next time, one of us should fake a limp so he'll go easier on us," Tori teases as we walk through the club toward the women's locker room after our lesson ends. Trophy cases line both sides of the hallway and I peer into a few, catching names that are familiar only because there are streets around Newport that carry the same titles.

Midway down the hall, I'm surprised to spot Nicholas in a framed photo propped against a trophy. He looks younger than he is now, but not a teenager. College age, maybe. He and his friend stand side by side, working together to hoist a large silver chalice up into the air. Nicholas beams at the camera, and I immediately think of my musings from Sunday. Apparently, he *does* know how to smile.

"That's Nicky and his best friend, Rhett," Tori says, coming closer so she can peer into the trophy case as well. "They were both there on Saturday night. Did you meet them?"

"Yes," I reply, studying the missing link between the boy in the painting and the man from the ball. I find it infuriating that he never had to suffer through an awkward stage. "Nicholas, not Rhett."

"Oh good. He's one of my best friends. Rhett is too, but I'm closer with Nicky."

The nickname—or perhaps the close bond it signifies—doesn't sit well with me.

"You're joking. What could you possibly see in him?"

She laughs, but when I turn to look at her, pressing for an actual answer, she shrugs. "He's loyal and kind."

I nearly clasp a hand over my chest in disbelief. "You're joking. Nicholas Hunt? Cornelia's grandson? *Kind*?! Are we talking about the same person?"

She cracks a smile. "He can be shy at times, sure, if that's what you're referring to."

Shy is not a word I'd use to describe that man. Arrogant, yes. One hundred percent.

Shy? *Ha.*

"How long have you known him?" I ask. Maybe it's a recent thing. Maybe she's never heard him speak before.

"My whole life. He's only a year older than me, and we all spent our summers in Newport together."

Well there goes that theory. Maybe he's different with her. It's understandable. She's of his world; I'm not.

"How old are you?" I ask, wondering more so about Nicholas' age.

"Twenty-eight." She jostles her shoulder against mine. "What did he do to you anyway? He seems to have left quite the impression."

"Oh, nothing. Just rubbed me the wrong way I guess," I say, moving away from the trophy case and hoping she'll drop the subject.

I compare myself to Tori while we're at lunch with Cornelia and her grandmother the next day. There're the obvious physical differences between us. I have curves where she has none. She carries her body in a delicate way, like she's a cloud floating above us, never quite touching earth. I seem to produce twice as much noise as she does at any given moment. Scooting in my chair, knocking my fork against my glass of water, jostling the tea cakes. I try to mimic her pin-straight posture and garner a curious stare from Cornelia.

"Are you all right, child? Quit fidgeting."

She's right. There's really no use.

"Nicholas will be in town this weekend," Lydia says, nodding to Tori. "Do you have plans to see him?"

She smiles sweetly. "Not yet. I'm sure we'll have lunch again on Sunday before he heads back to the city though, and he's sworn he'll take me out sailing again soon."

"If he does, you'll have to take Maren with you," Cornelia replies. "She's never been before."

A hearty, no-thank-you laugh spills out of me, and then I quickly clear my throat and offer an additional, "It's okay. It's not really my thing."

Being out on open water with Mr. I Think You Should Leave? *Hard pass.*

Tori smiles curiously. "Do you get motion sickness?"

I think back to the time Ariana forced me to sneak into a sketchy roadside carnival when we were teenagers. We rode every single death-defying ride twice thanks to the generosity of a weird carnie who enjoyed the way Ariana flirted with him. Leading him on wasn't one of her best moments. Thinking back, Ariana seems to have a lot of those. Anyway, my stomach was just fine the whole night.

"No, I have a stomach of steel," I say, reaching for another tea cake as if to prove it.

"Then you'll have to come." Tori beams. "It's an experience you'll never get anywhere else, and you couldn't ask for better yachtsmen. Rhett and Nicky have been sailing their whole lives."

I make a noncommittal show of acceptance and then go on sipping my tea while they make plans for a formal dinner this weekend. I assume I'm not included, but Cornelia clarifies on the way home that I'm expected to dine with them.

I don't even bother suggesting that maybe I should be *serving* the dinner rather than eating it. There's no hope where Cornelia is concerned. She's intent on treating me like I'm her guest, and I don't feel like continuing to fight her on it. I like her and I like living at Rosethorn. Besides, I've worked out an arrangement in my head. I'll continue to make myself as useful as possible to Cornelia, and in return I'll accept room and board. There's no refusing the clothing and gifts she seems intent on giving me, but I'll consider them on loan for the time being. It's not as if I'll take any of it with me when I leave. Why on earth would I need tennis whites back in the real world?

I've also decided I won't cash my paychecks. I still only have the one, but it's been burning a hole in my bedside table, taunting me. I know if I tried to give it back to Cornelia, she wouldn't take it. I could rip it up right in front of her, but I have no doubt there'd be a new one sitting on my bedside table the very next day, probably made out for twice the amount of the original.

Obviously, I could really use the money. I'll need it after I leave, but even knowing how far it could get me doesn't convince me that I actually *need* it. I can't accept it. I won't. She's giving me more than enough already.

I justify my decision by telling myself I'll leave here no better or worse than I was before my arrival. Actually, that's not quite true. I'll leave here with a whole array of knowledge I never possessed before, all of which pertains to a world I'll likely never enter into again. Formal dining, floral arranging, dress code for any event under the sun, party planning, hosting duties—it's all layering over knowledge I've used to survive until now. How long to nuke a bowl of ravioli without turning it into magma. How long a pair of shoes will last if you take good care of them. How far $5 will stretch at the grocery store.

At the very least, maybe Cornelia will give me a good reference for another job.

The next day, Vivien returns with garment bags filled with dresses, a dozen of them perfectly tailored to my measurements. I try on each one behind a silk screen in my room and then walk out to *oohs* and *aahs* from Vivien and Cornelia. There's a pale pink ball gown with lots of tulle. A blue strapless midi dress with a sheath skirt. A short flirty day dress with a light floral print. They're all impeccable and ridiculously well made. My favorite, however, is a silky dark green cowl-neck dress that gathers tightly around my waist before cascading like a waterfall down to the floor. The spaghetti straps crisscross in the back, dipping low, so that a traditional bra won't work with it. Vivien has me covered, though—naturally. She's also brought a myriad of lingerie choices, and I'm more than slightly horrified when she starts to pull them out.

Cornelia doesn't even bat an eyelash.

"You'll wear the green dress on Saturday for dinner. It complements you so well."

My stomach squeezes tight at the reminder of Saturday and who else will be present at the meal: the man I'm still not quite ready to see again.

12

MAREN

I shouldn't have worried about Nicholas. He doesn't arrive at Rosethorn on Friday like Cornelia was hoping he would. Work keeps him in the city through Saturday morning as well, and I'm forced to hide my devious smile behind a rose bush to keep her from asking questions.

In the late afternoon, I help her set the table with Diane. It's going to be a small group, and we set place cards for ourselves along with Tori, Lydia, and Dr. Reynolds, a humanities professor from Salve Regina University whom Cornelia thinks I'll enjoy talking to. We put a card out for Nicholas as well, just in case he arrives late, but Cornelia isn't very hopeful. Just in case, I make sure he and I are as far away from each other as possible, though it's not nearly far enough. Dr. Reynolds, as Cornelia's honored guest, has to take the seat at her right, and Lydia will fill the spot to Cornelia's left. I'm beside Lydia with Tori across from me, and then Nicholas will (hopefully not) be next to her.

We arrange centerpieces with the flowers we clipped from her gardens, and when we're done, Cornelia goes down into the kitchen to review tonight's menu with Chef. Everything is written in French, so I don't know why she insists I join her, but then it's probably because she wants me to learn. I do actually pick up a bit of what they're saying. The cherry pie will be stuffed with hen…or something like that. Who knows. The smells are delicious, at least.

Once that's done, I'm ordered back to my room to get ready. Why she thinks it should take me two hours to make myself presentable, I have no idea. Rita is a miracle worker, and she can somehow wrestle my hair into a romantic updo and sweep on some makeup in less than an hour. I use the extra time to sit in a robe in my bathroom, peering out through a small window that faces the gravel drive, praying he doesn't arrive. My stomach is a twisted knot of nerves as the sun falls completely away, leaving me with nothing but moonlight. Cars start to pull up to the house and I know I need to stand and put on my dress or I'm going to be late, but I stay there until the last possible second, convincing myself he won't show up.

After I dress, I walk downstairs to find Cornelia standing in the receiving room, greeting her guests. I'm introduced to the professor, who grips my hand in both of hers, greeting me with a wide smile.

"Pleasure to meet you," she says, and I find myself repeating the sentiment back to her.

She has long frizzy gray hair pushed back by a black headband, and large red glasses stand out against her thin face. Her brown and black plaid jacket is rolled up at the sleeves, revealing a surprising bright blue lining underneath. I like her immediately.

"Are you from the area?" she asks, keeping hold of my hand.

"No, actually. I grew up in Providence."

"So did I." She beams. "I only live here now because of my position at the university. Do you attend?"

At this point, Tori and Lydia have arrived as well and are listening in on our conversation. I don't mind. I'm not sure exactly what Cornelia has told them about me—I know they've heard bits and pieces—but I'd rather they know the whole truth.

My eyes widen. "University? *No*. No, I work for Cornelia."

"In what capacity?" Dr. Reynolds asks, curious.

Cornelia steps in to answer before I can, no doubt because she realizes I would botch the answer.

"She's my right-hand woman. She's helping me run Rosethorn, and more than that, she's a friend and guest in my home. I've taken her under my wing, so to say."

"How lovely. I can only imagine how difficult it is to manage one of these Gilded Age mansions. I've been telling you for years that you needed to take on a conservator."

Cornelia drops her hand to my shoulder. "Well, with any luck, Maren will fit the bill."

On our way into the dining room, Tori bumps into me with a wink. "You didn't tell me you work for Cornelia. I thought you were a family friend or grandniece or something."

I blanche. "Sorry, yeah. Yup." I rock back on my heels a bit awkwardly. "I'm her employee."

She laughs. "There's nothing to feel weird about."

I arch a brow, curious to push the subject. "You don't mind hanging out with *the help*?"

She looks horrified. "Do I seem that stuck-up to you? I'll have you know I work too. I manage an art gallery just up the road."

"That's awesome. I should come by sometime!"

"Oh, you like art?"

I shrug. "I think I do. Paintings and stuff?"

What's not to like?

"We deal primarily in contemporary sculptures."

"That too," I assure her, having absolutely no idea what she's talking about.

We all take our places at the table, and I'm doing an internal victory dance over the fact that Nicholas couldn't make it in time for dinner when I spot movement out in the hall. I look over, and my jaw drops. *How? How is he here?!* He's walking down the grand staircase, cinching his black tie tighter around his neck. He smooths it down against his chest and glances up, finding all of our attention on him.

He looks freshly showered and shaved, tan and horrifyingly handsome in his black suit.

How did he possibly sneak in here without me knowing?

"I'm sorry I'm running late," he says, strolling into the room and walking right behind my chair on his path to get to Cornelia. My breath catches in my chest, and I don't release a slow exhalation until he passes back into my line of sight.

He leans down to give her a kiss on the cheek, and she stares up at him adoringly as he rounds the table and takes his seat beside Tori.

"Nonsense. We haven't even started. You remember Dr. Reynolds, don't you?" Cornelia asks, extending her hand toward her guest. "From the university?"

"Of course. It's good to see you," he says, nodding in greeting.

Cornelia continues, "And Lydia and Tori, you know, of course. That only leaves our dear Maren. I hope you two were able to get acquainted last weekend, at the ball? I saw you talking outside."

My attention is on my place setting as I will my heart to slow down.

"Yes."

One word from him and my blood threatens to burst through my veins. I can't look up despite feeling everyone's gaze on me.

Collins and Bruce save the day with offerings of wine and champagne. Nicholas asks for a finger of whiskey, and I sit there, numb.

"And for you, ma'am?" Bruce asks.

His voice shocks me out of my stupor.

"Oh, water is fine. Thank you."

I don't trust myself with anything else.

"Tell me more about your upbringing, Maren," Dr. Reynolds goads. "I'm curious. What school did you attend in Providence?"

"I moved schools a few times," I say with a tight smile, hoping someone will pick up the conversation and run with it.

Alas, Lydia pipes up. "St. Andrew's is in Providence—didn't you have a friend who went there?" she asks Tori.

"Cassie, yes. She liked it a lot."

"I didn't attend St. Andrew's," I say, putting the question to rest. "Or any other private school, for that matter."

The table goes silent.

"And what about your parents?" Dr. Reynolds presses. "Did they not value your education?"

I laugh at the ridiculous question but then restrain myself once I see she's absolutely serious. "Of course they did. They simply couldn't afford to send me to any of those schools."

"What do they do for a living?" Lydia asks.

Had I known I'd be on the receiving end of 21 questions, I wouldn't have come down for dinner. Still, I force myself to answer, not wanting to offend Cornelia's guests. Besides, they're only curious. I would be too. It's obvious I'm the odd man out in this room.

"My parents were bohemians, I guess you could say. My mother was a writer, though she never had anything published, and my father was a musician. Between them, I don't think they had two nickels to rub together. I learned from them, though—more than I ever did at school. We were one of those odd families that didn't have a TV at home. Looking back, they probably couldn't afford it." I look up, somewhat expecting no one to be paying me any attention, but everyone stares, enraptured, so I continue, "No TV meant there was more time for everything else, reading, mostly. We had stacks of old books lining the walls in our living room. My mom had an arrangement with the public library. Every few months, she'd buy a box of books they were trying to get rid of for $5, sight unseen. It was so fun to open that box because we were never quite sure what would be inside. Cookbooks, children's books, old textbooks barely held together with tape, encyclopedias, erotica…" There are a few titters around the table and a pointed smile from Cornelia. "Anyway, we'd rifle through it together, laying claim. I wasn't picky. I couldn't afford to be, I guess."

"Sounds wonderful. You must have really fostered a love for the written word," Dr. Reynolds tells me with a smile.

"I did."

"Reminds me of my Nicky," Cornelia says. "He was such a voracious reader growing up. Sometimes we couldn't even get him to come down to dinner he was so absorbed in whatever book had caught his attention that day."

He doesn't speak up to confirm the statement, his presence a silent force so easily molded by my own insecurities. I take his quiet perusal of me as judgment, his stern expression to mean he was disappointed to have arrived and found me still here, in his realm. I feel distinctly *other* sitting at the table with the rest of them, unsure of myself as I reach for my water glass, embarrassed to find that my hand is shaky with nerves.

I only work up the courage to glance in his direction a few times during dinner, and it's only when I'm confident his attention is pulled elsewhere. I watch while he leans in to say something to Tori, and her resulting smile is an enigma to me. I want to lean forward and plead with her to share his words. *Tell me what he said. Tell me what it's like to sit there and have him lean in close to you like that.* I don't think I'd survive.

When the final course is cleared, Cornelia looks to me with a pleading expression. "Maren, if you're feeling up for it, I was hoping you'd play a song or two for us on the piano."

"Oh please do! I love the piano and I'm horrible at it," Tori says, clasping her hands together hopefully.

I look to Cornelia and nod. "Of course. I'd love to."

Everyone files out of the dining room, Cornelia and Lydia first, then Dr. Reynolds and Tori. I'm the last one in the room besides Nicholas. I think he hovers near the rear to be polite, but then I'm left with him trailing in my shadow down the long hallway between the dining room and the blue drawing room. I want to turn around and talk to him. I want to ask him if he really is shy and if that's why he didn't talk at dinner, or maybe he has something on his mind? His hatred of me, perhaps?

I don't work up the nerve by the time we reach the threshold of the drawing room, and then the moment passes as I'm forced to turn right toward the piano and he veers left to refill his glass.

Everyone starts to take their seats around the room as I adjust the bench in front of the piano. There's plenty of sheet music for me to choose from. Cornelia insisted she wanted to order a new batch of books from the local music store for the kids from St. Michael's to use, so I went and picked them out myself.

I choose a song called "Maribel" by Oskar Schuster, a contemporary composer I discovered thanks to the recommendation from the manager at the store.

I give everyone a chance to get comfortable while I arrange the sheets on the rack above the keys, but what I'm really doing is waiting for Nicholas to take his seat, annoyed when he chooses a chair in my line of sight, slightly apart from the rest of the group. In my periphery, I see him bring his glass to his lips, and I lift my hands and hover my fingers delicately above the keys.

The song starts out slow and sweet, a melody from a child's lullaby. As I continue to play, the song takes shape, growing into something complex and harder to untangle. My fingers fly, and even in the moment, I know I'm playing for him. I resent it. To be laid bare in front of a grand piano—I doubt there's anything more intimate than performing a piece of music to a quiet audience, all eyes locked on me. They watch unblinking, and their attention could be on my hands as they flutter across the black and white keys, or maybe on the back of my neck...my profile...my lips. I'm lost in the music and am therefore exposed, utterly. Like a doe in the woods standing within range of a hunter's arrow.

That's how I feel playing for Nicholas.

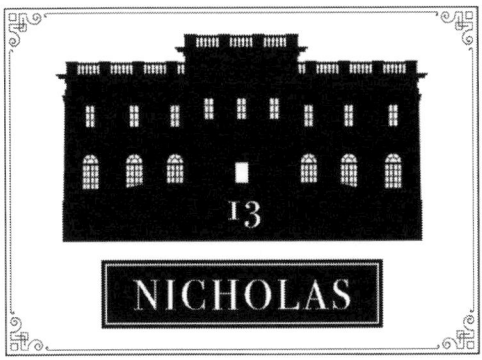

13
NICHOLAS

I've learned a lot about Maren this evening. She's a classically trained pianist, enthusiastic conversationalist, and wonderful addition to a dinner party. I find every detail about her to be more mysterious and confusing than the last. I've seen my friends, peers who grew up in the same life I did, sit at Cornelia's table and become shrinking violets under the steely gaze of my grandmother, but not "our dear" Maren. No, she rose to the occasion.

Even while bombarded by questions that seemed overly personal and rude, she kept her composure and won everyone to her side handily.

I trust her intentions even less now than I did before.

She sits there at my grandmother's piano, so stunning it would hurt to look away, and she reminds me of a wolf in sheep's clothing.

She begins to play a third song, and I glance over to see Cornelia dab at the corner of her eyes with her handkerchief. She's always been heavily influenced by music. A beautiful song played well has always softened her heart, and not for the first time, I worry how much she's coming to care for Maren.

I tried to speak with her again this week about letting Maren go. This time, she wouldn't even entertain the idea. I was halfway through pleading my case when she abruptly cut me off, told me she looked forward to seeing me at dinner on Saturday, and hung up the phone.

Maren plays on, and I stand to deposit my empty glass on a side table. I can't resist the call of my grandfather's antique cigar box, so I lift the lid. I haven't requested them in a while, but Collins keeps it fully stocked. I reach in to retrieve one and grab my grandfather's old lighter, carrying both to the French doors on the other side of the piano.

My footsteps accompany Maren's melody as I cross in front of her. She fumbles a note then quickly recovers and plays on. I doubt anyone else noticed, but I did.

So then I affect her like she affects me?

The thought makes my stomach churn. I'm sure she thinks I'm horrible after our exchange last weekend, but I'm not sure what she expects me to do.

I'm acting on behalf of my family, and I won't apologize for it.

I open one of the doors and stand on the threshold, inhaling the ocean air on impulse before I reach up and light my cigar, taking short puffs until the end glows dark orange in the night.

Standing here makes me think of the night of my eighteenth birthday, when my grandfather first showed me how to light a cigar. I can envision him clear as day, regal and sharp. Everyone knew him as the Commodore, and his legacy lives all around me. I see him in the trophy cases at the yacht club and the portrait gallery upstairs. I see him in the way I practice law, following in his footsteps. He was the one who taught me the difference between right and wrong, between acting for one's own personal gain and acting for the betterment of everyone. He was generous with his time and with his practice of the law but unyielding when it came to his beliefs. I think it's why so many people mistook him as severe, but no one who really knew him thought that. Under the surface, he was the embodiment of warmth.

I miss him as I listen to Maren's music, staring out at the dark churning sea. I ask myself what he would do in my shoes, if he would protect his family above all else.

I know the answer.

It's not much longer before guests start to depart. I send them farewell nods and continue smoking until Maren's music cuts off and she rises to leave the room along with everyone else.

"Maren, I'd like to talk to you for a moment."

Her footsteps stall near the door and, for a second, I'm worried she's about to ignore me.

"That doesn't sound like a request," she ventures.

"It's not," I say, flicking ash off my cigar.

"I can't imagine what you have to say to me now," she replies, pivoting to face me. "You've had all evening to talk."

I find it easier to keep my gaze off her, easier still if I pretend she's no one at all. She's merely a problem I'd like to eliminate.

"Has my grandmother told you about the reporters who've knocked on our doors pretending to be relatives and friends? Who've shown up uninvited to birthday parties and weddings? We've had long-lost cousins appear out of thin air, hoping to slice off a piece of inheritance for themselves. Nosey housekeepers. Thieving drivers. It seems we live with a target on our backs. Easy prey, some would think, especially as my grandmother creeps deeper into her 80s. I hope you understand."

"I do," she replies with a steady voice.

"It's why I can't have you in her life."

She steps toward me, her hand outstretched as if trying to convince me to look her way. "I'm not at Rosethorn to take advantage of her. I swear it."

"No? Then what exactly are you here for?" I say, finally giving in to the urge to turn and take her in from head to toe. A green-eyed siren. "What's your job title? Housekeeper? Assistant? Gardener? Do you have any experience tending soil, Ms. Mitchell?"

Her silence is all the confirmation I need.

"My grandmother is too kindhearted to send you off, but I'm not. My patience for leeches has grown thin over the years. I trust you know how to pack your bags and find your way?"

"I won't leave until Cornelia asks me to," she says with a venomous tone. "Contrary to what you may believe, I *am* of value to her, just not in the conventional ways. *No*, I don't till her gardens, but I eat dinner with her every night and I read to her in the afternoons. We take walks around the garden and we talk. We're friends."

When our gazes lock, she tips her chin up.

"I'm sorry to disappoint you, but I'm not leaving."

She turns and stalks out of the room, her footsteps the only thing I hear, even after she's long gone.

The following morning, I'm headed down to breakfast when I hear shuffling in my grandfather's old office. I know Cornelia has taken to using it in recent years and I expect to find her in there, sitting in his oversized chair, which is why I stop and peer in.

Instead, I find Maren rifling through papers behind the desk, visibly distressed.

"What are you doing?"

Her body tenses and she squeezes her eyes shut as if I frightened her. I probably did.

"Looking for your grandmother's glasses," she replies, not a hint of kindness in her tone.

"Well they're clearly not there in those papers."

She stops her search and glares up at me. "Are you insinuating something? If so, I'd rather you just say it."

I have the uncanny urge to smile and let her know I'm partly teasing. I don't think she's dumb enough to sneak around my grandmother's office in the middle of the day, especially while I'm still here. Besides, she didn't even shut the door.

When I don't reply, she continues her search, but not for long.

With a huff, she dips down to retrieve a pair of my grandmother's reading glasses that had fallen onto the ground. Mission complete.

"I wasn't snooping," she says as she brushes past me.

I have no choice but to follow after her, listening as she curses me under her breath.

We turn a corner and I could quicken my stride and catch her with ease, but I know she'd hate it. Instead, I speak up. My voice is deceptively casual, though we both know I'm trying to get a rise out of her. "You know we're going to the same place. There's no need to walk three steps ahead of me. I think we're capable of having a cordial conversation."

She laughs caustically. "We aren't."

Down in the breakfast room, my grandmother sits with the newspaper held up a mere inch from her face. When she hears our footsteps, she folds it down and sighs gratefully.

"I knew you'd find them, dear. Hurry along, I'm trying to read this story about azaleas and it's giving me eye strain."

Maren shoots me a pointed told-you-so smirk as she hands her the glasses before turning to the breakfast buffet.

"It looks like you picked up a stray on your way back down," my grandmother adds, winking at me.

"Not by choice," Maren murmurs under her breath as she starts to fill her plate with toast and sausage and eggs.

"What was that?" my grandmother asks.

"I said, 'What a glorious day it's going to be!'"

I smile despite myself and Maren catches it, her eyes going round as saucers.

I immediately drop it and clear my throat, moving along to fill my plate as well.

"What are your plans for the day, Nicky? Tell me you aren't running back to the city right after breakfast."

"I'm going to the club this morning to sail."

"You are? You should take Maren with you! We were just discussing the fact that she's never been before."

"No!" Maren says, shooting the word out of her mouth so fast it's a wonder I don't feel it whoosh past like a bullet.

"But Nicky's a wonderful yachtsman."

"I'm sure he is," she says, glancing at me. I swear she's sizing me up, but I can't be sure. "Even still, I'd rather not. Besides, you and I were going to prepare those baskets for the Boys and Girls Club, remember?"

I'm frowning, and it takes me a second to realize why exactly her answer annoys me so much. It's not like I want her to come sailing with me, but her adamant refusal doesn't sit well either. If her plan is to needle her way into Cornelia's life permanently, shouldn't she want to ingratiate herself to me, Cornelia's only grandchild, as well? She should be flirting and smiling and pretending to be a perfect angel.

I nearly choke on the thought. With her rich brown hair and sharp green eyes, angel is the last word I would use to describe her.

"It's better this way," I say, aiming my words at Cornelia. "Rhett and I already have a full boat, and I wouldn't have time to keep an eye on Maren."

"Who says you'd have to keep an eye on me?" she challenges, standing up a bit straighter.

"Spoken like a true sailing novice. Have you never seen a yacht in action? Injuries are extremely common with someone who doesn't know what they're doing."

"It's not as if I'd be the one tying the lines off, or whatever it is you do on a sailboat."

"No, you're right—you'd just be in the way."

Maren and I stand facing each other with our plates in hand, holding each other's gazes as if we've entered into some unnamed competition. Her eyes narrow and seem to say everything she's unwilling to give voice to. I cock my head in challenge.

"Why do I feel like I need to ring a bell and call for a timeout between you two?" my grandmother asks with a deep-set frown.

Maren is the one to look away first, so she can finish scooping some fruit onto her plate before carrying it over to the table.

"Ignore us. We haven't had our coffee yet," she says, smiling at my grandmother.

I finish making my plate and then pull out the chair across from Maren. We do a charming job of avoiding each other through the rest of breakfast, directing conversation through my grandmother. She must realize what we're doing, but she doesn't let on.

Maren is the first to finish and she rises, sweeping a hand down the front of her sundress to flatten the nonexistent wrinkles.

"If you don't mind, I think I'll ask Collins and Chef if they need anything from the market. I feel like going on a walk into town."

Suits me just fine.

I'd like to speak to my grandmother alone, to have one more chance to talk sense into her concerning Maren, though admittedly, as I get started and her eyes plead with me to drop it, I find I'm tempted to take her up on it. Even as I speak, there's less conviction behind my words than there was a week ago, and the thought is unsettling.

I want her gone. Don't I?

14
MAREN

I watch from my window as Tori and Nicholas talk on the driveway Sunday evening. Dappled sunlight spills through the trees, highlighting them from above. Tori is wearing a bright red sweater with a coordinating scarf tied in the French style around her neck. She smiles, and I can't imagine what they're saying. I even creak my window open a smidge, just in case their voices carry, but it doesn't work and I'm left feeling like a stalker.

Tori and a few of Nicholas' friends all arrived at Rosethorn just after breakfast to convene before sailing.

I stumbled upon their group on my way home from town and immediately froze, not wanting to cross paths with them. It's one thing to face off against Nicholas when his grandmother is present and another to do so in front of a group of his peers. If he insulted me while they all watched on, I'd probably throw up on the spot.

I told myself I didn't want to go sailing with them anyway as I circumvented the side of the property, grateful that Cornelia owns so much land surrounding Rosethorn. It was relatively easy to slip by them unnoticed as I trailed through an overgrown patch of trees. Sure, my legs got scratched up a bit from the brush and brambles in my path, but it was a small price to pay to save my dignity.

I passed the gardeners trimming an overgrown wall of ivy and sent them a wave, then I trailed back behind the house, hugging the wall until I made it to the entrance into the kitchen.

Chef was in there, preparing lunch, and I held up the sack full of ripe peaches I had promised I'd get him at the farmer's market. He had plans to bake them into a pie and I'm sure it's finished by now, but I sit up here, unwilling to move from my window seat.

Nicholas shakes his head at Tori and then motions back to his car—a ridiculous vehicle, by the way. Some kind of vintage Porsche, black and sleek and totally impractical. He leans in to give her a hug and a kiss on the cheek then they go their separate ways, Tori back to her grandmother's house and Nicholas back to New York.

I don't know why that makes me feel sick, but the feeling lingers into the next day and the next, until I arrive at the club for a second round of tennis lessons with Tori.

She greets me with a friendly wave and I try to forgive her for being friends with Nicholas. I try to separate them in my mind. Tori is nice; who cares if she's Nicholas' best friend? She's my friend too.

"Oh thank god," she says, sighing when she sees me. "I was worried you weren't going to show after last week."

"I almost bailed," I tease. "My arms are still sore."

She laughs as if I'm kidding. I'm not.

"Ah, here's our coach now. Don't smile—I have a feeling he feeds off of our happiness."

I can't help but laugh, but it doesn't last long. We're immediately thrown into our warm-up (which I would have previously thought of as a very intense workout on its own) and then it's thirty minutes of balls flying near my face as I try desperately to whack them away with a racquet. I succeed only twice. It's a shitshow, and worse, we have an audience.

Tori's cousin Barrett shows up toward the tail end of our session.

I haven't seen him since the ball two weeks ago, which means I still haven't had the chance to thank him for the flowers he sent.

He waits for us at the gate as we gather our bags, looking sharp in a white button-down and navy pants.

"You two might be the worst tennis players I've ever seen," he says good-naturedly as we walk toward him.

"Lay off, will you?" Tori says with a groan. "We're learning."

"Is that what you were doing? It looked like you were putting every effort into *not* hitting the ball."

She reaches over to shove him playfully but he leans out of the way just in time.

"I have to say, even if you do suck, at least you both *look* the part."

He's not wrong there. I can't imagine what all my gear cost Cornelia: my racquet and its designer bag; my zip-front tank and coordinating skort, both from L'Etoile, a brand I'd never heard of.

"Are you here just to annoy us or are you actually going to say hello to Maren? You know, the girl you've been asking me about nonstop for the last two weeks?"

I blush and look away, but Barrett doesn't seem to mind her disclosing his secrets.

"Yes, well, you haven't done a very good job getting us together. I thought I'd take matters into my own hands today," he says, coming forward to take my tennis bag before I can loop it over my shoulder. "Are you two heading in for lunch?"

"If I say yes, does that mean you're going to join us?" Tori asks, sounding annoyed by the prospect, though I think it's just her way of teasing him.

He grins. "Thank you for the invitation. I'd *love* to."

Barrett's already sitting at the table in the club's restaurant by the time we're done showering off. I changed into a simple blue sundress and flats then looped a scarf around my hair like a headband to keep flyaways from escaping my braid.

Tori's dressed similarly, and though it makes me feel silly to admit it to myself, I'm glad to see I'm starting to blend in so well.

We order drinks, me following Tori's lead with an Aperol spritz, and then I lean back in my chair and listen while she asks Barrett about his weekend.

"Weren't you in L.A. for your friend's birthday?"

"Yeah, Sam turned twenty-five. It was a good time. Small group. Kendall Jenner showed up for a little bit."

"Spare me the namedrops, please." Tori rolls her eyes. "You know I don't care."

He grins and cocks his head toward me. "Maren might."

"You think you'll win her over by bragging about celebrities you've partied with?"

She looks to me as if she expects me to roll my eyes too, but I don't want to be rude.

Instead, I pick up my menu. "What's good to eat here? I'm starving."

Barrett laughs and reaches over to share my menu. "For lunch, I prefer the lobster and endive salad or the grilled salmon, but get whatever you want—it's on me."

"Try all you want, but this isn't a date if I'm here," Tori comments as she browses her menu.

Barrett looks wounded. "As if I would bring Maren *here* for our first date."

I know it's just a game they're playing, trying to rile each other up, but it still leaves me shifting in my seat, unsure of what I'm supposed to do. Play along? Act offended? Flirt right back?

Barrett is cute, and I think if he asked, I *would* accept an invitation for a date, but not while we sit at a table with Tori. Fortunately, he's smart enough to realize that. Instead of pushing the subject, he asks his cousin about her weekend.

"Did you go sailing with Nicholas and Rhett?"

"Yeah, it was really fun. I hadn't been since last summer. It felt good to get back on the water."

"Did you and Nicholas hang out after?"

I frown, wondering what he means. I did see them talking outside of Rosethorn on Sunday evening.

Tori shakes her head, not bothering to look away from her menu. "No, he had to get back to the city."

Were they supposed to do something else? Go out together alone? My confusion must be evident on my face because Barrett laughs. "Maren, haven't you heard? Tori and Nicholas are a *thing*, at least on paper. She's practically been engaged to him since she was born. Cornelia and Lydia have been planning their wedding for years—Newport royalty. I hope I get a front-row seat at the wedding."

"Is that true?" I ask on bated breath.

I knew they were close, but I didn't realize it extended beyond friendship. Now that I think about it, though, it does make perfect sense. They've known each other forever. They had similar upbringings, and they clearly care a lot about each other.

Tori takes a sip of her drink, seemingly bored by the subject. "Oh sure, it's what everyone wants."

"Is it what you want?" I ask again, needing to know, as if the answer is suddenly a matter of life and death.

She laughs sadly. "No one ever seems to ask that question."

"Do you guys want to split an appetizer?" Barrett asks, completely disregarding the conversation at hand.

Tori's attention shifts out the window, to the marina with the sailboats bobbing gently in the calm water.

Her reaction to my line of questioning isn't at all what I would have expected, and her mood only seems to worsen through lunch.

It's not the first time I've noticed Tori draw inward. It's so obvious to me the way her face—with its angular jaw and fine bones—can sometimes look like a mask.

I try to catch her eye across the table, but she turns her attention to our waitress as she comes by to take our order. After that, the moment is gone, swept away by Barrett's antics. He's good at lightening a mood, and Tori lets him carry her blues away. She launches into a discussion about a garden party she's planning for Friday.

"You'll come, won't you?" she asks me. "Barrett can pick you up on the way."

"Yeah. We can get a drink beforehand, if you're up for it," he says, showing more sincerity than he has all lunch. I can tell from his tentative smile that he really wants me to agree, so I nod and then wonder what exactly I'm getting myself into.

At dinner that night, I bring up the garden party to Cornelia, to get her permission to go more than anything else. I know she likes that Tori and I have become friends, but I'm not sure where the boundaries lie—if there even are any—and I'd rather be cautious than presumptuous.

"If you need help with something that day, I don't have to go. Barrett mentioned taking me out for a drink beforehand, but—"

"Sounds like you're going to have a lovely time. We'll have to make sure you have something nice to wear. It's not too late to get something new. We can always have Vivien tailor it quickly for you."

I think of the ever-growing contents of my closet, and I can't imagine a scenario in which I don't have a single dress that could work for the party. If anything, I have too *many* options.

"I'll let you pick something for me after dinner," I assure her, confident that she knows more than I do about how to dress for the occasion. Before moving into Rosethorn, the only parties I attended called for denim cutoffs and a tank top. Something tells me that won't fly for this.

"I'm so happy you're getting settled here and finding friends. Everyone seems to like you as much as I do," she says, smiling warmly.

"Not everyone," I say, before I think better of it.

"Oh?"

I clear my throat and consider trying to evade her questioning gaze, but it's probably best that she knows the truth.

"I don't think your grandson likes me very much. He's made it clear to me on two occasions now." Three if you count our standoff at breakfast over the weekend.

She hums in understanding, not the least bit shocked.

"He's fiercely protective of me. Don't let him deter you, though. I want you here, and that's what matters. Besides, others want you here as well. Tori, for instance, and Barrett, not to mention everyone here at Rosethorn."

I'm glad she's not trying to persuade me into thinking Nicholas *does* like me. We both know that's not the case.

Though, since we're on the subject of her grandson, I can't help but ask. "Are Nicholas and Tori really betrothed?"

She laughs. "What makes you ask?"

"We talked about it at lunch today. Barrett made it sound like it was a done deal."

"I have *hoped* they would develop feelings for one another. I've known Tori since she was a baby and there are few people on earth as gracious as she is, not to mention that I think the match makes sense from a practical standpoint. You catch my meaning? The Pruitts are a very established family here in Newport. There would never be a question of one of them marrying solely for money. They each have their own."

I nod, realizing that's never something I've had to worry about. All the guys in my life have been just as dirt poor as me.

"Has he ever told you he has feelings for her?" I ask, training my voice so I don't sound overly curious.

She furrows her brow in thought. "He can be very English sometimes. He's like his father that way, always one to keep his lips buttoned, his heart locked away. I doubt he'd ever admit to catching feelings. To him, it's akin to admitting weakness."

Cornelia's words stick with me.

I wonder if Nicholas is really as closed off as she says he is. He does seem that way to me, but then I still barely know him. I run through our exchanges, turning them over in my mind and looking for any details I might have missed the first time around. I imagine him in the breakfast room, looking painfully handsome in a navy blue sweater and jeans—dressed down, but hardly.

I want to ask someone—Cornelia or Tori—if he'll be in town for the garden party, but I can't seem to work up the courage. What does it matter anyway? I won't let his presence deter me from going. Besides, I'm not going alone; I'm going with Barrett. I can't imagine what Nicholas will think of that. Will he accuse me of using Barrett too? Laughable. Barrett has made it perfectly clear that he's interested in me, and I find that I'm actually excited to go out with him as I finish getting ready for him to pick me up on Friday.

My short blue dress is thin, so I layer a cream cable-knit sweater over it. It's oversized and hanging off one of my shoulders in a flirty way that makes me feel confident as I walk down the steps of Rosethorn to meet Barrett. I saw on my way out that Cornelia, Rita, and Patricia are huddled in the window in the entry foyer, peering out at us.

"Have a good time!" Cornelia called as I swept past.
"You look beautiful!" Rita added.

I'm still smiling as Barrett gets out of the front seat of his silver Range Rover, coming around to greet me. His cocky smile is in place as he bends down to kiss my cheek.

"You look amazing," he says, holding my hand as he steps back to give me a once-over.

He's wearing khakis and a pale green shirt layered underneath a dark green sport coat.

"Thank you. I hope I don't get chilly. Tori said she was going to set up the table outside."

"Well it wouldn't be a garden party if we ate in the dining room," he quips, and I can't help but blush at my blunder. *Duh.* "But it doesn't matter—you can have my coat if you get cold. My pants too, if you want them," he teases, and I'm immediately put at ease.

There's something nice about Barrett's personality. Yes, he's cocky, but he's also self-deprecating and silly. He chats my ear off as he drives us toward a little wine bar he swears I'll love. Sure, most of what he says is filled with humble-brags or outright-blatant brags, but I don't really mind. I'm intrigued by his life, and I like hearing about it. It's fortunate, too, because he doesn't think to ask me about mine very often.

We spend an hour at the bar, splitting a bottle of white wine, and my mind wanders in a million different directions. I know I'm a little nervous about tonight. I haven't met many of Tori and Barrett's friends, and while Cornelia's have been welcoming to me, I'm not sure that will be the case with people my own age.

It doesn't help, as I realize after the fact, that I'm arriving with Barrett.

The first few people I'm introduced to mistake me for a girl he's been hooking up with in Boston.

"Are you Lauren?!" one guy asks enthusiastically, as if he's happy to finally put a face to a name.

I smile tightly and shake my head. "No, sorry. I'm Maren."

He doesn't even seem that embarrassed about the mix-up, writing me off instantly and turning to Barrett. "Honestly, I can't keep your girls straight sometimes, dude."

Barrett wraps his arm around my waist and tugs me closer as we walk away. "Sorry about that. He's a friend from college, and sometimes I think he forgets we've moved on from the frat house."

I force a smile, not wanting to make an issue of it. It's not like Barrett and I are dating or anything, and who cares if he's seeing some girl named Lauren, really?

While more of Barrett's friends wander over, I search the party for Tori, a task that proves to be harder than I expected. The Pruitts live in another Gilded Age mansion on Bellevue Avenue, one equal to Rosethorn in size, which means their garden is hardly a *garden* and more of a maze of sprawling hedges and fountains and creeping rose vines, all of which make it impossible to see if Tori is out here among the mingling crowd.

Near the house, where a bartender has set up shop to serve drinks, there's a long table with seating for twenty that's overflowing with flowers and candles and fine china place settings. People gather around there, and that's where Barrett leads me until I tell him I'm going in search of Tori.

"Don't worry, I'm sure she's around here somewhere. C'mon, there are some other people I'd like you to meet."

I'm forced into more introductions as "Barrett's date" rather than "Tori's friend", which leads to more questions about how we met and where I'm from and how long we've been seeing each other. It suddenly feels like too much too soon, so I use the good ol' bathroom excuse and find my way inside. The house is quiet compared to the garden, and the moment I make it through the French doors, I sigh in relief.

Then two feminine voices drift from down the hall.

"I just don't understand why it needs to be *today*?"

"You're not listening, Tori! It's not about it being *today* or *tomorrow* or *the next day*. It's about you breaking your word."

"You're upset, but I'm trying—"

Tori's voice trails off and I suddenly feel horrible for overhearing part of a conversation that seems very intimate, so I turn away, down a different side hall in search of a bathroom. I succeed in finding one, but when I finish and walk back out into the hall, I run smack dab into Tori.

"Oh!" she says, dabbing at her cheeks and hiding her face as if I won't notice she's crying.

"Hey, sorry. I just had to pee."

"There's another bathroom, closer to the garden," she says, pointing me in that direction.

I cringe and rock back on my heels. "Of course. Yeah, sorry. I wasn't…I mean…I didn't…" I frown and look away, down the hall, trying to decide how best to proceed. I sigh. "I heard you arguing before. I didn't mean to, but…"

Her eyes widen and then narrow accusatorially. "What? Are you serious?"

I hold my hands up in innocence. "It wasn't intentional. I just came inside to look for a bathroom, like I said. I didn't really hear much. I just wanted to make sure you're okay."

She sniffles and turns away, wrapping her arms around her waist.

"I'm fine."

"Okay, well, if there's anything you need, you know, I'm a good listener."

She nods but doesn't speak up, and I take the cue to walk away.

Any hope of salvaging the night dies a swift death in that hallway. I make it back outside in time to catch the vestiges of the sunset, and the candlelight on the dinner table holds more power now, turning everyone into softer versions of themselves—or maybe it just makes it difficult for people to realize I'm standing right behind them as they talk about me.

"What's with Barrett slumming it?" a guest asks her friend. "Did you hear that girl he brought works for the Cromwells? Like she's a *maid* or something."

"You're kidding."

"It's obvious what he's doing," a third guest chimes in. "She's a curiosity, something fun for him to look at. I bet it doesn't last more than a week."

"Excuse me," I say finally, trying to get through the bottleneck of people.

They turn toward me and burst out in awkward laughter, one of them whispering "Oh my god" under her breath as if she's never found something so amusing or titillating in her life. I look for Barrett and see he's near the bar with a group of guys. He holds up his hand to wave me over, and a flood of anxiety grips hold of me.

There's no way I can stay. In fact, I make my mind up as I walk toward him. "Hey, can I talk to you for a second?"

His brows furrow, and I'm grateful when he doesn't brush me off. "Sure thing."

Once we're out of earshot of his friends, I try on a smile. "Sorry to be a bore, but I'm going to head home. I'm just not up for a party tonight."

"Are you serious?"

My smile strains under the weight of his annoyed gaze.

"Sorry," he continues, shaking his head and easing his initial reaction. "I just really wanted to spend time with you. You aren't having fun?"

How do I put it mildly?

"Oh, you know, I'm just tired after a long week, and these are *your* friends."

"But they could be your friends too."

I'm not sure I want them to be, honestly.

"Maybe another night," I tell him, taking a step back as if to initiate my departure. If there were a button I could press to shoot me straight up into the air, I'd use it.

"Let me take you home at least," he says, looking for a place to set down his drink.

I shoot my hand out to touch his arm. "No, it's okay. Frank's outside."

"Really?"

There's disbelief in his tone, and well, there should be—I'm definitely lying.

Then one of his friends shouts his name, calling him back over to the group, and that's that. Barrett gives me a swift kiss on the cheek and promises to get in touch with me soon, and then I'm a free woman.

I try to spot Tori one more time on my way out, but she still hasn't come back outside. So, I curve around the side of the house and walk home along Bellevue Avenue with the gilded castles and marble mansions shining in the moonlight. My flats almost immediately start to chafe my heels, and now that the sun's down, the air is chilly. I hug my arms around my waist to ward off the cool air and pick up my pace, eager to get back to Rosethorn, my safe haven.

The imposing gates come into view and I skip ahead, waving at Neal in the guard house so he can buzz me through the small pedestrian gate that sits beside the huge one. I close it after I walk through and it locks automatically behind me. I sigh in relief as I turn to walk up the winding path that eventually deposits me in the driveway. Immediately, I look toward Nicholas' parking spot and hold my breath until I see that it's empty.

As I make my way to the house, shoulders slumped, I wonder if I left the party because I wasn't having fun or because he wasn't there.

15 MAREN

Nicholas didn't arrive at Rosethorn on Friday, and it leaves me continually on edge the next day, as if he's going to appear out of thin air at any moment. All day, I peer around every corner before I proceed down a new hallway, I make sure I'm always presentable when I go downstairs, and I try very hard to get my brain to concentrate on anything other than him. By sundown, he still hasn't arrived.

A small package arrives for me on Sunday morning. I assume it's from Barrett, but when I open it up, I find a handwritten note on personalized stationery. The letters VP are interwoven near the top in embossed ink. Below it, a handwritten message.

I'm sorry for how I acted on Friday. I was sad to find that you'd left the party early. Please say we're still friends? - Tori

Beneath the note, she included a new book of sheet music, and the gesture instantly eases my anxiety. At least I still have one friend in Newport outside of Rosethorn's gates.

I spend the evening playing songs from the book, aware of different staff members trickling in and out of the room to listen. Cornelia lets them have more flexible hours on Sunday, to go to church or see their families or just relax, so Collins and Frank and Patricia sit on the couches in the blue drawing room listening to me play until my fingers ache.

On Monday, Cornelia says there's nothing on the agenda for the day, so I keep myself busy on my own. I clip roses in the garden. I collect Cornelia's mail and bring it to her with her afternoon tea, then I read to her for a little while. I convince Chef to let me help prepare dinner while Cornelia lies down to rest. He doesn't really let me touch anything, but I'm allowed to bring him ingredients and watch him work *if* I keep a healthy distance.

Tuesday morning, a group of high school students arrive by bus to tour the first floor of Rosethorn and the surrounding grounds. Apparently, they do it every year. It's an arrangement set up through the Preservation Society in exchange for a small donation from the school district. Many of their students—like me—have grown up hearing about the Gilded Age mansions but have never seen them for themselves. Cornelia has me accompany her during the tour, and I watch the amazed expressions on the student's faces as they enter Rosethorn for the first time.

While I'm on the tour, Tori calls and leaves a message for me with Patricia.

Change of plans for our lesson today. Bring your swimsuit. Leave your racquet at home.

To say I'm relieved is an understatement. I'm beginning to *hate* tennis. Upstairs, in my room, I find a few swimsuit options in my closet, though I have no idea who picked them—someone who doesn't have boobs to support, apparently. Reluctantly, I grab a pale blue bikini and a cover-up, and I'm extremely excited to show up at the club to find that our tennis lesson has indeed been canceled for the day.

Tori waits for me near the courts wearing a colorful sarong and a wide-brimmed hat. She has two fruity-looking drinks in her hands with little umbrellas sticking out of the tops, and she holds both of them up with a smile.

"This is me apologizing for the weekend."

"You didn't have to do this," I say, accepting one of the glasses from her and taking a small sip. The piña colada is delicious.

"Sure, well, I figure we could use a break from tennis anyway. I really am sorry, you know. You caught me at a bad moment."

"Do you want to talk about it?" I ask as we approach the pool.

"What is it with you?" she teases. "Most people run from awkward conversations."

I shrug. "It's not a big deal if you'd rather keep things private."

"*Private.*" She groans at the word. "My whole life has been private. I can't breathe for risk that I'll accidentally spill all my secrets."

"Do you have a lot of them?" I prod.

"Just one," she says, looking away.

"You don't have to tell me," I assure her. "It's none of my business."

"I know, which is precisely why I want to tell you. You fluttered into Newport like some rare butterfly and

I fully expect you to leave just as quickly, so there's no real risk in telling you this *thing*. At least, it's not as risky as telling my family."

"You're making it sound like you've committed murder."

She studies her drink as we continue walking toward the pool. "It's nothing like that at all." Then she puffs out a breath and shakes her head like she's trying to build up her courage. "Right. Let's just think of it like a Band-Aid. How to…well…you know the other day at lunch with Barrett, when you were asking me about my relationship with Nicholas?"

My heart sinks and I do a small stutter step, enough to slosh some of my drink over the lip of my cup. Thank god she's too absorbed in her own confession to pay attention to me.

"Ye-yes, I remember."

"We've known each other for so long, and he's been wonderful to me."

I want to ask her for details—*How has he been wonderful?!*—but I sense it's not the right time.

"I think he and I would fit together so well, and you know our families would love it."

Just say it! I want to scream. *Say you're in love with Nicholas.*

"But I'm in love with someone else."

I stop on my dime.

"Someone else?" I repeat, dumbstruck.

She glances back at me. "Yes."

"*Who?* Do I know him?"

"Her."

"What?"

She smiles flatly. "Do you know *her* would be the correct question to ask."

"Oh. *Oh!*"

"There you have it. You don't need to look so surprised."

"I don't mean to. It's just that I really thought you were in love with Nicholas."

She laughs. "Yes, well, Nicky isn't my type."

"Apparently not." I think back to the party and the woman I heard her arguing with out in the hallway. "Was your girl—er…friend…was she at the party on Friday?"

Her light mood dissipates in an instant. "Yes, Mary Anne. Well, she was there in the beginning, and then she left before you."

"Because of the fight?"

"Because I was unwilling to do what I'd promised her. I had planned on introducing her to everyone that night as my girlfriend, but then I got cold feet. It's happened before. It's a lot…you know, to announce to a room full of people you've grown up with your whole life that you're not the person they thought you were. People expect me to adhere to a certain mold, and I'm ashamed to admit that I wasn't quite ready to come out to everyone. Mary Anne has been patient with me about it, giving me time."

"But she was upset you changed your mind?"

She cringes. "I know that paints her in a bad light, but you have to understand. Mary Anne has been openly proud of her sexuality for years. She flaunts it with pride, and she can't understand why I'm dragging my feet about it."

"If it makes you feel better, I certainly don't care."

Tori laughs. "I knew you wouldn't."

I stare at her for a moment, thinking back on the times when I thought she was reserved, now realizing how hard it must be for her to live two lives, pulled in opposite directions.

"Do you think your family won't approve?"

We reach a pair of pool chairs and she dumps her bag down onto one. "Honestly, I have no idea. My grandmother can be conservative at times, but I know she loves me. And well, my parents have both been divorced so many times, I don't think they have a leg to stand on when it comes to lecturing anyone about who they can and cannot love."

"Barrett will make a crass joke, I'm sure. Just prepare yourself now."

She rolls her eyes but smiles nonetheless. "I wouldn't expect anything less of him."

"And Nicholas?" I prod, curious to hear how she thinks he'll handle the news.

She smiles then. "Oh, Nicky has always known. He's the first person I told, actually, and he's kept my secret for me. I'm not sure what I would have done if I didn't have him to confide in for all these years."

She called him loyal weeks ago, and now it makes sense.

I frown in confusion, unsure of where to place this newfound knowledge about Nicholas. It doesn't exactly fit in the "I hate him" column I've been constructing so carefully, but it certainly doesn't make me like him either—or if it does, I don't admit it to myself. Opening my heart to a man like him feels like a dangerous game I'm not quite ready to play.

That day, Tori and I transition from acquaintances to real friends, ones with a secret bonding them together. We sit at the pool, sunbathing beneath the blue and white striped umbrellas, ordering drinks, and working through scenarios for how she could win Mary Anne back.

On Friday afternoon, I carry a tea tray toward the blue drawing room, surveying the careful arrangement. Patricia helped me set everything up down in the kitchen: cucumber sandwiches and bite-sized blueberry tarts on one side, the tea set on the other. In the middle, I placed a small bouquet of pale green hydrangeas from Cornelia's garden.

I think it looks nice, and I'm proud to carry it into the drawing room and share it with Cornelia. We have plans to continue reading *A Room With a View*. I hadn't read Forster before, but I've enjoyed his writing so much that I'm practically giddy with anticipation to pick up where we left off yesterday.

In the hall outside the drawing room, I hear Cornelia speaking, and then a beat later, Nicholas answers. My heart lurches in my chest.

I didn't witness his arrival at Rosethorn, and I curse myself for not keeping a better eye out. I glance down at my clothes and scrunch my nose. My loose cotton sundress, while extremely comfortable, isn't what I would have chosen for facing Nicholas again after two long weeks. The pale pink color makes me feel girlish and silly viewed through his eyes. I'm tempted to turn around, run up to my room, and change, but I don't want the tea to get cold and have Cornelia ask me questions about what took me so long. I wouldn't want to lie to her, even about something as trivial as this.

So, with a resigned sigh, I approach the doors and balance the tea tray on one hand so I can turn the door handle with the other, but then Cornelia speaks again, sharp and clear.

"Don't bother bringing it up again. I won't listen to you slander Maren. You're wasting your breath."

I frown, wounded that we're still on this same carousel, looping around and around as I continue to try to prove myself to Nicholas and he continues to think the worst of me. I've been here for over a month. I have two paychecks sitting uncashed in my bedside table. I've done nothing wrong except enter his world without his permission. Apparently, I'll never live down that crime.

With a newfound resentment for him, I push into the drawing room and pretend I haven't heard a thing.

Nicholas' response is cut off so I don't hear what he was about to say, but I have no doubt it would have been rude. I don't feign surprise at seeing him sitting on the couch across from Cornelia. Instead, I give him a curt nod and look away as quickly as possible, not that it helps. His image is burned in my memory instantly. He's sitting in tailored dark gray pants and a white button-down, the color contrasting sharply against his tan skin and midnight hair. He's frowning in consternation, but that's nothing new. It's the expression I'm most used to seeing from him.

He doesn't put on any airs or offer any greetings as I walk farther into the room. Instead, he watches me like a hawk as I cross in front of Cornelia and set the tray on the coffee table between them.

"Sorry for the interruption," I offer, sending the words in Cornelia's direction. They're for her benefit, not his.

"Nonsense. I was only just greeting Nicky. He arrived from New York not long ago."

"If I'd known, I would have brought another cup, but he's welcome to mine," I say, standing and stepping back from the table, preparing to leave them to it.

"You won't stay and chat with us?" Cornelia asks, sounding unhappy with the idea.

"No. I'm sure you two want some time to catch up. I was hoping to find some time to read today anyway."

"I don't care for tea," Nicholas says. "You might as well take it."

What kindness! Someone—quick—commemorate it with a plaque!

"Actually, this works out well," Cornelia says, nodding. "You two stay. I'm going to have a quick lie down as I feel more tired than usual today. I think it's the heat starting to creep in. Summer has found us, I'm afraid."

She stands and so does Nicholas, sharp and immediate, like a well-trained gentleman.

"No, no," she says, batting him away. "You sit down and entertain Maren. She's been running around all week, working herself to death, and I'd like you two to chat and get to know each other better."

I peer at Nicholas and it's clear she's just given him something akin to a death sentence, yet he doesn't leave.

I open my mouth to protest myself, but I realize it'll go over better after Cornelia leaves. We just need to wait her out.

She steals a blueberry tart off the tray, shoots me a wink, and flutters out of the room, not looking half as tired as she claims to be.

Once she leaves and closes the door after her, I stay standing, and so does Nicholas. Clearly, neither one of us is sure how to proceed.

I start to talk at the same time he does.

"You don't have to—"

"If you'd rather read—"

I laugh and shake my head, trying to break myself out of this shell of self-consciousness I'm trapped in any time I'm in his presence. It's the most ridiculous thing. I start by looking at him while he walks over to a side table to pour himself a small shot of amber liquor from an antique decanter, and I convince myself he's just a man. Tall and intimidating, sure, but no less mortal than the rest of us.

"Will this be a waste of time, do you think?" I ask, cutting through the bullshit. "If you're standing there with the same opinion of me you had a few weeks ago, I'd rather save my breath."

He laughs and tosses back the liquor before pouring himself another shot, this time sipping on it slowly as he turns to glance at me over his shoulder. His dark eyes hold me captive.

"Do you want a glass?" he offers, holding up his own.

"No thank you. I don't drink hard liquor this early in the day."

It's meant as a barb, and he takes it as one. "I don't either, except when I'm locked in a room with a feral cat."

I narrow my eyes. "You see that's rude, don't you? You can't expect me to like you when you say things like that."

He chuckles under his breath and shakes his head, turning toward me fully as he makes his way back to his spot on the couch. "Yes, well, you struck first with the insinuation that I'm an alcoholic, so neither of us has clean hands here."

I refuse to admit he has a point. Instead, I walk over to the side table to pour myself a small serving of the same liquor he's drinking, realizing I might need it. It's hardly a shot's worth, but still, when I take the first small sip, I know I won't be able to finish it.

"That's *horrible*," I hiss as it burns its way down my throat.

"It's thirty-year-old single malt whiskey. My grandfather's favorite."

Good thing he can't see the face I'm making or he might be insulted.

"Were you close with him?" I ask, venturing into polite conversation. We might as well *try*.

"Extremely. I spent more time with him and Cornelia than I did with my own parents."

"Oh? Why's that?" I ask, walking back across the room to take a seat on the couch facing his.

"Because, like you, I lost my mother and father when I was a young teenager."

"How?" I frown and lean forward, curious to gather pieces of humaneness from a man who seems to have so little.

His reply is issued with a clipped tone. There's no sentiment behind it. "Cancer took my mother when I was thirteen, and my father returned to England that same year."

"So he's still alive?"

"Yes, but we haven't spoken in years. To me, he's as good as dead."

His words rub me the wrong way.

"Spoken like someone who has a choice in the matter," I point out.

"Of course, compared to your position, it must seem cruel of me to say so, but our situations are entirely different. From what I understand, you were close with your father. I never had a relationship with mine, and what tenuous bond we did have disintegrated completely when he abandoned me to move back to England after my mother's death."

"You could have gone with him."

"I wasn't invited," he replies curtly before taking a sip of his drink.

My stomach churns thinking of Nicholas at the age he was in the portrait upstairs. A young man with no parents, not so unlike me.

"Was he upset about your mother?" I venture. "Is that why he left suddenly?"

I know people make poor decisions when they're grieving. It's not exactly an excuse, but maybe it's a reminder that we're all just humans trying our best.

He laughs, and it rings out harshly through the room. "Not in the least. My mother was a dollar princess. Have you heard the term before?" His bold dark eyes seek out mine, and I find I can't look away. "Her marriage to my father was arranged for very specific benefits. The

Cromwell wealth kept the Hunts' English estates afloat, and in exchange, my mother became a countess. Cash in exchange for a title."

"How sad."

His gaze pierces mine. "It happens every day. Don't delude yourself."

I sit back, wounded by his sharp rebuke.

He sighs and looks away to clear his throat, seemingly remorseful, though he doesn't say so. "Anyway, my father was glad for the freedom. No pesky wife and kid holding him back anymore."

"I'm sure he loved you in his own way."

"I gave up that naive hope a long time ago." He drains the rest of his drink. "And no matter. I had more family than I knew what to do with, my grandparents and everyone here at Rosethorn. I didn't miss him all that much."

"How lucky for you."

I didn't share the same luxury, and no doubt from his conversations with Cornelia, he knows it. Realization seems to dawn on him, and he glances back to me. For a moment, we sit silently staring at one another, and for the first time since we met, I feel like there's a tether within reach if only one of us would grab it.

He frowns, his eyes holding mine captive.

"I can't figure out who you are, Maren," he says, tipping his head to the side. My heart hammers painfully in my chest as his eyes search mine for answers. "Are you a con artist with a devious plot or an innocent lamb continuously thrashed by unfortunate circumstances?"

I know which way he's likely to lean. Too many people have come before him, expecting the worst of me. I don't have tolerance for it anymore.

I stand and give him a sour smile. "The wonderful thing about my situation here at Rosethorn is that it doesn't matter who you think I am. Your opinion is of no consequence."

Then I turn and leave the room.

16

NICHOLAS

Before dinner, I go out on my boat to clear my head. It's a futile endeavor. The wind doesn't take me far, and I still have energy to burn when I return to the marina. I drive fast on the way home, taking Ocean Drive around the long way, angry with tourists for keeping me from speeding along the winding road. It takes me a long time to get home, but I'm no more satisfied with myself as I loop my car into my parking spot and charge in the back door.

Rich smells waft out from the kitchen, and I'm reminded that I'm likely running behind. I still need to shower before the meal, so I take the stairs two at a time and head straight for my room.

Bruce has already pulled out a dark blue suit for me to wear, hanging it on a hook outside of my closet with an accompanying white shirt. No tie tonight.

I fly through my shower and take the time to shave my five o'clock shadow, knowing my grandmother will appreciate the extra effort. I comb my hair back and slip on my jacket, staring at my harsh expression in the mirror.

It seems my afternoon with Maren is bleeding into the evening. I wonder if she's still upset from this afternoon, but I'm not left with the question for long. We run into each other out in the hallway on our way to the grand staircase.

She's wearing a tight off-the-shoulder dress that's the exact same shade as my suit. It hugs her body and draws my gaze down her curves to the slit that cuts up and exposes one of her tan legs.

I hold out my arm for her to take. It's the polite thing to do. We're both going down to dinner, and if she were anyone else, I'd offer the same gesture.

She reluctantly accepts.

"About this afternoon—" I begin to say as we start to walk, but she cuts me off.

"I hope you're not about to apologize, because I have no intention of accepting a peace offering from you."

"I wasn't going to offer peace," I say, dropping my hand over hers on my arm to keep her in place beside me as we turn toward the stairs. Her hip brushes against me and I'm aware of it on a molecular level. Her scent is so strong. I think it's her shampoo and I'd like to find out, to inhale a deep breath and get a chest full of it.

"Good, so we're on the same page? It's war from here on out?" she asks, and it almost feels like a game. "I'd like to know so I can stay armed."

I stifle the urge to laugh for fear that she'll move away from me. Her hand on my arm is barely there as it is, and I'm worried she'll withdraw it if I say the wrong thing.

"Are you two coming down any time soon or do I have to stand here forever?" Rhett asks, drawing my attention to where he stands in the foyer.

Crap. I forgot I invited him to dinner tonight. Rhett's my closest friend, but I can't say I'm glad to see him, especially when his gaze shifts to Maren and his eyes widen with intrigue.

I can't even begin to unravel my reaction to him. I tug Maren an inch closer. I don't even smile when he looks my way again. I even consider, for one second, marching right to the front door, throwing it open, and telling my oldest friend to get lost. It's absurd.

"And who might this delicate flower be?" Rhett teases, beaming up at Maren as we descend the final few stairs together.

"His name is Nicholas," Maren quips, stepping away from me. I have no choice but to let go of her hand. "Be careful though—he's not a delicate flower. More like a Venus flytrap if you ask me."

Rhett barks out a laugh. "I like you. You're Maren, aren't you? You have to be."

"Yes. And you are…?"

"Rhett," I answer for him. "My oldest friend, who surely won't forget where his loyalties lie."

Rhett extends his elbow to Maren so he can pick up where I left off. "Do you hear something, Maren? An annoying gnat?"

"Nothing at all."

Rhett throws me a grin over his shoulder, and I do him one better by flipping him off.

My grandmother sees and tells me to mind my manners. Then she turns up her charm to greet our guest.

"I'm so happy you could join us for dinner, Rhett. I've been anxious for you to meet our dear Maren."

"I've heard so much about her," he admits, escorting her to the seat to the left of my grandmother. Before he can pull out the chair beside her, I yank it out myself—a tad too hard. Three pairs of eyes fall on me as I sit down and scoot my chair forward with an audible screech.

"You needn't be such a brute about it, Nicky," my grandmother says. "I was going to ask Rhett to sit on my right. Your seat beside Maren was never in contest."

I feel the closest thing to a blush I've felt in twenty years.

"If Nicholas is anxious to sit by me, it's only so he can keep a close eye on me during dinner," Maren assures Rhett. "To make sure I don't steal any of the salad forks."

He laughs and turns to me.

"So she knows you're suspicious of her?" he asks, a twinkle of excitement in his eyes. He looks absolutely delighted by tonight's turn of events.

I groan. "If I am suspicious…or *was* suspicious," I say, correcting myself because I'm not certain which one is more accurate at this point. "It was for good reason."

"Oh heavens, I need a glass of wine," my grandmother says, looking back at Bruce, who hurries to fulfill her wish.

"Nicholas thinks I'm a con artist," Maren says, turning to me with a thoughtful brow. "Is that what you called me this afternoon? I can't remember. I try so hard to forget every word as soon as you say it."

"*Maren*," my grandmother chides, but there's no need. I don't need her help fighting my own battles.

I lean in close to Maren, to be sure she's listening. "That's not what was said and you know it."

She shrugs and turns away to accept the glass of wine Bruce just finished pouring for her. "Close enough. You insinuated it was a possibility."

"Let's change the subject, shall we?" Rhett asks. "Maren, do you have a boyfriend?"

I scowl at him, but he doesn't pay me any attention.

"Not at the moment. Why, are you in the market?" she teases.

"Are you three going to go on like this through the entire dinner?" my grandmother asks, fanning her face. "I feel faint already."

"Believe me, Maren," Rhett says, grinning from ear to ear. "I'd take you up on the offer in an instant if I didn't think Nicky would lop my head off with that butter knife."

To his credit, I *am* gripping it a tad too hard. I drop it back on the table as a gesture of goodwill. *See? I won't kill you, Rhett.* At least not in front of my grandmother.

"I ask because I heard you and Barrett Knox went out on a date last week," he continues. "I was curious to hear your side of it."

"Why does it sound like you've already heard his side?" Maren wonders, sounding coy.

Rhett laughs and leans back in his chair, trying to dig himself out of the hole he's put himself in. "Yeah, well, Barrett isn't one to keep quiet about a pretty girl." He holds his hands out quickly, to nip in the bud the line of thinking we were all heading down. "Not that he's been spreading intimate details or anything. As I hear it, the two of you just went to get a drink before Tori's garden party."

What the hell? Why am I just now hearing about this?

"That's absurd," I interject. "Barrett's too young for her."

"We're the same age," she points out with an amused smile.

That can't be possible.

"Yeah, well, let's just say you're a lot more mature than he is. I worry for any woman who seriously considers dating him."

"That's rude. I had a good time."

"I agree with Maren, Nicky," my grandmother adds. "I think you judge Barrett too harshly. Sure, he has a bit of growing up to do, but I was here, watching, when he picked Maren up, and he was very gallant about it. Reminds me of when boys used to come here to take your mother out."

"You *allowed* her to go out with him?"

"I didn't just allow it—I encouraged it. Since when do you have an issue with Barrett anyway?"

Since this moment apparently.

Maren turns to Rhett. "Now you have me curious. What else has Barrett been saying about me?"

"Oh, you know, just the telltale signs of new love. He thinks you're the prettiest woman he's ever laid eyes on, *yada-yada*."

She laughs as if it's absurd.

It's not.

I could use a drink, something a little stronger than this wine.

"And what about Barrett? Do you find him handsome?" my grandmother asks.

"Of course. What's not to like?"

"I prefer blondes myself," Rhett adds, no doubt referring to himself.

She laughs and shakes her head. "You know, actually, Nicholas," she says, turning to me, "if you and I hadn't gotten off to such a rocky start, I think I would have found *you* very handsome."

"He looks just like his grandfather," my grandmother says with a proud smile.

"But now?" I ask, forgetting we have an audience.

She shrugs. "It doesn't matter."

Bullshit.

I've never wanted to draw the truth out of someone more. I want to touch her chin and turn her head toward me and look into her eyes for signs of denial.

It *does* matter.

Salmon tartare is served as the first course, and my grandmother tries to steer the conversation toward upcoming restoration work at Rosethorn. She doesn't succeed.

"Nicholas broke a lot of hearts when we were growing up," Rhett tells Maren, continuing the game they're playing at my expense. "He's a tough nut to crack, but that didn't stop girls from trying. In fact, they only tried harder."

"That doesn't surprise me at all," Maren says, as if she has me completely pegged. "I'm sure he loved it. Did he take them out on his sailboat? *Woo* them on the open seas?"

"Only a few girls were that lucky."

"Lucky?" Maren teases.

I toss my napkin onto the table and screech my chair back to stand. "Maren, could I speak with you out in the hall?"

I'm already yanking her chair back, so she doesn't really have a choice in the matter.

I almost expect my grandmother to speak up in protest, but she must recognize something in my expression because she stays perfectly silent as I step out into the narrow side hall, opposite the grand entry on the other side of the dining room. It's dimly lit compared to the rest of the house, a small passage we rarely use.

Maren follows a beat after me with her head held high, fury reigning in her eyes.

My heart races in my chest and the overwhelming urge to reprimand her and leave her there in the hall feeling like a petulant child fades once she and I stand eye to eye.

"Am I in trouble?" she asks, cocking one delicate brow.

I step closer and lower my voice, aware that we haven't gone that far from the dining room.

"That's enough."

"Oh c'mon, even your friend is—"

"You're encouraging him."

"I'm teasing. I think it should be allowed, don't you? Dinner would be so boring without it."

"You've made your point. You wanted to punish me and you have."

She laughs and steps closer to me to ensure I'll hear her whispered words. "I highly doubt that. *You*, the great Nicholas Hunt, champion of your house—you're inherently *un*punishable. You wear so much armor I doubt I could say a single thing that would hit your heart."

She's wrong. Each mocking word she's said tonight has fallen onto my heart like a drop of burning oil.

My silence doesn't sit well with her. She sighs and lets her hands fall to her sides in defeat. "Oh fine. I won't say another word. How about that? I won't even open my mouth unless you tell me to. Surely I can't do any harm just by *being* in the room—"

I take her then, wrapping my hands around her trim waist and hauling her flush against me. I have no idea what I'm doing. Maybe, initially, I wanted to knock some sense into her, force her into the realization that her silence would solve nothing. She could hide under the table and I'd still be too aware of her in that room. Now, though, her green eyes are closer than they've ever been, and I give in to the wild urge to bend my head toward hers.

Her hand shoots up, not striking my cheek but good and ready to do so.

"Don't you dare," she hisses, letting her hand fall to my chest so she can wrap her fingers around the lapel of my coat.

Our hearts beat together wildly as our lips stay within reach. She's rigid in my hands, a piece of glass ready to break, and then another second passes and she softens at the exact moment that my sanity snaps back into place.

I let go of her and step back swiftly, rubbing a hand across my forehead.

No amount of apologies would suffice, so I don't bother.

Instead, I give her the space to push past me and reenter the dining room.

I go through the side hall, down into the kitchen, and out into the chilly night air.

I started off hating Maren on principle, and though there are many reasons to forgive her past transgressions and grant her the benefit of the doubt, beneath it all lies the obstinate determination to go on hating her. I can hardly consider the scenario in which I might have made life harder for a person who's already dealt with more than her fair share of hardships. It leaves me with a burning ache in my chest, an insurmountable amount of shame.

17
MAREN

In the morning, I take my coffee out into the back yard, wrapping my sweater tighter around my shoulders to block the ocean breeze as I approach the edge of the property. It's a perilous drop from where I stand down to the rocky shores below, but an ornate wrought iron fence holds me back. Still, I don't lean on it too much. Years of exposure to the elements has given it a patina, and I worry there might be some structural damage as well.

I sip my coffee and glance down below. There's a break in the drop, midway down, a flat walkway that cuts through the jagged rocks, parallel to Bellevue Avenue. It's Newport's famed Cliff Walk, and though I've never traversed it myself, I've seen quite a few tourists accomplish the feat. On a Saturday morning, with weather as beautiful as it is today, I'm not surprised to see it's already busy with casual hikers.

They look up and wave to me, and I wave back. I wonder what they think of me standing up here, if they mistake me for one of the Cromwells. I can't imagine.

I hear approaching footsteps in the damp grass behind me, and I glance back to see Nicholas walking toward me from the house. My stomach squeezes tight and I feel immediate unease. He never returned to dinner last night and a part of me worried he'd gone back to New York, but this morning, when I peered out my bathroom window, his car was still parked outside, causing a dangerous feeling of hope to blossom in my chest. It's still there even as I try to quash it.

I turn back to stare out at the ocean, and each passing second while I wait for him to reach me is a short millennium.

He stops beside me, and I can no longer hear the roar of the ocean over my own heartbeat.

He's the first to speak.

"When I was a child, there was no fence here."

"I can't imagine."

Even just thinking about it makes me take a small step back, more in line with him.

"It wasn't as dangerous as you might think. There were never any injuries. People were smart enough to stay back. The fence is only there now because of the Cliff Walk. My grandfather didn't want tourists to mistake Rosethorn for public property."

"Why was the Cliff Walk first built? Why would you all have agreed to let them take a portion of your property?"

"It wasn't ours to give. It's the law. No one has ownership of the ocean."

It's a beautiful sentiment. I tell him so and he nods, staring out at the sea as the breeze ruffles the dark strands of his hair. He looks so beautifully severe this morning, so much like his portrait. His sharp profile begs to be touched and I almost open my mouth to apologize about last night, but then he speaks and the words die on my tongue.

"I won't repeat my actions from last night," he says obstinately.

My heart lurches in my chest.

"It was inappropriate, and I hope I didn't offend you," he continues.

Yes, my initial reaction was offense. It's why my hand shot up to protect myself, but then once realization set in, once my body recognized Nicholas' strong hold, warmth spread through me like a slow-moving trickle of lava. I would have let him kiss me if he'd tried. I would have begged him to continue, and maybe it's for the best that we didn't start at all. How different would this morning's chat be if he were here telling me he regretted his actions, saying he didn't mean to get my hopes up or string me along. How mortifying would it have been if he wanted to take back the kiss altogether instead of just the *possibility* of a kiss?

This is better.

This way, my dignity is spared.

"You're welcome at Rosethorn as long as you'd like to remain here," he says before turning back toward the house.

Wetness gathers in the corners of my eyes, and I dab it away with a sharp, forceful inhalation.

A house as big as Rosethorn seems to magnify every emotion. There's no escaping them in the cavernous halls and quiet rooms. Loneliness seeps in Saturday afternoon, so dark and all-consuming I can't shake it. Cornelia and Lydia have plans to eat out for dinner tonight, and Nicholas isn't home either. I go downstairs and find most of the staff playing poker, laughing around their dining table, and I know better than to interrupt. I go back up to my room and try to call Ariana, but she doesn't answer. I'm not surprised. She hasn't taken any of my calls since I arrived here. I worry about her, wondering how she's faring since we last spoke. I'm tempted to leave her another message, but I don't bother.

I put on jeans and a light t-shirt then head into town just to have something to do. I've never seen the shops on Bellevue so busy. Tourists bustle around on the sidewalk, licking ice cream cones and taking pictures in front of the overgrown hydrangea blossoms. I pass the wine bar Barrett took me to last week and am surprised to find Nicholas and Rhett sitting outside among friends. It's a group of eight or so, a few of whom I recognize from Tori's garden party. A petite blonde sits to the left of Nicholas, chatting animatedly. I force myself to look away and keep walking.

My goal is to reach Tori's gallery, and I make it there just as the sun is starting to set. I peer through the windows to see if she's busy and find her near the front, standing beside a dark bronze sculpture of a thin, distorted figure. Her patrons study it as Tori talks, and then her eyes glance past them, seeing me out on the sidewalk. She smiles and waves and I do the same before continuing on so I don't distract her from making a sale.

Though it's dinner time and every restaurant I pass sends out tempting smells, I continue to walk, enjoying the feeling of being in motion. I don't stop until I've reached Miantonomi Memorial Park. I have no clue how far I am from Rosethorn, but I don't worry about it. My feet carried me here; they'll carry me back.

I turn back around to head home, staying on well-lit streets now that night has fallen completely. Somewhere along the way, I become aware of a small shaggy dog following along behind me. It looks like some kind of terrier mix with dirty brown hair sticking up in every direction.

"I don't have any food," I tell it, turning my pockets out as if to prove my point.

It wags its tail and I groan, turning back around to continue my walk.

It follows, growing cockier as the minutes pass. Eventually, he's right beside me, trotting along.

"Do you have a home?" I ask, fully expecting an answer.

He barks back, genius dog that he is, and I can't help but smile.

Even without further invitation, he continues along beside me until we pass another street and step under an especially bright lamp post. I stop and use the light to bend down and search for a collar. He whirls around in excitement, barking and lapping at my hand as I pat his head. I start to part some of the fur at his throat, expecting to find a collar under the matted mess, but he releases a low warning growl right as I spot a dark angry wound, barely scabbed over. No collar in sight.

"Oh, you're hurt," I say, moving my hands away so I don't irritate his cut.

He licks my palm, as if in apology for the growl, and I stand up, patting my thigh for him to come along. He's very dutiful, never wandering far, even as we pass through the busy streets with tourists flooding out of restaurants. One especially tall man crosses into my path and the dog jumps in front of me, growling low and menacing.

"It's okay, c'mon."

He listens, but not before issuing another growl in the stranger's direction.

When we arrive home, I tell him to wait on the other side of the gate for me and then pass by Neal. I make it halfway to the house before I realize the dog snuck in after me, looking very proud of himself.

He issues another bark and I shush him. "You're going to get yourself caught. Now, you need to stay outside. I'll go in to get you something to eat and something to clean that wound with. It looks close to getting infected, I think."

I tell him to sit when I reach the kitchen door and he stays standing, tipping his head to the side as if confused. I roll my eyes and slip through the door, closing it quickly behind me just in case he gets the idea to come into the house after me. He barks once and I wince, hoping no one heard it.

Patricia is in the kitchen tidying up.

"Oh, Maren. Barrett called while you were out, a few hours ago."

I nod, not really caring. "Thanks."

"Are you hungry? Chef made a light dinner. I could heat something up for you?"

Her kindness feels like too much to bear on a day like today.

"No. Thank you, Patricia. I'm just going to get some water and a snack."

"All right. Good night," she says, giving me a warm smile before she grabs a load of dirty dish towels to carry off toward the laundry room.

I wait a beat to be sure she's gone then start to raid the refrigerator, looking for something a dog could eat. Chef keeps everything perfectly organized, so it isn't hard to hunt down some sliced chicken and cooked sweet potato mash. I search around desperately for a paper plate and find nothing. In the end, I settle for the most worn-looking pot I can find and scoop a little of the chicken and potatoes into it. Then I add some dish soap and water into a mixing bowl and toss a towel over my shoulder on my way back outside.

The dog isn't there when I open the door and my heart immediately sinks, but then I see him out on the grass rolling out and having a jolly ol' time.

"Dog," I hiss under my breath.

He leaps to his feet and trots back over, and I lead us toward a corner of the house with the fewest windows. I put the pot of food down for him and he immediately goes to town on it. While he's distracted, I pour a little of the soapy water onto his neck. He doesn't even notice as I work the towel into the matted hair, carrying away dried blood so I can properly clean the wound. He licks at the pot, trying to get every last morsel of food while I continue my work, and when we're both done, I sit back on my heels, unsure of what to do now.

"You have to go back home," I tell him. "You have a home, don't you?"

He doesn't look like it, and if he does have owners, they weren't taking very good care of him. He really is a scruffy little thing. There's a little chunk missing from the tip of his right ear, and when I reach out to feel his side, his ribs stick out, further proving my suspicions.

"Okay. Fine. You can stay here, but you can't come inside. I know I'd get in trouble."

He scratches at his back for a second then turns in a circle a few times and snuggles up in front of my knees.

I pat his head reassuringly. "I doubt I'm supposed to keep you here, but well…I'm a stray too, you know. Maybe we were supposed to find each other."

I sit there for a little while, soothing him, and then I finally stand to dump the rest of the soapy water into the grass and refill it with fresh water. After that, I go in search of one of the huge towels Frank uses to dry the cars after he washes them. Once I'm back outside, I fold it in half, and then I fold it again and plop it on the ground beside his water bowl.

His head pops up and he looks at me curiously.

"You have to sleep out here, okay?" I point to the makeshift towel bed. "You can't come inside."

He makes no complaints as he curls up on the towel and rests his head on his paws.

I think we might actually get away with the arrangement until I'm awoken in the morning by shrieks coming from downstairs. I leap out of bed and run down the steps, cringing as Chef's French-accented English rings out of the kitchen.

"Why is there a dirty *chien* in my kitchen!?"

Oh god.

I arrive to find a complete disaster. Patricia and Chef have the dog cornered in the kitchen. Patricia holds out a broom in defense; meanwhile, Chef has a whisk and a frying pan.

The dog cowers with his tail between his legs.

"Don't hurt him!" I shout, rushing past them to leap in front of him.

"Don't go near him!" Patricia warns. "He's vicious—he tried to bite my hand!"

"He's not vicious," I argue, petting his head to calm him down. "He's scared. Look at you two!"

They glance at each other, only now realizing they look like a pair of cartoon villains. Patricia slowly lowers her broom. Chef sets his frying pan on the nearby counter.

"How did that dog get in here?" Cornelia asks.

I turn to see her and Nicholas standing in the doorway. Cornelia's tying her robe closed over her silk pajamas, but Nicholas came down shirtless in a pair of black pajama pants. His dark hair is a ruffled mess, and I am momentarily dumbstruck by the sight of him.

"It rushed in when I opened the door," Patricia explains. "I couldn't stop it. It must have been sitting there, waiting on the other side."

"How did it get on the property?" Chef asks.

"There are a few gaps in the perimeter fence," Nicholas replies. "We've had animals sneak through in the past."

It seems they're all likely to buy his explanation of events and I know I could stay silent, but it'd still be a lie of omission, so I sigh and force myself to look back down at the dog.

"He came in with me last night."

"Into the house?!" Chef asks, horrified.

"No, just onto the property."

"Why?" Patricia asks.

"Because he was in bad shape. He has a cut on his neck and was really hungry…he found me during my walk home and I didn't want to leave him all alone."

"Maren," Cornelia scolds.

"What was I *supposed* to do?" I say defensively. "Just leave him to fend for himself?"

"Precisely," Chef says. "It's what mutts do."

I glare up at him. *Why don't you go a couple of days without food and see how much you like it?*

"Maren, that dog cannot stay," Cornelia says with a tinge of remorse in her tone. "Though I don't think it would hurt if we gave him a proper bath—*outside*."

Thirty minutes later, the dog is splashing around in a huge metal tub filled with water and soap. Cornelia attacks his left side, I get his right, and together, we scrub as much as we can for as long as he lets us. He barks and leaps, sloshing water over the side so that my t-shirt and shorts are soaked through.

"He's not brown at all." Cornelia laughs in amazement. "He's white!"

She's right. He had so much dirt and grime caked on, we couldn't tell.

"He'll look much more dignified once we've got him cleaned off," she continues. "Like a proper gentleman."

As if he understands her, he gives her hand a few hearty licks.

"All right, okay. Don't get carried away now." She grins, giving him a formal pat on his head. "Just because I said you're handsome doesn't mean anything will change. You still aren't allowed in the house, you hear? Outside only."

"What? He can stay?!"

"Outside," she says, leveling me with a warning glare. "If I see him in the kitchen again, I'll banish him for good. I don't want to be awoken by Chef's girlish screams for a second time."

Her threat doesn't pack much of a punch when she says it in a baby voice while rubbing behind his ears.

"Still…he's not at all my kind of dog," she adds as we dry him off. "My family grew up with purebred standard poodles."

"Well I think he's perfect. Small and rambunctious."

"What are you going to call him?" Nicholas asks.

I glance up to find him walking toward us in workout shorts and an old Yale t-shirt. He has three towels folded in his arms; hopefully one of them is for me. I have soap smeared across my face and soggy clothes sticking to my skin.

"Louis," Cornelia replies confidently, not even considering for a moment that I might want some input. "It's a name fit for a king. Now hand me one of those towels."

Nicholas hands us each one and then helps us dry Louis. He gets two good swipes with the towel before the dog takes off like a rocket across the yard, shaking out his fur as he runs.

Patricia brings out a little bowl filled with breakfast for him.

"Did you make that, Patricia?" I ask, eyeing the food. There's brown rice and ground meat as well as carrots and zucchini. *I* would eat it.

She laughs. "No. Chef whipped it up. Apparently, he thinks the bags of dog food they sell in stores aren't fit for a dog staying at Rosethorn."

Nicholas laughs before whistling for Louis. He dashes back over, smells the food Patricia's holding, and immediately starts twirling around and around in circles, as if trying to impress her.

Cornelia tuts. "What unseemly behavior, Louis!"

She tries to get him to sit. He doesn't. She pushes down his little rump until he gives the *impression* of sitting, but when she moves her hand, he jumps right back up. I'm laughing and I glance over to find Nicholas doing the same. Our eyes lock and a little zing runs down my spine. My smile fades as I turn away, blinking away the rush of anxiety filling my stomach.

"Right, well," Cornelia begins as she wipes her hands clean. "First thing tomorrow, I'll have a trainer here, *and* a groomer. You'll see—in a week's time, he'll know thirty commands in English and French!"

"I look forward to seeing it," Nicholas says, stepping forward to kiss her cheek. "I've got to run back to the city."

"So soon?"

"I'll be back next weekend," he assures her.

I take the knowledge for myself as well. I sleep with it that night, knowing I won't have to wait too long before I see him again. Of course, it doesn't even occur to me until the morning that I shouldn't *want* to see him, but by then, the feeling of anticipation has already grown roots.

NICHOLAS

I don't normally mind summers in the city. Sure, the stifling heat can get unbearable, especially compounded by the hordes of people out in droves, sweating their way from one tourist destination to another, but there's a newfound excitement in the air too, spurred by life having been kept shuttered during the winter months. Kites fly overhead in Central Park. Ice cream vendors perch on street corners. Children splash through sprinklers.

Monday morning, I walk the short distance from my apartment to work and try to bring my mind back to the appeal cases we have on our plate, all of which need my full attention. Usually, I have no trouble getting my brain on track, but now I'm wondering about inane things instead: if Louis has found his way into the house again, if Cornelia actually intends on going through with the trainer, if Maren is happy she convinced a household of people to bend to her will so easily. They all want to make her happy and I find, surprisingly, that I'm among them.

There's a small voice inside my head criticizing me for falling into her trap. It's self-preservation and usually I'm glad for the instinct, but it seems it's no longer founded in Maren's case. At least I hope not.

In my office, a few eager interns and associates are already at work. They wave to me as I pass by and head into my office, and one brings me a cup of coffee as I turn on my TV to catch an early news broadcast. The stories about my family have dried up, partly because of threatened lawsuits from my lawyers and partly because the "salacious insider information" Michael Lewis promised the world wasn't all that noteworthy. Tidbits about my grandmother's comings and goings from Rosethorn didn't elicit the fiery excitement he was hoping for. *And then—get this—she goes to the yacht club to eat lunch!*

I mute the news as I reach for a stack of mail sitting on the corner of my desk. We get a lot, especially concerning the defendants we're trying to exonerate. After I slide my letter opener through the top of an envelope, I press play on my answering machine. I have an assistant who fields calls from the general office line, but I usually have one or two messages from people who know my personal number.

Today, the first message is from a person I can't immediately place. I glance over at my phone as it continues to play.

"Hi, Mr. Hunt. This is Mrs. Buchanan from Holly Home. You called me a few weeks ago inquiring about one of our past employees, Maren Mitchell? On that call, I mentioned a theft that had recently occurred here, and I insinuated that the blame should be placed on Ms. Mitchell. I'm embarrassed to admit that I was wrong about those circumstances I described to you. The item in question was found in another employee's locker over the weekend. He's confessed to the crime and has since been terminated. Anyway, I wanted to be sure to contact you in case you were still considering hiring Ms. Mitchell. As I said before, she was a good employee, and I feel bad if my earlier accusations might have swayed you against her. Sorry for the misunderstanding. Call me if you have any other questions."

The message ends and I sit perfectly still, absorbing her words.

My first instinct is to get angry at Mrs. Buchanan, but how can I? We're guilty of the same crime.

It's ironic, especially considering my line of work. If anyone should know better than to wrongfully accuse someone, it's me. I close my eyes and pinch the bridge of my nose, burning up with anger I can't redirect onto anyone else.

I want to call Maren and apologize, but for what exactly? How do I apologize for the amount of wrong I've done to her? And why should she even listen?

There's a knock on my door. "Mr. Hunt? Do you have a second to go over this timeline for Antonio Owens?"

I sigh and drop my hand, pushing thoughts of Maren away for another time.

"Of course. Come in."

19

MAREN

"Wake up, Maren. We have a plane to catch!" Cornelia exclaims, coming into my room and throwing back the heavy drapes. Her dramatic moment is thwarted by the fact that the sun isn't even out yet. It feels like it's still the middle of the night, and my head is foggy with the urge to go back to sleep.

"What are you talking about?" I groan, rolling over onto my stomach so I can stuff my face into my pillow.

"We're going to be late to the airport if you don't hop to it," she says, strolling over to turn on the lamp on my bedside table.

I burrow deeper into my covers. "Airport...? Where are you going?"

"Where are *we* going, dear, and I can't tell you. It's a surprise."

Immediately, I'm intrigued enough to pop my head up off my pillow and turn toward her. When I first started at Rosethorn, Cornelia had me apply for an expedited passport. It was the same day she had me sign the non-disclosure agreement, so it didn't really stick out in my mind. At the time, she waved off the reasons.

"Oh, I travel every now and then and I'd like you to accompany me. You can't do that if you don't have a passport."

A fist knocks on my bedroom door and then Patricia strolls in with a breakfast tray. She carries it toward my bed and stands there until I push myself up to a sitting position. Then she smiles and drops it on my lap.

"Eat up while we pack," Cornelia orders. "Frank will have the car ready in an hour."

"Where are we going?" I ask again.

Cornelia grins. "You'll find out soon enough. Patricia, would you mind having Collins bring up one of my trunks? I realize now Maren doesn't have any sufficient luggage."

"There's a duffle bag in there somewhere," I say before lifting a slice of toast to my mouth.

Cornelia levels me with a reproachful stare. "One doesn't take a *duffle* to Paris."

"To PARIS?!" I ask, nearly choking on my bite.

She laughs and rolls her eyes. "Ah, well, that secret didn't last long. Now eat up quickly so Patricia can help you get ready. You need to look presentable for our day of travel."

Louis runs into the room then, barking up a storm.

As promised, the groomer and the trainer arrived yesterday, along with a mobile vet.

The vet finished his check-up and microchip scan rather quickly. The groomer worked her magic in an hour; the trainer…not so much.

"I'll need two weeks with him if you want to see progress. He's very set in his ways."

Cornelia agreed.

Then she promptly picked him up and carried him into the house as we all watched on silently.

"I don't want to hear arguments from any of you," she called back to us. "I heard it's supposed to be unseasonably cool tonight. I don't want him to catch a chill. Also, he's still recovering from his wound."

The wound, which by the way, has proved to be no more than a scratch, really.

So now Louis has house privileges, or he's had them for one day, at least. I'm not sure they'll last. We spent all day yesterday running around, making sure he wasn't chewing on anything he wasn't supposed to. I nearly had a heart attack when we found him playing tug-of-war with the edge of an antique rug, but Cornelia just shrugged.

"I never liked that thing much anyway."

His name fits him now that he's been groomed. His fur is trimmed short and his face is much more handsome. He's wearing a red collar around his neck that Cornelia and I found in a shop in town on Sunday, and in his mouth is a plush toy in the shape of a Starbucks cup. I almost can't remember what he looked like a few days ago.

He leaps up onto my bed and turns in a circle to lie beside me. I'm not sure where he slept last night, but I have a pretty good guess.

"How long will we be there?" I ask Cornelia as I rub his back.

"Two weeks."

The first thing I should think is *TWO WEEKS IN PARIS?! What a dream!* but the thought that strikes me first is *What about Nicholas?*

It's so startling and frankly disturbing that I decide to retreat into it curiously. Why would I care about Nicholas and the fact that we won't see him this weekend or next? Why would he pop into my head at all? When he left to go back to New York on Sunday, I barely noticed. I was busy *not* noticing as he loaded up his car and disappeared down the long drive.

He won't miss me, I remind myself, and with that, I push aside my breakfast tray and comforter and leap out of bed.

We leave Rosethorn with three full Louis Vuitton trunks that Bruce and Frank have to hoist into the back of the Range Rover together. I'm wearing fitted black pants and one of Cornelia's old Chanel blazers. An Hermès scarf is knotted loosely around my neck and my hair is pulled into a sleek low ponytail. I asked Cornelia why I needed to dress so nice just to sit on an airplane, and she replied, "It's just how it's done."

I'm more glad than ever that while she wasn't watching, I stuffed a pair of pajama pants into my carry-on bag. Just in case.

I realize on our drive down to New York City that we aren't actually headed straight to the airport. Our flight isn't until tonight, but Cornelia wanted to wake me up at the crack of dawn because she had a few errands to run in the city first. We stop in to visit a gallery so she can inspect an abstract painting she previously commissioned. We stay and talk to the artist and the gallery owner for a little while, looking at other paintings before Cornelia requests to have one other piece delivered to Rosethorn along with the first. After that, we head to lunch at Eleven Madison Park. We're the only ones in the sprawling dining room, which I find odd considering how amazing the food is. Cornelia doesn't mention until we're on our way out that the restaurant has routinely been rated the best in the world and carries three Michelin stars to prove it. They only do dinner service, but today they opened up early just for us as a *favor* to Cornelia.

After that, we walk through Bloomingdale's so Cornelia can pick up a few last-minute travel items, one of which is a designer bag she hands to me as we're walking out of the store. The sales consultant offered to wrap it up and put it in a gift box, but Cornelia said there was no need. Apparently, she plans on using it.

I assume she's handing it to me because she wants me to carry it, but then she says, "I'd like you to transfer everything you have in your ratty red purse into this bag so you can use it as your carry-on."

"Are you crazy?" I ask, holding it out at arm's length as if it's a snake that might try to bite me. "I saw what this cost! It's more than most people make in a month!"

"I think most people would just say thank you."

"I can't—"

"Frank, let's head over to the airport. I'd like to relax for a little while before our flight this evening."

Just like that, the discussion is over. My red pleather purse with its zipper that doesn't quite zip anymore and its cross-body strap that's been knotted together since it split in two a few months back is left in the back seat of the car when we arrive at the airport.

We're met at the curb by a concierge from Air France. She leads us to an awaiting golf cart that whisks us from the entrance of the airport, through a private security screening, and then right past all the normal folk, straight to the La Première first class lounge.

I feel guilty as I walk inside, aware of the fact that I probably belong out *there*, loitering between the Auntie Anne's Pretzels kiosk and Sbarro, next to the dude clipping his toenails in public. In the private lounge, there's a full restaurant and bar, as well as a spa. Cornelia sits down in a quiet corner with a book, so I do the same, but I don't do any reading. I people watch, glancing around me at all the lounge-goers and wondering how they can possibly afford to travel this way. They're all dressed up. Most of the women are in heels and dresses with perfectly coiffed hair. There's an air of respectability about them, and I'm suddenly grateful that Cornelia didn't let me wear pajama pants like I wanted to.

We stay in the lounge until our flight boards. Another golf cart carries us straight to the tarmac, and then I'm escorted to a private cabin inside the plane. I'm visibly confused as I turn back to the flight attendant.

"How many other people will I share this with?"

She frowns in confusion. "This is your private suite."

"But this is a *room*…in an airplane. It has a bed and a TV."

"Is it not to your liking? I have one other suite available, but it's slightly smaller and you won't be across the hall from your travel companion."

"Are there not just…like…normal seats? In a row?"

"Not in Première class. I'm sorry."

She's sorry. I almost laugh at that as she tells me she'll be right back with champagne and a warm hand towel.

Wonderful, because of course I need a warm hand towel. How could I possibly travel to Paris without a warm hand towel!?

I think I'm going crazy.

I sit down in the chair across from the bed and look around my cabin in disbelief. Nothing about this makes sense. No one deserves this life, no one—least of all me. It's why I fight Cornelia tooth and nail about every little luxury she tries to toss my way. It feels like too much, and while it's nice, it's not necessary. It doesn't change who I am at my core.

When the flight attendant returns with the amenities she promised, I ask her how long it will take us to get to Paris.

"Flight time is around seven and a half hours. We should arrive at 8:15 AM Paris time. If you need anything during the flight, press that little black button beside your bed and I'll be happy to assist you."

I don't press that button even once, too scared to bother her. I make do with the snacks that came pre-loaded in the cabin and the complimentary candy I swiped from the airport lounge. After I flip through the TV channels aimlessly for a little while, I search around the space, opening cupboards and doors. There's a pair of pajamas with the Air France logo on them, brand new and freshly laundered. I slip them on and lie down on the bed, trying to ignore the feeling of anxiety starting to creep in.

I've never been out of the country before. I always thought I'd love to go explore the world someday, but now that it's actually happening, I feel slightly uneasy. I know it's silly. I know I'm likely just overly tired and a little homesick, but I can't shake the dark cloud hanging over my head as I toss and turn on the bed.

I don't want to spend the whole time in Paris worrying about my troubles back home. Two weeks abroad with Cornelia is a dream—one I know I'll never experience again—so with newfound resolve, I decide to let myself enjoy it completely.

No feeling guilty. No worrying about life afterward.

In Paris, we're staying in a two-bedroom suite at the Mandarin Oriental. Cornelia tells me she has plans to visit the spa, so I have the morning to myself if I want to catch up on sleep or go out and explore. I opt for the latter, swapping my flats for a pair of sneakers. I wander with no destination in mind, grateful that our hotel is in the heart of the city. I exchange a few of the euros Cornelia handed me at the hotel for a map from a street vendor and use it to traverse the 8th arrondissement, ultimately ending up at the Arc de Triomphe. I follow the signs leading to the underpass that carries pedestrians underneath the chaotic traffic circle surrounding the arch, and then I start to climb up the 284 steps.

Outside, at the top of the arch, I find a sunny view of Paris waiting for me. It's remarkable how classical the city has remained, how short it all is compared to the skyscrapers in Manhattan. I overhear a tour guide explaining to his group that Paris chose to outlaw towers so the nineteenth-century structures could remain the tallest in the city. Among them, most prominently, is the Eiffel Tower.

Everyone around me has their phones out, snapping photos, but I have nothing but my memory to commemorate the moment, so I stand on the ledge, against the iron rail, and I stare for as long as I can bear it, trying to memorize the view from every angle.

Tourists flutter around me, most of whom aren't speaking English, so it's rather easy to find myself alone in the crowd. I like it.

I linger until my stomach growls and then I start the trek back down the stairs and out into the city. Along the Champs-*Élysées*, I purchase an assorted pack of macarons from Ladurée and eat them while I walk, convincing myself that they make a perfectly decent lunch if you're in Paris. I window shop and force myself to slow down whenever my pace creeps back up. I have plenty of time to get back to the hotel, and there is a finite number of minutes I'll get in this city. I want to embrace every single one of them.

A young couple with matching leather jackets walks up the sidewalk toward me, hand in hand. The girl pulls a face at something the boy says and then tries to extricate herself from his hold in an act of defiance. He leaps behind her and wraps his arms around her waist, not letting her get away, holding her tight as she laughs and puts up a weak fight. It's obvious she doesn't really want to get away from him, not even a little bit. I smile, living vicariously through them as they pass me by, completely unaware of my presence. I realize I should be sad that I don't have a boyfriend with me here, but I'm not. It's the exact opposite. I've never been filled with so much hope and excitement for what the future holds. Here, no one knows who I'm supposed to be. My past is an ocean away, and I don't need a man to make my trip special. I'll have a love affair with Paris instead.

Over the next few days, Cornelia and I take turns setting the agenda. We have no plans we're beholden to, which means there's never any reason to be anywhere at any given time. We stroll through the Louvre slowly on our second day and barely make it through half the exhibition halls, so we decide we'll go again the next day. Obviously, I can go at a much faster pace than Cornelia can, which is why we make the perfect pair. I speed her up and she slows me down.

For an entire afternoon, we sit outside a cafe on the bank of the Seine and watch the restoration work at Notre Dame while we switch from coffee to wine, reading when we feel like it, chatting when the subject strikes us.

She asks me if I've ever been in love and I'm embarrassed to admit I haven't, not unless being in love with the memory of my parents counts.

She tells me of a time she summered in Paris when she was a teenager. She had a French tutor who was only a few years older than her and extremely cute. As her understanding of the French language deepened, so did her feelings for him. By the end of summer, she was convinced she was wholeheartedly in love with him and she *needed* to remain in Paris instead of returning to the States.

"What did he say?"

"He gave me my first kiss, patted my head, and told me there would be someone much better for me down the line."

"Was there?"

"Oh yes, though it would be years before I found him."

"Nicholas' grandfather?"

She smiles fondly and nods. "Edward was not at all my type when we first met. In fact, I thought he was a little rude. He didn't like me much either. I wasn't afraid to speak my mind in an age when most women would have happily zipped their lips and married a nice boy from a nice family."

"What happened?"

"Oh, he fell hopelessly in love with me, of course. I know I might not look it now, but I was a great beauty."

"You still are."

She smiles like she's humoring me. "It was so fun to have him wrapped around my finger in the beginning. I could have told him to jump off a bridge and he would have done it."

"Sounds like you had quite the evil streak," I say with a laugh.

"I didn't let myself get too carried away. I eventually put him out of his misery and proposed."

"You proposed to him!?"

She laughs. "That's about the same reaction he had. You should have seen his face, this proud, arrogant man staring down at me on one knee—I'll never forget it."

"Maybe I'll do the same one day when I fall in love." I shake the silly thought from my head. "Or better yet, maybe I'll never marry and I'll just stay with you forever."

I see her frown out of the corner of my eye, though I was expecting a smile. "Nothing would break my heart more."

"Why?" I challenge with a furrowed brow. "Women can be happy without a husband, without children."

"Yes, my dear. You're right. Could you though?"

I take a moment to think about her question, glancing back across the Seine.

"I hate to admit it, because it feels like I'm giving in to some preset societal demand that I *have* to become a mother just because I'm a woman, but the truth is, I've been on my own since I was thirteen. Nearly every person and every place in my life has been temporary, and I want something permanent. I want a real family and a home, wherever and with whomever that may be."

She reaches across the table to touch my arm. I stare down at her elegantly aged hand and the emerald wedding ring she never takes off.

"I understand your grief, Maren. I do. Nicholas' mom, Judith, was my only child, and she passed away far too young. Being with you reminds me of what it's like to be a mother, to care for and dote on someone simply because you love them and want the very best for them."

My chest tightens as tears collect in the corners of my eyes.

I sniffle and try to lean back, but she tightens her grip for a split second.

"You know I adore you. I'd keep you with me forever if I thought it was for the best," she says, patting my arm and then releasing me so I can slyly turn back to the Seine and wipe my tears with my napkin.

Our first week rolls into the second, and we journey out of Paris to explore Versailles and its surrounding gardens. We stay too long, admiring Marie Antoinette's "cottage" as our guide walks us through what life was like for her at Louis XVI's court before the French Revolution. At first glance, it would be easy to compare her to Cornelia considering they've both experienced what it feels like to have the world at one's fingertips, but I can't imagine Cornelia ever acting in line with the late French queen. The guide explains to us that the popular phrase *Qu'ils mangent de la brioche*, what we know as "Let them eat cake", isn't an indulgent anthem, but rather an example of how little regard Marie Antoinette might have felt toward her subjects who were enduring a famine and had no bread to eat. Her flippant disregard for their suffering isn't at all how Cornelia feels toward the struggles of others, and I'm a prime example of that.

The next day, Cornelia needs to rest, so I stroll through the city on my own, venturing into the Musée d'Orsay early enough that I'm alone in front of Vincent Van Gogh's haunting self-portrait. His intense gaze seems to pry into me, digging beneath layers as I stand in the quiet room studying him studying me. In other rooms, I stumble upon people with sketchpads and easels, set up in front of famous paintings by Monet and Degas, recreating them in their own way. I wish I had even one artistic bone in my body so I could do the same. It's inspiring to be in a city like this, and it makes me miss the piano at Rosethorn. I've gotten so used to having it at my fingertips whenever the mood strikes.

As I'm leaving, a flash of dark hair catches my attention, and I think for one wild moment that Nicholas is here, at the museum. He's come to Paris. I whip around to get a better look, lips parted in shock, and then my heart sinks when I find it's just a man, slightly shorter than Nicholas, whose pale features look nothing like his. My wave of shock gives way to a confusing crash of disappointment. I'm left with residual butterflies that work themselves into knots in my stomach as I walk across the bridge over the Seine, back toward our hotel.

Cornelia and I spend the next day getting pampered at Institut Dior. After we relax in the serenity room, they place us in separate treatment rooms so we can each get a massage and a facial. From there, I'm whisked into the salon so I can get a much-needed haircut. I've never actually had someone give me a styled cut. When I was young, my mom trimmed my hair every so often, and as a teenager, I just had Ariana do the same. I'm surprised how long it takes. I guess it takes time when you actually know what you're doing. When the stylist is finished and I glance up at myself in the mirror, I see what I was missing. My long hair has been trimmed a few inches on the bottom so it looks healthy and shiny, and there are subtle layers to help better accentuate my features.

When we're done, Cornelia asks me where I'd like to go for dinner, and I tell our driver to take us back to the Mandarin Oriental.

"When's the last time you put on a hotel robe, ordered room service, and watched a wildly overpriced pay-per-view movie?"

She considers the question with a laugh. "Never."

"Then tonight will be a first for both of us."

I know two weeks abroad can't rewrite who I am. Solo walks in the early afternoons through the streets of Paris and explorations inside landmarks like the Musée d'Orsay and the Eiffel Tower don't rearrange my biology, but I do feel like the experience has given my self-consciousness a much-needed shakeup. I was a complete stranger in a foreign place and no one cared. No one asked if I belonged there. There was a sense of freedom, and in that freedom, growth. On the drive back home from the airport back in Newport, I realize I've never felt more comfortable in my own skin.

It doesn't fade either.

In the days that follow, I finally feel like I belong at Rosethorn. It's a subtle change, the courage to lift my head and speak my mind and gain a real foothold in day-to-day life there. I'm no longer relegating myself to the sides of the halls, worried to get in anyone's way. I walk Louis in the mornings, I confirm Cornelia's appointments for the day with Diane, I sit in on planning meetings and lunches and teas, I meet Tori at the club and I manage to play, if not great, at least mediocre tennis. I exist in a way that feels loud and confident and resolute, because for once, I'm not apologizing for being who I am.

⊙✧⊙

Nicholas arrives on Friday evening, three weeks after I last saw him. When I hear his car stir up the gravel drive, I rush down the stairs and fly through the kitchen and out the back door. It's impulsive and out of character. I've never shown this much excitement at his arrival. I've never come out to greet him like this and I know he's about to come inside, but everyone will be in there and how will we talk when there's such a crowd?

I don't have a plan as I walk down the stone stairs and wait for him on the gravel. He's preoccupied as he reaches in to grab a brown leather bag from his back seat, but when he closes the door and stands to his full height, he finally turns toward me and stops.

Three weeks haven't dulled him in the least. He's as sharp and handsome as ever.

He's wearing his clothes from work, I think, though he's rolled his shirtsleeves up to his elbows and undone his top button. If he's had a long day—and I'm sure he has—I can't tell. Everything about him still looks so perfect. But no, that's not right. When I look closer, I see his hair is a little mussed up and his shirt is untucked. His eyes are narrowed as they take me in. He's not perfect; he's just Nicholas.

"You're back," he says by way of greeting as he finally starts to walk toward me.

I nod and wring out my hands as he draws near, aware of every inch that disappears between us. "Yes. We got in on Tuesday."

He stops when he's only a few feet away from me, his height blocking some of the landscape lighting so that I'm thrown into shadow.

"Did you come out here just to greet me?" he asks with a bemused tilt of his head.

"I was looking for Louis," I say suddenly, narrowing my eyes and glancing around as if in search of the dog. "You haven't seen him, have you?"

"No."

I swallow forcefully, aware that he's studying me curiously. I let my gaze make its way back to him, and I venture to ask a question I'm curious about.

"Did you miss us while we were gone?"

"Newport didn't feel the same," he replies, not giving me the answer I wanted.

I huff out an annoyed laugh and step to the side, giving him the opportunity to walk past me, up the stairs, and into the house.

He doesn't move. "You've changed."

"I got a haircut," I say, as if that explains everything.

He shakes his head. "I don't think that's it."

He doesn't elaborate, and I'm forced to stand there while he takes me in. His silent judgments have always had the uncanny ability to split me in two, but this time, instead of weakening under his gaze, I turn to him and hope to shock him out of his careful study with the truth.

"Is it a crime? I hope I *have* changed. I wanted to set fire to my old life and return to Newport as one of you. I wanted to become just like everybody else."

His eyes flit up to mine, holding me captive.

"You'll never be like everybody else."

His words are a poison dart, draining me of all my newfound confidence. I only barely manage to keep my lip from quivering as I nod and turn to precede him inside.

We don't say another word as I slip away and hurry back up to my room.

20
NICHOLAS

I'm smoking a cigar on the patio outside later that night, stewing, when my phone rings in my pocket. I tug it out as Tori's name flashes across the screen, and without hesitating, I swipe my finger to answer it.

"*Nicky!*"

I wince at the loud music pulsing through the phone.

"Where are you?" I ask, curious as to why I didn't get an invite.

"Out with Maren! You know, the girl you *hate*!"

I frown. "Are you drunk?"

"Abso-*fucking*-lutely, Nicky boy. It's why I'm calling. Are you sober?"

"Yes."

"Great! Can you come pick us up? Maren is flirting with Barrett and it's making me want to gag. I don't think I can watch it for another second or I might actually throw up."

I have a hundred questions, but I settle for the most important one.

"Where are you guys?"

She gives me the name of the bar and I stub out my cigar.

"I'll be there in a few minutes. Keep Barrett away from Maren."

I sound menacing even to my own ears, but Tori doesn't call me out on it. Instead, she laughs. "Easier said than done."

I drive like a bat out of hell on the way to pick them up. This evening has been a disaster ever since I first arrived. I was jittery with nerves on my drive from the city. I was anxious to see Maren again after three weeks without her, but after our brief talk outside, she decided to skip dinner. When Patricia attempted to take up a tray of food to her, she returned moments later with it still in her hands, informing my grandmother and me that Maren wasn't in her room. I had no clue where she went, but apparently it was out to a bar with Tori and Barrett.

With it being full-blown tourist season, parking outside the bar is insane, and Tori won't answer her phone. Eventually, I find a spot a few blocks north and then head toward the crowded entrance.

Inside, I'm annoyed to find it's packed from wall to wall. Rowdy college kids shout over the music, and out of respect for my hearing, I head out to search the back patio that overlooks the water, but when that proves fruitless, I snake back through the tables inside for a second time. I have my phone pressed to my ear as I call Tori yet again, and I'm about to give up when bodies shift and a clear path to the bar opens up, right to where Maren sits on a stool with Barrett's arm wrapped around her waist. Her head rests on his shoulder.

An uncomfortable ache settles in my gut as I pocket my phone and head straight for them. I have half a mind to pry them apart myself like some overbearing ogre, but instead, I aim my sights on Tori. She glances up as she sips from a straw then does a double take when she realizes it's me.

"Nicky!"

I drag a hand through my hair, nodding my head toward the entrance. "Hey, are you ready to go?"

Maren's back stiffens at the sound of my voice. Then she looks over her shoulder and throws her hands up in the air.

"Look who's here! The asshole himself!" She waves toward the bar. "Hey, bartender, can you give everyone free shots courtesy of my pal, Nicholas Hunt?"

The few people around her hoot and holler as if free shots are actually coming their way. I shake my head at the bartender and he grunts, moving along to another group of patrons at the other end of the bar.

Barrett cracks up.

Maren turns away from me, and Tori claps me on the shoulder.

"Thank god you're here. Maren, let's go. Nicky's taking us home."

Maren doesn't turn around. "I'm fine. Thanks."

"I can just take her later," Barrett volunteers, smiling down at her like he can't believe his good fortune.

"Nah, let's go," I say, reaching out to touch her arm.

She tries to pull away from me, but the momentum has her slipping off her stool. I leap to catch her before she tumbles to the ground and then instead of propping her back on the seat, I use my grip on her to help her stand, already directing her toward the door.

She tries to yank free, but it's easy enough to keep ahold of her. I should feel bad, but I don't.

"What the hell!" Barrett shouts behind me.

"I take it you can get home safely?" I ask him, not actually caring what his answer is. Then I turn to Tori, who's still sitting dumbstruck on her stool. "You coming?"

"No, she's not coming—and I'm not either!" Maren protests.

I push her toward the door, and when Tori catches up to us, Maren shoots daggers at her. "Is this your fault? Did you call him?"

"Yes. We needed a ride home."

"I just spent two hours talking shit about him. You could have called someone else."

Tori grins up at me. "It's true. She really did have a lot to say about you."

I push open the door of the bar and make sure to lead Maren out in front of me. "I have no doubt. I'm curious, though—what's the root of her issue with me?"

"*Her* issue with you is that you're an arrogant asshole with no regard for the feelings of others!" Maren replies passionately.

"I sound like a real prick," I agree as we turn the corner. "My car's a few blocks that way."

More than ever, I wish I'd been able to secure a parking spot closer to the bar. Tori and Maren aren't stumbling drunk, just tipsy enough that they're prone to wander. Every shop we pass seems to catch Tori's attention. "Oooh, I love the way they styled that bookshelf! Do you think they'd let me buy that lamp?"

I double back to prod her along. "Sure. Why don't you come back in the morning and ask?"

"Good idea."

Maren walks behind us with her arms crossed and her eyes narrowed. There's no cooling off between the bar and my car. When I open the passenger door and hold it for her, she huffs something under her breath and climbs into the back.

Tori slides into the front seat and shoots me an angelic smile. "Nicky, you're a lifesaver."

"To be clear, I never asked to have my life saved," Maren says in a disgruntled tone. "I was having a perfectly good time with Barrett at the bar."

"Yes, I'm sure he loved hearing you groan about Nicholas all evening," Tori replies, and I can't help but smirk at that—though it fades quickly when Tori continues, "You are aware that you agreed to be his date to that gala next weekend, right?"

"What?!" Maren asks in shock. Then she catches sight of my face and tightens her arms across her chest in defiance. "Oh, yes. Sure. I'm excited."

I slam the door and round the back of the car to take my seat, wondering if her words are even partly true. I start my engine and study her for a moment in the rearview mirror, but when she catches me, she throws up her eyebrows and prods me to get going. "Did you yank me out of that bar just to keep me here all night?"

Tori laughs under her breath, and I tell myself to focus on driving.

On the way to drop Tori off, she chats enough to cover up the fact that Maren continues stewing in the back seat. I don't register a single thing she says, but I become aware of her absence as soon as she's gone. After she hops out of the car and wishes us both a good night, the silence looms heavy and Maren doesn't seem anxious to fill it.

"Do you want to move up here?" I ask, glancing back at her in the rearview mirror.

She's made herself small in the corner of the back seat, as far away from me as possible.

"No thank you."

I sigh and turn back out onto Bellevue Avenue to head toward Rosethorn. The drive only takes a few minutes and then we're pulling into my parking space. Maren undoes her seatbelt and I'm about to get out when my hand hesitates on the door.

"Tell me why you're so angry with me."

"I'm tired," she says stiffly. "I don't have it in me."

"*Maren.*"

She lets her forehead smack against the back of the passenger seat.

"Are you going to keep me prisoner in here until I tell you?"

The ludicrous idea makes me smile. "If I need to."

She doesn't share my humor. She sighs and sits back against her seat, staring out the window.

I turn back to face the front, unsure of what we're doing here. If she's not going to talk, I can't force her to sit here all night. I glance up and watch her in the mirror again, trying to determine how close she is to giving in.

Time passes and the silence in the car continues.

Neither one of us moves, and the minutes stretch on. I'm about to open my door and surrender even though I don't want to. I want to press her for the truth at all costs, but I know it's not right. I don't want to make her even more upset.

Then she speaks.

"Do you even realize how cruel you can be sometimes?" she asks me, turning her head to meet my eyes in the rearview mirror. Her words feel like a rare bird that will startle at the smallest motion. Left alone, however...what then?

I don't respond, and a few moments later, she continues.

"I was so happy in Paris, so free and confident. I wanted to bring those feelings home with me, but then you arrived today and in a matter of seconds, you wiped all that confidence away."

"How?"

She shakes her head. "You don't even remember, do you?" She turns away and speaks softly, repeating my words back to me. "*You'll never be like everybody else.*"

"That was meant as a compliment, Maren."

"Oh really?" She grunts sarcastically. "Then I guess you don't really know me at all. I'm a girl who's spent her whole life feeling distinctly apart from the world around her, never truly blending in, never a part of anything. Those words weren't a compliment to me."

"I'm sorry."

She leans forward, searching in vain for the mechanism she needs to pull so she can push the front seat up and out of her way. After a moment, she groans in defeat. "*Please* let me out of the car."

I don't listen. I'm too struck by what she just said, too angry that she might not understand where I was coming from.

"If you feel apart from the rest of us, Maren, it's not because you can't measure up—it's because you float above us. You're the most..." I frown as my sentence trails off, unsure of how to continue. "You're so much—" I sigh, angry with my inability to articulate my feelings to her. "You're different in the best way. Don't you see? It was a compliment."

"*Please*," she says, her voice close to breaking.

I open my door without a moment's hesitation and round the car to let her out. I pop the seat forward and hold out my hand for her to take, but she ignores it as she awkwardly climbs out of the car on her own.

I slam the door closed and watch her walk toward the house, paralyzed by competing voices in my head. *Go after her! Give her space.*

Ultimately, I let her walk away, and I hate myself for it.

21
MAREN

Last night comes back to me with an accompanying flood of shame when I wake up in my bed in the morning. Ordering drinks at the bar with Tori and Barrett...stewing over my hatred for Nicholas...drinking...more drinking...agreeing to be Barrett's date for a gala next weekend...acting like a brat when Nicholas arrived at the bar...fighting with him in his car.

To say I could have handled myself better is an understatement. I should find Nicholas immediately and apologize, but I don't. I stay tucked beneath my comforter, staring up at the beautifully painted ceiling and praying my life will work itself out without me having to do anything.

Maybe it's not as bad as I'm remembering? Maybe I didn't make a *complete* fool of myself?

That luxurious thought carries me on a cloud for a few minutes, and then I remember the first thing I said to him in the bar.

"Look who's here! The asshole himself!"

My cheeks are on fire as I roll over and stuff my head under my pillow.

I have no clue what time it is.

Time to get up, that's for sure. Sunlight pours into my room and sounds from the house filter past my bedroom door: Louis' bark, Cornelia's laugh, someone's footsteps approaching then pausing before continuing down the hall.

I want to put off the inevitable, but I also can't just laze around in here all day; I'm already hungry.

I dress slowly in jeans and a white blouse. I throw my hair in a braid and creak my door open, glancing both ways down the hall. The coast is clear, so I pad on light feet down the stairs and toward the kitchen. That's my first stop.

"Where have you been?" Cornelia asks from behind me once I make it to the threshold.

I leap out of my skin and whirl around to face her. "Jesus! You could have given me a heart attack."

She laughs. "I wasn't the one being sneaky. I was merely turning a corner. *You* were the one tiptoeing around like a mouse."

"I was just trying to be quiet."

"You were trying to be *silent*—there's a difference. Who are you hiding from?" she asks me with a curious smile.

"No one."

"Nicholas?"

I act like the idea is totally preposterous. "Why would I hide from Nicholas?"

"Oh, just a guess. Not a very good one, apparently. Anyway, if you're curious, he went sailing with Rhett. He'll be gone all day."

I simultaneously want to jump for joy and sit down to sulk. Such is my life where Nicholas is concerned.

"Also, a girl came looking for you earlier. When was it?" she asks herself before waving the question away. "9 or 9:30. You really have wasted the entire morning in bed."

"A girl? Tori?"

"No, she was a stranger to me." Her features pinch together in thought. "Short with very bright blonde hair. I asked if she wanted to come in and sit while I fetched you, but she said she'd just come back another day."

My heart drops. "Did you catch her name?"

"She left before I could ask."

"Was she about my age?"

"I think so."

Ariana? Is she in Newport? She knows I'm here—I've left messages on her phone with Rosethorn's number and address in case she needed to reach me—but she hasn't called me back. Why would she just show up here unannounced?

My curiosity is piqued enough that I offer to go into town to pick up a few groceries for Chef, and on the way, I stop in at a few hotels—not the fancier ones. I can't imagine Ariana could afford any of them, but then again, I don't have any idea what her finances are like these days.

At the front desks, I describe what Ariana looks like and ask the hotel staff if they know of a guest who's currently staying there that fits that description. Some of them are willing to tell me they haven't seen her, but most explain that they promise their patrons a certain level of privacy and they can't disclose personal information.

"Okay. Thanks anyway," I tell the last one before drumming my fingers on the front desk and turning back for the door. It's getting late and I'm not sure if Chef is waiting on any of the items I promised I'd pick up, so I give up for the day and head to the grocery store.

Right when I get home, I check the leather-bound notebook where we take down messages in the foyer in case there's something from Ariana. There's one waiting for me from Tori, inviting me to go to the beach with her tomorrow, but nothing from my old friend. When I drop off the grocery bags in the kitchen, I ask Chef and Patricia if anyone has come by looking for me.

"We haven't had any visitors since you left," Patricia says. "Were you expecting someone? Should I add a place setting for dinner?"

I smile glumly and shake my head. "No, thank you."

I haven't seen Ariana in a few years, and though there are times when I miss her, she's always been such a wildcard in my life, wreaking havoc and leaving me to pick up the pieces. Still, she's the closest thing I have to real family, so I won't give up on her. If she's in Newport, I hope she comes back to Rosethorn.

Sleep doesn't come easy that night, and I'm relieved when Tori swings by the next day to drag me to the beach. I need to get out of my head. I need to stop thinking about the fact that Nicholas apparently didn't get home from sailing until really late last night and was still sleeping when I went down for breakfast with Cornelia. I need to stop thinking about him, period.

We fly down Ocean Drive in Tori's car with the windows down. Wind whips my hair and I close my eyes, relishing feeling the sun on my face.

We wind along the road toward a private beach club Tori's been going to since she was a little girl. I don't quite understand its purpose.

"Can't we just go to a normal beach? With normal people?"

"It's not about the *people*. It's the fact that, for all the water surrounding Newport, there's not all that much sandy beach access. The public spots will be so crowded by now we wouldn't even be able to find a spot to put our stuff."

Well, when she puts it that way…

The private beach actually isn't as nice as I was expecting. There're no real amenities other than the fence that blocks tourists from overcrowding the area and the fancy restrooms where we change into our bathing suits. There's also a small cafe that serves burgers and fries, but we won't need to eat there thanks to the picnic basket Chef sent me off with this morning.

"Eat the charcuterie early. It won't keep all day."

Of course, because who doesn't take a premade charcuterie board to the beach?

There's fruit salad and croissants and lemon cookies too. I have enough food to feed everyone here.

The other perk of Tori's membership at the club is the fact that there're already beach chairs and umbrellas, as well as rolled towels, waiting for us near the water. No schlepping lawn chairs back and forth from the car. No breaking a sweat while you set up camp for the day.

We arrive at a secluded section of beach, set the picnic basket and the small cooler with drinks between two lawn chairs, and then I survey our spot. It's perfect. Ten steps and we're in the crystal blue-green water. I have my sights aimed there. My fingers are poised at the bottom of my cover-up when Tori catches my attention.

"Hold on, let me ask that attendant to push all these chairs together," she says, pointing to the cluster of beach chairs to our right.

"Why?"

"There're some other people coming."

My heart drops.

"Who? The people from your garden party?"

Please say no.

"Just some of the guys probably. I invited Mary Anne too, but I doubt she'll show up."

I grimace and let my cover-up fall back in place. "How are things going with you two?"

"Oh, it's not really *going* at all. She hasn't broken things off with me completely, but she's still not convinced that I'm prepared to tell everyone the truth about who I am. I'm almost thirty—Jesus, how long can I go on pretending just to please others?"

"What's holding you back? You're not…I mean, your family wouldn't cut you off, would they?"

"What? No. *NO*. It's nothing like that. I was given control of my trust when I turned twenty-five, but even if that *was* a concern, I wouldn't let it hold me back. It has more to do with tradition. Y'know, life as I know it will end. Some people are going to judge me."

"But why would you care about their judgments? Put yourself in Mary Anne's shoes. You staying silent probably makes her feel like you're ashamed to be with her."

"I'm not!"

"I know that, but—"

A beach ball comes sailing our way and lands lightly in the sand at my feet. I glance back over my shoulder to see Barrett and another guy I don't recognize making their way toward us. Barrett shoots me a lopsided grin and a big wave.

I haven't seen him since Friday night, and the first thing I do after he introduces me to his friend, Max, is apologize for getting so drunk.

"What? You were tipsy. *Barely.*" He jostles my shoulder. "It was fine. C'mon, don't worry about it."

I smile with relief.

"But you do remember agreeing to be my date for Friday night, right? To the gala?"

I nod enthusiastically. "Sure. Yeah. It'll be fun."

I'm tempted to put a stipulation on his invitation and clarify that we're just going as friends, but he looks so happy when I agree and the sun is shining and the waves are calling my name. It's summer in Newport and not everything has to be so damn hard. I can just have fun.

I whip off my cover-up and toss it on my chair then pick up the beach ball, walking backward in the sand.

"You coming in?"

He grins and reaches back to tug his t-shirt off over his head. He drops it next to my cover-up and then I turn and race toward the water with him on my heels. I crash into the waves first, but then he's there wrapping his arms around my waist, and I squeal as I try to break away from him. We both go under, and when I surface again, I'm laughing so much I can't breathe.

We stay out in the water, tossing the ball back and forth and trying to keep it from touching the water, until I glance back to the shore and see that more people have arrived. Tori's waving them over and I don't want to be rude, so I reluctantly head back toward the shore, wringing the water out of my hair as I go.

"C'mon, let's go say hi," I say to Barrett, and he falls in step beside me. "I'm thirsty anyway."

"They have good drinks here. You want something from the bar?"

"After Friday? I'm good," I say, tossing him a teasing glare.

He laughs and shakes his head. "I swear you weren't all that bad. Well, not until Nicholas got there. Speak of the devil…"

My gut clenches and I follow his gaze to find Nicholas and Rhett talking to Tori and Max. Rhett waves excitedly as he sees us walking toward them. Nicholas does not. He narrows his eyes, glances between Barrett and me, and then turns back to Tori to ask something.

She shrugs.

"Hey everyone," I say with a weak smile once we reach the group, unable to meet Nicholas' eyes. Our argument from Friday still feels fresh, especially considering the fact that we haven't seen each other since then.

"Hey Maren," Rhett says, coming over to give me a side hug.

"Hey!" I hug him back and then step away, apologizing for getting him all wet.

He laughs. "Well we are at the beach, right?"

I blush and nod, propping my hands on my hips and hoping someone else will lead the conversation from here so I can sink into some quicksand.

"Maren? Will you do my back?" Tori asks, waving a bottle of sunscreen out toward me from her perch on her beach chair.

"Yeah, but you'll have to return the favor. I forgot to put any on before I went in."

There's shuffling as everyone begins to claim seats. Tori and I are already in the center, and Barrett's quick to sit down on the chair beside mine, lying down and closing his eyes to dry out in the sun. Nicholas sits on the other side of Tori, dropping his bag and reaching back to take off his shirt. I watch with rapt attention, unblinking, unmoving, as he pulls it up and over his head. I saw him shirtless the morning Louis first made his appearance for everyone at Rosethorn, but not for long, and not like this. The sun beams down onto his tan muscled chest, and there's a sprinkling of black hair leading down to his navy swim trunks.

Sailing has clearly kept him in great shape over the years.

God bless sailboats, I think with a tiny smile.

Then he reaches down to grab his sunglasses off his chair and turns suddenly, catching me staring. It's comical. There's no way for me to avert my eyes quickly enough or convincingly enough, so I just laugh instead. It's an awkward, please-don't-hate-me-for-checking-you-out laugh, but what he says in return has my cheeks burning bright red.

"Now you can't blame me for doing the same," he says, walking over to take the sunscreen right out of my hand so he can squeeze some out onto his palm.

My mouth is a fly trap as he gives the bottle back to me and walks away toward the water so he can dip his toes in while he rubs sunscreen onto his face and shoulders.

"What the *hell* was that about?" Tori asks.

I have no answer for her.

22
NICHOLAS

Maren in a sky blue bikini might send me to an early grave. Lush curves, tan skin, long wet brown hair. If I manage to look away from her at all, it's only for a moment and only because her body is still burned in my mind even when my attention is on something else.

Rhett's been talking to me about a yacht race he wants us to enter in a few months, and *who the fuck cares, man? Can you please stop talking?* My brain can only handle so much at one time, and watching Maren walk out of the water is priority number one right now.

"Why don't you just ask her out already?" Rhett prods, having successfully followed my gaze.

I jerk my attention back to him. "Because last I checked she and I weren't on great terms. Why would she say yes?"

"Because you're the second best guy I know—after myself, of course."

I laugh and brush him off. "You're an idiot."

"Well, if you're not going to do something about it, Barrett will."

"He already has."

"It was only one date, and it didn't sound all that serious."

"No, but they went out with Tori on Friday and Barrett asked Maren to be his date to the ballet gala next weekend. She said yes."

"No shit? Sorry man."

"It's fine. Even if we were better friends, I don't think it's appropriate. I don't want her thinking I'm trying to take advantage of her position at Rosethorn, like she *has* to say yes to a date with me or something."

"What a damn saint. If I were you, none of that shit would matter."

With his motivating words in mind, I push off my chair and head toward her.

She's at the ocean's edge, by herself, burying her toes in the sand.

I keep a healthy distance as I come to stand beside her. She stills for a moment, then continues stirring up the sand. "Having a good time?" I ask.

She peers up at me from beneath her wet lashes. "Yes, actually. Are you?"

"It's a little awkward…after Friday night."

She nods and nibbles on her bottom lip before tossing me a shy smile.

"Yeah. Obviously, I'm sorry for the way I acted. It wasn't one of my finer moments."

"There's no reason to apologize. I'm not sorry you said what you did. In fact, I'm happy we cleared the air."

She laughs and shakes her head.

"What?" I prod.

"Oh, nothing. It just…doesn't really feel like the air is *clear*. Does it?"

Our gazes stay locked together, and I'm not sure what we're talking about—Friday night or everything that came before it? Our feelings about our fight or our feelings, period?

"Are you into Barrett?" I ask suddenly, consequences and awkwardness be damned.

She smiles and then teasingly replies, "Are you jealous?"

"I've never been the type."

She shrugs. "Then you have nothing to worry about."

I don't like her evasiveness. I step closer and catch hold of her green eyes, which are brilliantly bright in the sunlight. "I don't see you two together."

"Oh? I didn't realize you were psychic. Tell me, who should I be with if not Barrett?"

"Someone more mature, for starters."

"Hmm, mature…does that mean someone *older*?"

I continue on, ignoring her question. "Someone intelligent. Witty."

"Wow." She grins. "You don't think much of Barrett, do you?"

"I just want the best for you."

"And what about you? Are *you* on the table?"

I take a beat, thinking over her surprising words, and it's just enough time for her to regret them. She shakes her head and turns to walk away. I reach out and catch her arm, keeping her near me.

"Hey, do you like me?" I ask, brows furrowed.

"*Like you?* How could I possibly like you when I'm so busy hating you?" she teases.

"Don't do that."

I hate the games. I want honesty.

"Maren! Nicky!" Tori shouts, cutting off our intimate moment. "You guys want to play volleyball?"

I keep Maren in my sights, trying desperately to drag us back to where we just were. *Screw volleyball. Screw everyone else. Let's keep talking.*

But Maren blinks and turns away, agreeing to play before dashing off away from me.

Around five, everyone starts to pack it in. We're all a little tanner than we were at the start of the day, and a little sandier too.

I watch Maren tug on a short white dress over her bikini, and I think I can finally release the breath I've been holding in all day.

"Maren, you ready to go?" Barrett asks, nodding toward the exit.

"She's with me," I say, like a goddamn brute.

Barrett laughs. "This again? What do you have against me driving her home?"

"Nothing, but I'm headed there already, so there's no need for you to take her."

"She can always come with me if she wants," Tori adds, not helping the situation.

"Wow. I've never had so many people offer to drive me somewhere." Maren laughs. "How'd I get so lucky? Barrett, Tori, thanks for the offer, but I agree with Nicholas. It's just easiest."

Tori winks like she doesn't quite believe Maren's reasoning. Barrett shrugs and walks over to give her a kiss on the cheek. I'm pretty sure he whispers something about how excited he is that he'll be her date next weekend, but I can't be certain. I'm too busy trying to convince myself not to pull them apart. What was I saying earlier about not being the jealous type? Turns out I was wrong.

I nod to Max and Rhett. Rhett gives me a sarcastic salute.

"Let's go," I say, grabbing Maren's picnic basket for her and starting to head for the parking lot.

"So *grumpy*. What did I do to you?" she asks, running through the sand to catch up to me.

"I'm tired and I've still got to get back to the city tonight."

"Well, if you're that tired, I can just go home with someone else."

"No."

She laughs. "All right, then let me drive."

"Do you have a license?"

"No. Never got around to it. In fact, I've only been behind the wheel of a car twice."

"And you expect me to hand over my keys?"

"No." She laughs. "I know you'd never let me. I just wanted to test the theory."

I toss my keys so she has to think fast to catch them. "Let's try it out."

She stops dead in her tracks. "Are you crazy? I could never afford to fix your car if I wrecked it!"

"You won't wreck it. I'll be in the car too. Let's go."

She has to pick up her pace to keep up with me. "Are you going to lay a towel down or something on the front seat for me? I'm still wet and I don't want to mess up the leather."

"I'm not too precious about my car. Just get in."

"I could take my bikini off."

Jesus, the thought nearly kills me.

I don't think I even utter a verbal response, just an animalistic grunt and a shake of my head.

Leave. Your. Clothes. On. *Please*.

In the parking lot, I pop my trunk and toss our stuff inside, then I round the car and open the driver's side door so I can adjust the seat for her. She's shorter than me, so she'll need to be closer to the pedals.

"Try it out," I say, pointing down to the seat.

She does as she's told, gripping the steering wheel and adjusting her posture. "I think it's good."

"And the rearview mirror?"

She tilts it a smidge lower. "Perfect."

"Then let's go."

I take my seat opposite her and buckle my seatbelt. When I glance over, she's drumming her thumbs on the wheel and wearing a shit-eating grin.

"You look mighty confident for someone who's only driven a car twice."

"It's nerves."

"Uh-huh. Start 'er up. Let's go."

The thing about my car is that it's an older, restored model. It's not as responsive as new Porsches on the road today, both with steering and with braking, and Ocean Drive has a lot of curves. We're only two minutes into our drive and already I'm rethinking my decision to let her drive.

"Brake. Brake, brake, *brake*!" I tell her as we go around a bend in the road, careening toward a stop sign at the bottom of a hill.

The brakes squeal as Maren slams her foot down harder. I'm prepping for impact just as the car comes to a sudden, jolting stop in the nick of time.

"Oh my god," she says with a wild laugh. "I thought I *was* braking!"

"Not hard enough."

"*Clearly.*"

I glance behind us and am glad to see there's no one else on the road. We have a second to catch our breath.

"You can let go of my thigh now," she says, drawing attention to the fact that my hand is gripping her leg.

I look down to find my fingers are digging into her, and I don't move them right away. I register the feel of her smooth skin beneath my palm, the fact that her white dress has slid up to just below the edge of her bikini. She's a dream, sitting there in my car, barely clothed, and I have to fight the urge to slide my hand up higher before I take it away completely.

"It's not too late, y'know. You can drive the rest of the way if you want," she teases.

"Just keep going. You're doing fine."

Fine is a relative term, however, and after another near-death experience, I tell her to pull over.

"Right up there. See that private driveway where there's a clearing in those trees?"

She turns off the road slowly and puts the car in park, letting her forehead fall against the steering wheel. If she's anything like me, her heart's beating a mile a minute right now.

I glance up at the old gate in front of us, blocking the rest of the gravel path that leads to parts unknown. Overgrown ivy does its best to conceal the KEEP OUT sign dangling from the gate, which is redundant anyway; it's clear no one's tried to come here in a long time.

"That was…exhilarating," she whispers.

I laugh and glance over at her.

Her head is tipped toward me, and she's smiling like I've never seen her smile. A big wild grin spreads from ear to ear, dimpling her cheeks and creasing the skin near her eyes. My chest tightens as I take her in, green-eyed and glowing. She's otherworldly. A nymph. A siren. I'm there on my seat one second, and the next I'm leaning over the gear shift, wrapping my hand around her neck, and drawing her toward me so I can kiss her.

It's the least smooth I've ever been. There's no proper lead-in, no preamble. It's not my fault though. I didn't initiate this. It just…happened.

She freezes up at first, no doubt in shock, but her lips are so warm and soft and she shivers when my hand snakes up into her hair. I goad her into kissing me gently. I do the exact thing I told Rhett I wouldn't do earlier—I take advantage of a girl I want more than my next breath.

Eventually, she softens in my arms, and those gentle kisses turn hungrier. My hands are in her hair, around her neck, cradling her chin so I can tilt her just the way I want her.

She reaches down, and there's the telltale sound of a seatbelt releasing then an awkward scramble of limbs as I tug her off her seat. There's barely any space for us to move, but I get her on me, her knees on either side of my thighs.

We're wedged on the seat together, and if there's pain, I don't feel it. I feel her on me, moving, grinding, sweeping her hips in time with our mouths. I grab ahold of her waist and it must be painful how tightly I grip her, how relentlessly I hold her down onto me…how much I want to keep her.

My mouth seeks hers again, harder this time, and she moans.

The sound sends blood south and I know she can feel me there rocking against her. Hard. Wanting.

We're careful to keep reality at bay. We don't break apart. We don't talk. We consume each other until my car feels like a furnace, like she and I might combust.

I take it further and wait for her to stop me, to give some signal that I've crossed an invisible line. My hands find the hem of her flimsy dress and then they slide underneath, up against her smooth thighs, her taut stomach, quivering with nerves. I slide my hands up higher until I feel her bikini-clad breasts fill my hands.

Every curse word known to man flutters through my mind. *Holy-fucking-hallelujah.* I tease her and I grip her and then that smooth material is tugged up and out of my way so I can feel her bare skin in my hands, the real thing.

There are things in life that feel so good you know they must be bad.

Touching Maren feels like that, like I'm defiling an angel, kissing my way straight to hell.

We should stop, I think fleetingly, right before she moans again. My palms brush back and forth over her breasts, and she must be sensitive there because I feel her tiny flinches of pleasure and the way her legs tighten around mine instinctively. I rock up against her, trying to alleviate my aching need.

More, more, more, we seem to say with our mouths as we continue. Why should this moment ever end? Why shouldn't I die just like this? With her sensual body on top of me, reminding me what it feels like to be alive?

Her mouth kisses a path along my chin, to the spot just below my right ear. I lean back and let her have better access to me, and it's the sexiest thing I've ever felt—her taking control, grinding on me and swirling her hips. I thrust up against her like a teenager, close to coming just from this.

"*Maren.*"

Her name rushes out of me on a whispered moan, and suddenly, she stops moving.

She's perfectly frozen against me, her breath hitting my neck before she pulls her mouth away from my skin.

I don't move. I wait to follow her lead.

Her chest shakes and she releases a heavy exhalation. My heart splinters and I reach down to grip her face so I can pull her back and ask why she's crying, but when I see her smile and her eyes squeezed shut, I realize she's laughing.

"Oh my god. Did we seriously just do that?!" she asks, adorably blinking one of her eyes open to inspect me. I have a feeling she was hoping I would have disappeared before she looked again.

I don't answer. Words fail me at the moment.

Then she glances down at herself—at where I can't help but continue to look too—and sees her heavy breasts straining against her nearly see-through dress, and she laughs even more.

Fucking *hell*.

"Oh my god!" she repeats as she reaches up to fix her bikini top so it covers her again. I have half a mind to argue with her, but I don't think it would go over well.

"Are you upset?" I venture.

"Upset? *No!*" She looks baffled by the idea. "Are you?"

"Of course not."

Jesus, I'm still hard. Upset isn't even in my vocabulary at the moment.

It's like I've telegrammed my thoughts to her because her cheeks turn into two bright cherries as she fidgets on my lap.

"Oh. Oh, right. Here, let me get off of you."

I catch her hand and open her palm so I can drop a kiss to the center of it. "Or you could stay?"

Her eyes flutter for a moment and then she shakes away the feeling.

"Here? Like *this*? I think I've already lost circulation in my left leg—it's really shoved up against the door. You can't be comfortable either."

She must not know the meaning of comfort. Her body is a comfort to me, one I'm sad to lose when she reaches for the door handle and pops it open. She nearly tumbles out of the car, laughing as she catches her weight and stands to wipe her hands down over her dress.

If she's trying to make it look like we didn't just fool around in my car, it's futile. The beach had already turned her hair into a curly mess, and my hands only made it worse. Or *better*, depending on who you ask. I'm biased.

"Don't look at me like that," she groans, burying her face in her hands.

"Like what?"

"Like we just…did that. C'mon, hop to it. You need to drive me home."

I slide out of the seat and adjust myself in my swim trunks. I wince and she looks away, her blush deepening.

Her reaction has me curious. "Maren, have you had sex before?"

Her eyes widen into saucers as she whips back around to face me. "Of course! Just not with anyone like you."

"Am I so different?"

"You're a man and it's obvious in every way."

I give her a cocky smile. "I'll take the compliment."

"You should," she says, walking toward me so she can prop her hands on my shoulders and push me along to my side of the car. "That was some very nice kissing."

I can't help but laugh.

"So then why'd we stop?" I say, leaning my weight back against her so she can't continue to push me around the hood of the car.

"Like I said…my leg was falling asleep…"

Her words sound weak.

"Do you regret what we just did?" I ask, turning halfway to face her.

She looks down at the ground. "No, I don't, but I also didn't want it to continue. Does that make sense?"

Not really. I want to press her on her meaning, but when she glances up at me again, there's a vulnerability in her gaze that I don't want to abuse.

"Can you just take me home? I'm getting cold in this bathing suit."

I nod and turn away, dragging my hands through my hair while I give myself a little mental pep talk to rein it in. Visions of laying her down on the hood of my car and continuing where we left off aren't exactly helping cool my blood.

I roll my neck and vow to keep my eyes off her on the way home. Unfortunately, I don't succeed.

Any time she moves, breathes, talks, I look her way and take her in like I'm hoping the sight of her will sustain me for days to come.

She's talking about the beach, telling me how pretty it was, how cool that it was tucked into a cove like that, hidden from the rest of the world. She wants to take Cornelia there, and I laugh. I can't remember the last time my grandmother visited the ocean, but if anyone could get her there, it's Maren.

We pull into my parking spot at Rosethorn and I kill the engine.

I don't move at first—not quite ready to leave her—but Maren hops out of the car and goes around to try to pop the trunk. After a few failed attempts, I get out to help her.

She laughs when she sees how simple it is.

"Oh, right, you pull the lever. Why didn't I think of that?" she says lightly as she reaches in for the picnic basket.

The back door opens and Louis bounds toward us, barking excitedly. Cornelia stands at the door, admonishing him.

"Louis, no jumping on Maren!"

"It's okay. He must have missed me today," Maren says, leaning down to pick him up. He licks at her face over and over again. "Enough, Louis. Jeez." She laughs. "Can't a girl catch her breath?"

"Did you two have a good time at the beach?" Cornelia asks. "Chef is just about done with dinner. Nicholas, I'm assuming you can't stay?"

"I'll go up to shower, but then I need to head back to the city and get some work in before tomorrow."

"Of course. Come along, Maren."

She sets Louis back on the ground and turns back toward me. "I probably won't see you before you leave, so have a safe drive back to New York. I'm sure it'll be less eventful than the one you just experienced."

Cornelia hums. "What's that supposed to mean?"

Maren laughs as she starts toward her. "Nicholas was brave enough to let me drive his car."

"You're kidding," she says, wrapping her arm around Maren's shoulders as she reaches the door. They turn away from me as she continues, "He worships that thing."

"I'll have you know I was very good at it," she replies.

"Why don't I believe that?" Cornelia asks as they disappear into the house together.

I stand in the shadow of Rosethorn, racked with indecision. Feelings churn inside me: longing, shame, anger at myself for not pressing her for the truth. What just happened rocked me to my bones, but Maren seems wholly unaffected by it.

Is she truly?

Are we not in this together?

Falling?

23

MAREN

I'm sad I have to shower before dinner. Standing under the stream, I resent having to wash away Nicholas' scent. I lather up my skin and linger, putting my hands in the same spots where his were, trying to feel what he felt. I grip my thigh like he did when we were careening down Ocean Drive. I slide my hand into my hair and twist it like he did, taking a fistful of it in a painful grip. Tugging. Wincing. It's not the same though, and when I turn off the hot water and step out to wrap a towel around my shoulders, I catch my reflection in the mirror and smile.

Shame might be a common emotion in a situation like this, but I don't feel it.

I feel heated and happy and devious.

It must be what Ariana felt all those years ago, doing something bad and getting away with it.

I know there's no going back from what we just did in his car. There are so many possibilities open now. You can't kiss the way we kissed then expect nothing to change, but I can't seem to care. I'm too delirious, even now.

I choose a silky dress for dinner, something that glides over my skin like his hands did. I'm still worked up and on edge. He started something and I stopped him before he could finish, so I only have myself to blame. I know that, and still...

I take my bottom lip between my teeth and skate my hand between my thighs, rubbing the silk against my overly sensitive skin.

I want to continue like this—getting carried away in our bad choices—but I'm late for dinner and I can't keep everyone waiting, so with a sigh, I drop my hand and tug open my door, wandering down the hall.

I know Nicholas already left; I heard his car pull away as I was dressing after my shower. There's no hope of him slipping through my bedroom door and joining me tonight, no potential for him to greet me with a knowing smile in the morning. He had to get back to New York City, and I have to get back to my life too.

I play the piano for Cornelia after dinner, and I don't stop until my fingers ache.

I use up all my energy there, expecting to walk upstairs later and find that I'm spent, but Nicholas creeps back into my mind as soon as I close my door. My dark room beckons dark thoughts. I wonder if he's thinking of me too as I take my dress off and hang it neatly back in my closet. I'm left in a lacy bra and panties and normally I would change into a comfy nightgown, but tonight I slide between my sheets just like this and feel the cool fabric rub against my skin, the lace against my breasts.

If I knew Nicholas' number, I'd call him just to hear his voice.

Maybe I'd ask him what he was doing. Wearing. Thinking.

Where do you wish I touched you today?

Were you upset that I stopped us or are you glad we have something to look forward to for next time?

Next time.

What a tantalizing thought.

I know I'm strategically leaving out half the truth. Uneasy thoughts are tucked under a rug, worry about what comes next, waiting to trip me up when I least expect them to. Does Nicholas just want to fool around? And what do I want? What happens when Cornelia finds out?

The thing is, those thoughts are easy to sweep away because today doesn't feel quite real.

It was a dream, right?

It had to be.

My week follows a remarkably normal pattern after that Sunday on the beach. I teach piano lessons to the children from St. Michael's. I play tennis with Tori. I work in the garden with Cornelia. I think of Nicholas. Fantasize about him, really. His touch haunts me in a way that makes me anxious for the weekend, anxious for the moment his wheels hit the gravel drive.

So anxious and preoccupied, in fact, that I completely forget about the gala and my date with Barrett. He sends flowers Friday morning, an overflowing vase of red roses and a little matching corsage I'm apparently supposed to wear to the event.

I should find it silly and juvenile, but I didn't go to prom or any other school dances that would have required a corsage, and even if I had, it wouldn't have been as delicately arranged as this one.

"He called earlier in the week, asking about your dress color," Cornelia reveals with an admiring tone. "He did a good job matching it."

I smile. "You didn't mention anything."

"I know how to keep a secret, thank you."

"Yes, well, I wish you *had* said something. I sort of forgot about the gala."

"How?"

Oh...just...been busy dreaming about your grandson.

"Must have just slipped my mind," I say instead.

I wonder if I had remembered, if I would have called to cancel my plans with Barrett. I'm not sure. I don't want to hurt his feelings, and there's no harm in attending the gala with him, really. He's just giving me a ride. *And flowers*, my conscience reminds me.

"Let's have Chef keep this cold so the petals don't wilt," Cornelia says, picking up the small box that holds the corsage nestled in tissue paper.

I turn to follow after her just as the doorbell rings behind us. Normally, someone else would reach it first—usually Collins—but we're already in the foyer. Cornelia nods toward the door and I walk over to open it, blinking slowly as my old friend comes into view for the first time in years.

"Ariana."

My voice isn't excited so much as shocked.

"Maren?"

Her confusion—accompanied with a slow once-over of my outfit—instantly churns my stomach. There's no doubt I look *very* different than the last time she saw me, but it's a good different. At least it is to me.

"You're all grown up," she says, and I can tell she's settling on those words instead of something else. I wish she'd just say what she really means.

"So are you," I say, stretching a tight smile across my face.

It's true. The Ariana I remember in my head isn't standing on Rosethorn's doorstep. Her bottle-blonde hair is brighter than she used to keep it, trimmed short so it barely reaches the base of her chin. Her brown eyes look heavy and tired, but maybe it's just the dark makeup she's wearing. Her low-cut jeans and lacy tank top leave a few inches of her midriff exposed, and I'm disappointed to see that she's thinner than she used to be.

I have an overwhelming urge to reach out and hug her, to ask her how she's been and *where* she's been, but I don't get the sense that she'd welcome my touch. Her brows are furrowed as she glances behind me, into Rosethorn's foyer. I'm sure she's shocked by the splendor of the house, the same way I was the first time I saw it.

"Maren?" Cornelia says gently. "Invite your guest inside. It's rude to keep her on the doorstep like that."

I blanche and step back, opening the door wider so Ariana can walk past me.

She hesitates for a moment, then comes in. She stops a few feet in and looks up at the ceiling that extends up to the second story. It's meant to be an impressive room, but I find I'm slightly embarrassed by it when Ariana laughs quietly under her breath.

"Should I take my shoes off?"

I look to Cornelia, who smiles and shakes her head. "No need. Now, tell me, what's your name, dear?"

"Ariana Barnes."

"I'm Cornelia Cromwell." She comes forward and extends her hand, which Ariana takes awkwardly. "It's a pleasure to meet you. Are you a friend of Maren's? I recognize you from the other day, when you came by asking for her."

"Yeah, well…in another life, I guess, we were friends." She gives me another shy once-over.

I frown. "We still are. We just haven't seen each other in a while."

"Why don't we all go into the drawing room?" Cornelia suggests, smoothing over the awkwardness with her genteel hospitality. "I'd love to get to know you better, Ariana, unless…" She pauses and looks between us. "Do you have something private to discuss with Maren?"

Ariana glances over at me like I'm a perfect stranger and then shakes her head. "No, it's fine. We can all talk."

I feel wary falling in step beside Ariana behind Cornelia.

"I'll meet you two in there. I need to drop this off with Chef," Cornelia says, holding up the corsage. "And I'll ask for refreshments. Ariana, we just had a late breakfast not too long ago, but are you hungry, dear? I can have Chef make you something."

"I'm fine. Thanks," she says, somewhat gruffly.

Cornelia doesn't notice Ariana's tone, and when she turns toward the kitchen, I'm left to lead Ariana toward the blue drawing room.

The moment we're alone, she turns toward me. "What the hell is this place? A castle? A museum?"

"It's a private residence."

She snorts. "Listen to yourself. *Private residence*—who talks like that?"

I bristle at her tone. "You don't need to be rude. Cornelia is extremely kind. You'll like her if you give her a chance."

She nods, strolling around the room, touching things that don't belong to her.

"Sounds like you have a nice setup for yourself here. I always forgot what a suck-up you were, always had your nose so far up Nancy and Bob's ass I'm surprised you didn't walk around smelling like shit."

"Stop."

She slices her eyes over to me and shrugs. "Whatever."

I uncurl my fists at my sides and force myself to forgive her rudeness. "How are you? Really? Are you still living with Drew?"

"We broke up," she says, flicking the pedal of an orchid before she sits down on one of the couches near the fireplace, making herself at home.

"I'm sorry to hear that."

"Are you?" Her eyes slice up to mine. "You hated him."

For good reason. He was horrible to her, manipulative and emotionally abusive. I warned her to leave him years ago, and she never did. It's the reason we grew apart, though now, seeing her here, I wonder if that's really the only reason.

"I'm still sorry. I know you loved him."

She sniffles in distaste and looks up at me. "Doesn't matter now."

I want to ask her why she's here. The question is poised at the tip of my tongue, but I can't work up the courage. It seems so rude, as if she couldn't be here just to see me and catch up. I want to give her the benefit of the doubt, so I do. I force myself to walk across the room and close the gap between us, sitting beside her on the couch and taking her hand in mine.

She's stiff, but she doesn't fight me.

I squeeze her hand and smile.

"I'm happy you're here."

She narrows her eyes. "Are you?"

"I've missed you. And you know I worry about you."

Her gaze softens. "I worry about you too."

Cornelia strolls into the room with Louis on her heels and finds us there, with our hands together. She smiles.

"I'm so happy to meet one of Maren's friends," she says to Ariana. "She's so quiet about her past, I feel like she was born the day she arrived here at Rosethorn. Tell me, how long have you two known each other?"

"Since we were teenagers," I answer. "Living in the same foster home."

"I see. Was that the family you were with in high school? Before you turned eighteen?"

I nod and turn to Ariana, eager to change the subject.

"Where are you staying?"

She shrugs. "I took a bus down from Providence this morning."

"Do you have plans to return today?" Cornelia asks. "You're welcome to stay here. There's plenty of room."

"We have the gala later," I remind her.

"Yes, of course. Ariana can come with us if she'd like. I'll arrange it with the host. I'm sure she won't mind one bit."

Ariana isn't given the chance to decline Cornelia's offer. Almost as soon as it's issued, Cornelia's on the phone confirming Ariana's attendance and then hauling us both up to my bedroom so we can pick a dress for Ariana to wear. It's not easy. She's slender where I'm curvy, so most of mine don't fit her, and of those that do, only two are fancy enough for the event.

We land on a blue sleeveless dress with a slit up the left leg. The tie back makes it so we can tighten it around her chest and make it fit more snuggly. The lace overlay is beautiful against Ariana's pale skin.

"Perfect," Cornelia says, stepping back to admire my old friend. "Let me go make some more calls, and I'll send Rita up in a few hours to help you both with hair and makeup. If I were you two, I'd rest until then. It's going to be a long night."

Once she's gone, Ariana stays standing in front of the mirror, turning in a circle and looking at herself in the dress from different angles.

"Do you like it? You can pick something else if you want."

She shakes her head. "It's fine. Not really my taste, but I guess this thing we're going to is pretty fancy?"

"I'm not sure. I've never been."

"Right." She angles her back to me. "Will you untie this?"

I help her out of the dress and turn to give her privacy while she puts her clothes back on.

"I know this probably feels sudden, but I think you'll enjoy coming with us tonight," I offer, aware of the fact that she's probably close to bailing on the whole thing.

"If you say so."

She finishes changing then walks past me toward one of the windows that looks out onto the rose garden. She pushes the drapes back with her finger and studies the view before shaking her head and looking at me.

"So what are you doing here, exactly? Is this the room you stay in all the time?"

I nod, suddenly a little embarrassed by how fancy it all is. "Yes. I live here."

"And you work here? Isn't that what your messages said? That you were *hired* here?"

I wring my hands together. "Yes."

"Why aren't you wearing that rose uniform like everyone else? And how come that old lady is so nice to you?"

"*Cornelia*," I say, emphasizing her name. "And that's just her nature. She's nice to everyone."

"Yeah right." She scoffs. "You know she's only being nice because she feels sorry for me. I can tell when she looks at me."

I don't agree. "I think she cares for me and wants me to be happy, and she knows you're my friend. I wouldn't read too much into it."

"She *cares* for you?" She huffs out a laugh. "She's your boss, isn't she? Don't kid yourself."

I know it'd be impossible to explain to Ariana the nuances of my position here at Rosethorn—it's not exactly black and white—but my silence gives her the wrong impression.

"You remind me of that little white dog she carries around," she says with a laugh of disgust. "You think these rich people give a fuck about you? You're a pet to them."

"You're being rude," I bite out harshly.

"No, I'm being honest. Wake up, Maren. What are you really doing here? Playing dress-up? Pretending to be one of them? It's pathetic."

Ariana has always had the uncanny ability to beat me back into a corner so that my voice and my opinions become too small to give life to. I know she's wrong. I know it, and yet I stay silent as she walks toward me and forces me into a hug.

"I know that sounds harsh, but I just don't want you to get hurt when they're done with you, okay? That's why I'm here, actually. It's perfect."

"What is?"

"We can leave here together. Go back to Providence, find an apartment."

I frown and pull away so she's forced to hold me at arm's length. "Do you have a job?"

"Not yet."

"How are we going to afford an apartment then?" I prod her, reminded of all the reasons we used to butt heads in the past. Ariana lives for impulse decisions and wild rides. It doesn't matter to her what the aftershocks entail.

"We'll figure it out. Aren't they paying you pretty nice here? Hell, we can probably sell that stupid blue dress they want me to wear tonight and make two months' rent right there."

I bristle at the idea, but she doesn't notice.

She steps back and sighs. "Think about it. Okay?"

Later that evening, after Rita's finished curling my hair and applying my makeup, I sneak down to the kitchen in my robe so I can get some water and a quick break from Ariana. She's being so bossy with Rita, telling her exactly how she's supposed to be applying eyeshadow and mascara, as if Rita isn't an absolute genius at this sort of thing.

I take my time walking back up to my room, strolling through the upstairs corridor at a snail's pace, taking a moment to admire paintings I might have glanced over quickly in the past. Footsteps sound down the hall behind me and I turn in time to see Nicholas arriving with his leather bag in tow. He must have just come in from the city, still wearing black pants and a white button-down. His brows are pinched together as if he's still carrying the weight of his work on his shoulders.

He looks up and catches sight of me, and I freeze on the spot. His hard expression lessens as he continues toward me, dropping his bag when he's only a few feet away.

"Hi," I say, smiling shyly up at him.

"Hi," he says, reaching out to wrap a hand around my arm so he can tug me close. My question of how he and I would act when we saw each other again is answered for me. Our foreheads touch and my eyes flutter closed.

I inhale a deep breath—maybe the first I've taken all day—surprised to find it's Nicholas' scent that calms the nerves I've had ever since Ariana first arrived.

"I missed you this week," I admit, giving him the gift of honesty.

"I missed you too," he says, picking his hand up off my arm to cradle my neck. His thumb brushes my skin and I shiver on impulse. "Normally, I visit Newport once or twice a month in the summer. Recently, I can't seem to stay away."

"Why have you been coming so often?"

"Because of you."

His confession, said so quietly, sends butterflies rushing to my stomach.

I open my eyes and lean back so I can see him. He's so handsome, rough and dark and severe. He's the same Nicholas he's always been, only now, I think I understand him. And yet…I want to understand him *more*.

I want to kiss him. My eyes even fall to his lips longingly, but I hold off, unsure of where we should take this reunion.

"Are you still going to the gala with Barrett?" he asks, rubbing my arm.

"I wish I weren't."

He doesn't let go of me, though I brace for his departure and his anger. If the roles were reversed, I'd be upset if he were going with someone else.

Instead of leaving, he presses a kiss to my cheek and whispers against my ear. "If he hadn't beat me to it, I would have asked you. I would have had you on my arm the whole night. I would have snuck you away to a private corner and taken full advantage of you."

His thumb drags slowly down my neck, accompanied by his words.

"And now?" I ask, voice breathy.

He moves his head so he can look down at me.

"Now, I suppose I'll respect Barrett enough not to steal you away, though I'm not sure how I'll feel once I see you in your dress. What color is it?"

"Dark red," I tell him as warmth spreads through me.

"Is it modest?"

"It might have been if I were less…"

Endowed.

"Maren…" He sounds like he's in pain.

I smile and press a kiss to the edge of his mouth before slinking away from him. "I have a feeling we'll both be suffering tonight."

"I don't intend on suffering long," he promises, and then I turn and rush back to my room.

24

MAREN

Cornelia claps her hands excitedly as Ariana and I join her in the foyer. "Oh, this is perfect. Look how our group has rounded out. Now that Nicholas has arrived, he can accompany Ariana. That way you won't have to walk in alone, dear. Here, I called over to my florist and had them send over a corsage to match your dress. You both look so lovely."

Ariana takes the corsage and slips it on her wrist, but she forgets to say thank you, so I do it for her, appreciating the lengths Cornelia has gone to ensure she feels welcome and included.

Barrett arrives then, strolling in through the front door past Collins, wearing a black tuxedo with a dark red bow tie that compliments my dress.

He looks handsome—and a tad too cocky—and I can tell Ariana agrees. Her brows shoot up in shock as he walks in and kisses me on the cheek before turning to her.

"Barrett, this is my good friend, Ariana."

He grins and reaches over to shake her hand. "Ariana. Awesome. Nice to meet you. You're coming with us tonight as well, I assume? Either that or you're extremely dressed up to stay in and watch Netflix."

She laughs and sidles closer, adopting a flirty tone when she replies, "Of course I'm coming. I wouldn't miss it."

If I were interested in Barrett, her overly enthusiastic greeting would likely bother me, but instead, I'm relieved to see she and Barrett become friendly so quickly. I don't want her to feel lonely tonight.

Nicholas is the last to come downstairs, concentrating on fixing the cuff-link on his sleeve so that he doesn't register the crowd waiting for him until he's upon us. I drink him in slowly, appreciating his midnight black tuxedo and the way it seems to intensify his good looks. His dark hair is princely perfect. His tan jaw is smooth and clean-shaven. He's never looked more handsome or more out of reach.

"Barrett, good to see you," he says, not bothering to offer his hand before he turns to me, sliding his gaze up my dress slowly so that I have to fight to stand still. Our eyes lock, and longing spreads low in my belly. I force a swallow before I speak.

"Nicholas, this is Ariana. My friend."

Nicholas frowns in confusion, flicking his gaze to her as if only now noticing there's another person standing beside me.

"Nice to meet you," he says with a nod. "How do you know Maren?"

"We go way back," she says, knocking her hip against mine. "We're like sisters."

"Ariana arrived in town just today," Cornelia volunteers. "Surprising us all."

"You should have seen the shock on Maren's face when she saw me." Ariana laughs. "It's like she almost forgot where she came from living in a fancy place like this."

Nicholas hums in response, and I can tell he isn't happy with the turn of events. Fortunately, Barrett is there as a buffer. It's like he doesn't even notice the tension in the room as he leans in to talk to Ariana.

I walk over to Cornelia to thank her again for including Ariana and for going to the trouble to order her corsage, and I feel Nicholas' presence behind me even before his hand hits my lower back.

"Nicky, would you be kind enough to escort Ariana to the gala?" Cornelia asks him with a pleading look in her eyes. "I think she'd feel so much better walking in on your arm, especially since Maren has Barrett to escort her."

"That's fine. Maren, can I talk to you for a moment?"

"Later," Cornelia admonishes. "We're going to be late. Come, let's go. Ariana, you can ride with Nicholas and me. Barrett and Maren, we'll see you there."

I've almost grown accustomed to the glitz and glamour of Newport—the houses commissioned by rich families and constructed by world-renowned architects; the sprawling gardens and accompanying greenhouses featuring rare and exquisite varieties of flowers; the Italian-constructed marble sculptures and paintings, direct replicas of Renaissance favorites—but when we pull up to the mansion where tonight's event is being held, I find I'm once again awestruck by the sight in front of me.

It's the largest mansion I've seen here.

"This home used to be owned by the Vanderbilts," Barrett tells me as he opens his door and hands off his keys to a waiting valet.

Of course the Vanderbilts lived here. Why wouldn't they?

I step out of the car and take in the marble porte cochère stretched above us. It has to be three stories high, at least. A tiled mosaic covers the ceiling, and I'm spinning in a circle, trying to take in the mythological scene depicted there when Barrett comes around to lead me toward the front door. There's a sign on either side of the entryway, announcing tonight's cause. All of the money raised will fund scholarships and grants for students at the School of American Ballet. I'm sure it might seem frivolous to some, but as a child who used music as an escape from a life riddled with difficult situations, I'm happy that tonight will help aspiring dancers who need it the most.

I stroll in on Barrett's arm, through the massive doors manned by suited attendants holding trays of champagne. Barrett takes a glass and hands it to me before retrieving one for himself as well.

We're ushered through the beautiful house (if you can call it a house) toward a rectangular ballroom, and I'm struck by how similar it looks to the Hall of Mirrors at Versailles. Along one of the long walls, large floor-to-ceiling French doors open out to a lush garden. Across the room, mirrored panels reflect a stage where young dancers twirl while nearby onlookers watch entranced. Against the back wall, a silent auction is underway, and that's where Barrett leads me.

"What should we bid on? A weekend getaway to the Caymans? A trip to the Italian Alps?"

I laugh and shake my head. "You're serious, aren't you?"

"Of course. What guy wouldn't want to whisk you away for a weekend? Especially after seeing you in that bikini on the beach. Forget the Alps—let's go to the Caymans."

My hand tightens on his arm, trying to slow him down.

"Barrett, you know I only think of you as a friend, right? I like you, I do. It's just…"

He groans. "Oh, c'mon. You don't have to do that. I can tell, you know? I mean you haven't exactly seemed overly enthusiastic about my advances. I've been taking it slow, trying to get you to warm up to me, but I can see there's no use."

"Please don't be mad."

"I'm not. I'm…surprised." He releases a dejected laugh. "You know, it's been a while since I've felt this feeling."

"Sadness?"

He laughs and shakes his head. "Rejection."

I roll my eyes teasingly. "Good. It'll probably do wonders for all the women who come after me. Maybe it'll knock your ego down a peg or two."

He winks. "Not likely." I can't help but chuckle, and he tugs me toward the auction tables. "Well, still, come help me pick what to bid on. I trust your opinion."

There are a lot to choose from: private dining experiences at the best restaurants, one-on-one sessions with celebrity trainers, dozens of vacation rentals spanning every inch of the globe from Dubai to South Africa. We've only just started browsing the various auction packages when Ariana finds us in a huff.

"Jesus, I hate that guy."

"Who?"

"Nicholas. Who does he fucking think he is? The entire ride over here he grilled me. He's such a rich snob, you can tell. No offense," she says, aware that Barrett is listening to her.

"None taken." He smirks, continuing to browse through the items up for bid.

I reach out for Ariana's arm, trying to calm her down. "It's not like that. He's just protective of his family."

"So why was he so preoccupied with my relationship with *you* then? Whatever." She looks around, in search of something. "I'm getting a drink. This place better have an open bar. Are you coming?"

I don't really want to, but I also don't want to leave her alone. I tell Barrett I'll be back and then I accompany Ariana over to one of the bars nearest to us. The line moves quickly, and when we get to the front, Ariana's quick with her order.

"Can I get a shot?"

The bartender laughs, clearly surprised by her question. "Sure thing."

"Tequila? With lime?"

He prepares it for her and she downs it immediately before asking for another one.

"Ariana," I hiss under my breath.

"*What?*"

"Pace yourself. We just got here."

She rolls her eyes and asks for a Seven and Seven after taking the second shot.

"You expect me to deal with all these stuffy people stone-cold sober? Yeah right."

The "stuffy people" can hear her loud and clear considering she's not trying to muffle her voice at all.

I look around the room in search of Nicholas as if he'll somehow be able to help the situation, but a commotion near the door catches my attention first.

Tori is here, and she's not alone.

She's standing at the entrance of the ballroom wearing an iridescent gold gown that cascades down her lithe figure. On her arm is a woman I can only assume to be Mary Anne, and I'm not the only one whose attention is on them. It seems like half the ballroom has turned in their direction, curious about their arrival.

Tori, aware of all the eyes on her, turns to Mary Anne and whispers something in her ear then kisses her on the lips before boldly strolling into the room. She might as well have just shouted about her relationship from the rooftops, and I'm thrilled.

I'm wearing a grin so big my cheeks hurt. I want to thrust my hand into the air and shout, *About damn time!*

The crowd parts for them, and for half a moment, I wonder if no one will stop to talk to them, as if they're possibly ashamed by what Tori just did. Immediately, I start toward them. To do what? I'm not sure. Offer my support? Hook arms with them? Issue congratulations?

All I know is I want to be by their side right now, but Nicholas beats me to it.

His dark figure slices through the crowd so that right as Tori and Mary Anne reach the center of the ballroom, he's there to intercept them.

He hugs Tori then extends his hand to Mary Anne. She laughs and ignores it, pressing up on her toes to hug him instead. Cornelia is on his heels, joining the group so she can chat with the pair as well. Pride swells inside me.

I know how influential the Cromwells are in Newport, how much their opinion matters. It's old fashioned and ridiculous that one family should have so much sway over society here, but in this instance, I'm glad for it.

It's as if a magic wand is waved and everyone returns to minding their own business, not all that shocked to find that a woman brought another woman as a date tonight. It's like HELLO, we're living in 2020, not 1620.

Ariana and I reach them, and Nicholas steps over to make room for us. Tori grins when she sees me.

"Maren! You have to meet Mary Anne."

"I'd love to," I say, extending my hand to her.

She's stunning, like punch-you-in-the-gut, can't-look-away beautiful. Her long blonde hair is tugged back into a low chignon, and her designer tuxedo with its feminine cut looks like something a celebrity would wear to the Oscars. I tell her so, and she laughs.

"It's custom Chanel, but don't tell anyone," she says with a wink.

"I don't mean to be rude, but I see a few guests I need to say hello to," Cornelia says. "Mary Anne, it was a pleasure to meet you. Tori will have to bring you to Rosethorn next week for dinner. Maybe on Friday? Let me know!"

Tori shoots Mary Anne a winning smile as Cornelia leaves us.

Then the circle shifts, and Tori finally notices Ariana in our ranks.

"Oh, hi. I don't think we've met."

I want to kick myself for being rude.

"I'm sorry. Tori, this is my friend, Ariana. Ariana, this is Tori and Mary Anne."

Ariana waves and then cuts in before anyone can say a word.

"Since I know you're about to ask, Maren and I know each other because we were in the same foster home when we were in high school."

Tori's dark brows shoot up in recognition. "Of course. Maren's mentioned you to me before."

Once, over lunch at the club after tennis had wrapped up, Tori managed to get me to talk a little bit about my past. She asked about my friends, and I was embarrassed to admit I only really ever had one. Ariana.

"Has she? I'm surprised."

I frown, not quite catching her meaning. Does she think I'm ashamed of her? I'm not.

"What was Maren like back then?" Tori asks curiously.

Ariana chuckles and shakes her head. "A quiet goody-goody. She never spoke up at first, but we shared a bunk and eventually I forced some conversation out of her."

"I wasn't that bad."

She arches a brow in contest. "You were a total dweeb." Then she shrugs, as if slightly regretting her words. "Sorry. Was I supposed to lie? I mean, you loved playing piano and reading and shit. God, it took so much arguing to convince you to come out with me. It's like you lived and breathed by our house rules. God forbid we ever broke curfew."

"I liked Nancy and Bob. They were good people. I didn't want to make them worry about us."

"We were seventeen!" Ariana argues. "What do you think they expected?"

"Were they strict?" Tori asks.

"They had to be with Ariana," I say, giving in to the urge to tell the truth.

Ariana takes a sip of her drink before replying with a gloating tone, "Yeah, whatever. I've never been good at following rules, but Maren always covered for me, didn't you? Said I was in the bathroom when they'd come to do bed checks at night. Helped me climb back in the window when I'd get home from sneaking out."

She laughs at the memory. Meanwhile, my stomach clenches tight. Those nights were horrible. I sat up, worried she'd be caught, counting the minutes until I'd hear her rocks hit the window. It was the rudimentary signal system we'd devised so I'd know it was time for me to open it and help her back inside.

"Sounds like you were a wild child," Mary Anne notes curiously.

Ariana smiles, obviously proud of the title. "Oh my god, Maren—do you remember the night of JJ's party? That feels like so *long* ago."

She laughs at the memory, and I'm visibly taken aback. How can she bring up the subject so casually? How is she not more remorseful after all these years? The crap she put me through still stings, and I'm surprised to find pain stirring inside me, fresh as ever, even now.

Nicholas' hand hits my lower back and he leans toward me.

"Come outside with me for a moment."

I open my mouth to respond, but he's already directing me away from the group, nodding toward the others while pushing me along.

His hand slides around my back, holding on to my waist, and to anyone looking, it's obviously an intimate gesture, protective and loving.

I stutter-step and he grips me tighter, glancing down at me with concern.

"Are you all right?"

I nod but stay silent as we slip out of the ballroom and out into the warm air of the garden. It's deserted since it's still so early in the evening. There's so much to take in inside that people haven't found their way out here yet, no one but us.

"Why did you whisk me away?" I ask after he leads me down a shallow bank of steps and toward a bench, hidden from the French doors by a row of Italian cypress trees.

"You looked like you needed it."

I hum and drag my finger along the smooth marble seat beneath me. Is everything here so perfect? Even the garden benches are pristine white.

"What's wrong, Maren?"

I sniff and beat back the emotions threatening to overflow, glancing up at him standing in the shadows.

"Does no one cry here, either? I suppose there's no need to, in heaven," I quote.

He smiles softly, recognizing the words. "Wharton."

"Cornelia's favorite."

He nods.

I glance back down at the bench, aware of the fact that he means to extract the truth out of me eventually. I might as well make it easy for him and for myself. "I guess I'm sad to realize Ariana isn't who I want her to be, even now."

"Isn't she your friend?"

"Oh, I'm not sure she ever was."

"I'd like to hear what happened between you two. Will you tell me?"

"What do you mean?"

"When was the moment you realized she wasn't your friend?"

I laugh bitterly. *The* moment? There are too many to count. He's intuitive, though. There was a specific night that hurts more than the rest, that damaged me more than the others.

"You heard her mention a party just now, and you must have seen my reaction…that's why you pulled me out here. If you listen to Ariana, it was the best night of our lives. Wild. Hilarious…" I laugh sarcastically. "I remember it a little differently."

He stands perfectly still, listening to me with earnest eyes.

I realize as I begin to talk that it's the first time I've told the story to anyone. No one's ever asked about it before, or even *known* to ask.

The words feel clunky at first, like I'm pulling them out of disuse after years of being stuffed away in the recesses of my hurt locker.

"I had just turned eighteen and Ariana wanted me to celebrate. I didn't feel like it. I was a few weeks away from graduating out of the foster care system, and I didn't have a place to go yet. My foster parents had offered to let me stay on at their place, but I knew I was keeping a bed from someone else, and besides, I didn't *love* their house. It was tiny and all the kids had to share one bathroom. I was…ready to get out. I just didn't quite know where I'd land yet." I shake away the tangent and return to the important part of the story. "Anyway, Ariana convinced me to go with her to a party she knew about. I rarely went with her when she wanted to go out. I knew she was into some pretty hard stuff, and I'd met a few of her other friends. They seemed like a bad crowd to me.

"I mostly agreed to go so I could keep an eye on Ariana and make sure she got back home on time. She'd been getting into trouble a lot at the house lately—bad grades, bad attitude—and I'd heard Nancy and Bob threaten to kick her out if she screwed up again. I thought they were pretty serious about it, but Ariana didn't really seem to care."

"So you went with her?"

"Yeah. The party was fine, bigger than I was expecting. There was a DJ set up in the living room and the bass was shaking the walls. I couldn't think, let alone talk to anyone. Ariana slipped off somewhere early on and I just stayed in the living room because it felt like a safe zone. There were a lot of people in there. Nothing could happen to me, I thought."

I rub my forehead, trying to ease the tension there. "Sorry. I'm rambling. None of that's even important. It's just the bass was so loud, like I said, so I didn't hear the police cars pull up. Everyone scattered like they had some preset plan in place for how to get the hell out of there. I could have run out a side door easily enough, but I stayed to look for Ariana and eventually she came barreling down the stairs, clearly high as a kite. She took my hand and pulled me out into the back yard. We ran for the fence and tried to hop it, but it was too high. I helped her over, and her backpack fell off onto the ground. I picked it up and swung it onto my shoulder without thinking.

"I remember her being more worried about it than she was about me. She kept shouting, 'My backpack!' instead of, like, 'Hey Maren! C'mon, hurry up!'

"Once I told her I had it and not to worry about it, she hopped down onto the other side and the cops found me there, trying to get over the fence by myself." I scratch the center of my palm to give my brain something else to concentrate on. "I got into a lot of trouble."

"There were drugs in her backpack, weren't there?"

I look away, out through the maze of cypress trees.

"Yeah. Quite a lot, apparently. I didn't realize she'd been dealing some on the side. She never told me."

"Why'd you take the fall for her?"

"Because like I said, if she got into trouble again, she'd get kicked out of the house. I figured I had a clean record so I could take the hit. Also, naively, I assumed I could just tell the cops the backpack wasn't mine and they'd believe me."

That wasn't the case. Lesson learned.

"It's still on my record."

He walks over and takes my hands so he can pull me up off the bench. He's too close, pressed against me; if I wanted to look at him, I'd have to tip my head back. It's nice to have that excuse to keep my gaze pinned on his chest instead, feeling his arms wrap around my waist. He bends low and kisses my cheek once. Then again. It's an invitation, and I can't resist the urge to turn my head so our lips can finally meet.

He tightens his hold on me and our kiss grows from something soft into something more, like he's trying to rewrite a wrong, trying to draw the pain out of me like it's venom.

I curl my hands around his neck, along the base of his hair, feeling the short, soft strands as his tongue touches mine. I'm hungry for him to take it further. I want his touch on my skin, under my dress, inside my panties.

I can feel him getting carried away too. The farther he pushes me back into the shadows of the garden, the faster my heart beats. His hands are everywhere, on my shoulders and bare arms, tracing along the strapless V-neck of my gown. Lower they slide, pressing the tulle skirt between my thighs. There're so many layers and still, I feel him there, still react with a sigh and a plea.

His kiss turns punishing as he rubs me through all the fabric, faster, harder. I claw at his arms, angry that this is as far as we can go. Angry that, for all his wealth and lineage and arrogance, he can't whip up a bed for us right here out of thin air.

"Let me take you home," he whispers, and I'm nodding my head in agreement before he even finishes the request.

MAREN

He leads me through the party, walking so fast I nearly have to run to keep up. We slip by everyone as if we aren't really there, past ballerinas twirling on stage and dozens of conversations flitting in and out of earshot. Nicholas ignores the few people who call his name, and we must look so bizarre fleeing from the gala, like two criminals on the lam.

We're near the entrance of the house when I blurt out, "Nicholas, I have to tell Ariana I'm leaving. And what about Cornelia?"

He groans as if annoyed to hear their names.

I laugh. "We can't just abandon everyone."

"Why can't we?" he asks, actually picking *up* his pace.

"Nicholas," I protest with a laugh, tugging him back. "We can't just leave."

"But you agreed in the garden," he says, turning back to face me with a wicked look in his eyes.

"Yes, well, I was under duress."

He grins at that, leaning in to kiss me on the mouth. I lean into him too so that when he pulls away, I have a millisecond where I feel like I'm falling and no one will catch me.

His arm comes around my waist and he sighs. "Fine. If you think we have to stay here, we'll stay."

"Do you plan on keeping me pinned against you all night?"

"If I have to. Have you seen yourself in this dress?"

He looks down as if in pain.

"I warned you about it."

"You didn't warn me *enough*."

I try not to look like I'm gloating as we whirl back into the ballroom. Nicholas keeps his hand on my back as he leads us toward the bar. After he orders, he takes a long sip of his drink, gets another good look at me in my dress, and then downs another sip. I can only smile.

It doesn't take long for our party of two to get interrupted. Cornelia finds us soon enough, glancing down at where Nicholas' hand is still on my back. She doesn't issue any commentary, but she is intrigued enough to arch one of her eyebrows.

"Maren? Can I steal you away from Nicky for a moment? I'd like to introduce you to a friend of mine. Her grandson goes to St. Michael's, and he's been raving to her about his new piano teacher *Ms. Mitchell*."

"Of course. Nicholas won't miss me too much," I tease, hurrying to follow after her.

He tugs me back for a moment, pressing a kiss to the back of my hand as his eyes narrow on mine. His look says, *Hurry back...or else*, and it sends a shiver down my spine.

Cornelia locks elbows with me as we walk across the room, her shrewd gaze trying to catch mine.

"Should I ask?"

I shrug. "If you do, I won't have an answer for you."

"I was worried that might be the case. I do hope the two of you know what you're doing. I can't think of two people I care about more."

"Would you be upset if—"

"I'd rather you not even finish that question. It's insulting. You know how I feel about you. I'd love nothing more than to see you with Nicholas."

"What about Tori?"

"Yes, well, I think we all know that match was never meant to be. Tonight proves it."

"I don't want you to think Nicholas and I are anything serious. You know him—I have no idea what he's thinking at the moment."

"I'd rather not get involved. I'm not sure whose side I would take, and if he treats you badly or you break his heart, I'd rather not know the gritty details. I can't imagine picking one of you over the other."

"But he's your family," I press.

"And so what? I've fallen in love with you just the same. You're my dear Maren, and please don't forget that."

I'm surprised by how busy I'm kept for the next hour. Cornelia introduces me to her friend, who wants to introduce me to *another* friend. Then Tori and Mary Anne catch up with us and we three sneak away to the dessert table. I search for Ariana, wondering where she might have gone off to, and accidentally lock eyes with Nicholas across the room. He's standing with Rhett and a few other guys, but he's angled in my direction.

I blush as he lifts his drink to his mouth, and I'm unable to look away.

We should have never left the garden, I think, flicking my eyes to the French doors.

The subtle tilt of his mouth tells me he agrees.

"Are you hopelessly in love with him yet or what?" Tori asks, following my gaze.

I laugh as if the idea is insane and turn my back on Nicholas to face the desserts.

"Of course not."

"Why not?"

"Because I'm still not convinced we can sit in a room together for longer than five minutes without wringing each other's necks."

"I think you two might just want to tear each other's clothes off."

I hum as if the idea hadn't occurred to me and reach for a little cup of chocolate mousse. "You guys haven't seen Ariana, have you?"

"Last I saw she was headed out to the garden with Barrett."

"Really?"

"Yeah. Is that weird? You don't like him, do you? You were just sending Nicholas some pretty heavy screw-me eyes."

I'm quick to defend my reaction. "No, I don't like him like that. I'm just surprised…"

"Oh, wait, there's Barrett," Tori says, nodding her head toward a group of people not far from us. "But no Ariana."

"I'm going to go check outside."

I don't want her to feel like I abandoned her here. I know so few people, which means she knows even fewer. I reach for another cup of mousse as a peace offering and carry it to the French doors, relieved to see a blonde girl leaning against the thick stone railing that divides the porch from the garden beyond.

"Ariana?"

She turns over her shoulder and sees me approaching, but there's no accompanying smile.

"Do you want some dessert? It's really good."

I hold out one of the cups for her, and she accepts it before placing it down beside her hand so she can prop her elbows back on the rail and glance out at the garden.

"Are you having a good time?" I ask.

"I'm not sure."

I frown and put down my dessert, mimicking her posture and staring out at the grounds before us. We stand there, quietly surveying the sprawling landscape, and the tension in the air seems to grow thick with things unsaid.

"Is the sea right there?" she finally asks. "Beyond those cliffs?"

"Yes. Can't you hear it?"

"No. The party's too loud."

"Yeah, I guess you're right. Why are you out here all on your own?"

Ariana doesn't succumb to moments of introspection often, or at least she didn't when we were teenagers. She was always in a rush to go somewhere, do something, cure the inevitable boredom of teendom. I'd bring up something serious—like what we were going to study in college—and she'd groan in agony. *Who cares?! We're young. Can't we just worry about what we're going to do this weekend?*

It's unsettling to stand beside her now, unsure of where her mind's at.

"This isn't really my scene."

I smile. "Yeah. I'm not sure it's mine either."

"Don't do that."

I flinch at her hard tone. "What?"

"Don't try to make yourself small just to comfort me. You do belong in there."

"Well if I do, it's only because I've made the effort to get to know people, to put myself in their world. I'm sure if you stayed here, you'd start to feel the same."

She snorts under her breath and shakes her head, looking down.

"I'm not staying here."

I frown. "Why not?"

She doesn't answer right away, and I listen as she scuffs her high heel against the ground over and over again. I put my hand on her shoulder but she shirks away in disgust.

"Don't."

I let my arm drop to my side as the sharp pain of her rejection momentarily paralyzes me.

"I don't deserve your comfort. *Believe me.* You know, Barrett hit on me tonight, and I encouraged him." She continues scuffing her shoe. "You know *why*?"

I shake my head.

"It felt good to take something from you."

There's no malice there, her tone so dejected. I stay quiet and hope she'll keep talking, wanting to hear what she has to say once and for all.

"It hasn't always been easy to be your friend," she continues, and I immediately want to cut her off.

My friend? *MY friend?!*

I was the best friend she ever had. I was the one who put my neck on the line for her time and time again.

"You were so fuckin' smart and talented and better than the rest of us. I don't think I had one boyfriend in high school who wasn't more interested in you than me. They thought they were being so clever, too, always trying to hide it. *Is Maren coming out with us? Hey, just wondering, is Maren seeing anyone?*"

My first instinct is to refute her, but shutting down someone else's feelings doesn't make them go away.

"I don't remember it that way," I say instead.

She hums wistfully. "You were always too lost in your own world to pay much attention, trying to hatch a plan to get yourself out of the hellhole we'd found ourselves in. Had you opened your eyes and looked around, you would have seen that the world wanted you. They put up with me so they could get close to you, but you never let anyone get too close. I should have warned them they were wasting their time."

"You never said anything…"

"Because what would have changed? You would have only felt bad for me, and the absolute last thing I need in life is another person's pity."

"Well, still…you must have resented me for it."

"Obviously I still do. It's why it felt so good when Barrett flirted with me. I wanted it to be real. I wanted him to want me more than he wanted you, but then I saw you with Nicholas and realized, yet again, I'm second best. The consolation prize."

My heart breaks for her. "*Ariana—*"

"I just said I don't want your pity, Maren, so if you're about to launch into some apology about how you didn't realize you were the pretty one or the sweet one or the one who never broke the rules, I don't really want to hear it."

"Then what do you want from me?"

She shakes her head and looks out toward the ocean. "I don't even know anymore. I thought maybe now things would be different. I had good intentions coming here and I meant what I said about us being roommates again, but it's probably for the best that we just stay away from each other."

"What are you *talking* about? You're my family."

"Yeah, and look at how I've treated you. I let you take the fall for me over and over, with our foster family and with the cops."

I hold my breath, unsure how deep into this subject she's willing to go.

"I know I ruined your life." Her features pinch in pained regret. "If not for those charges, you could have gone to college. You wouldn't have had to struggle to find a job. That's on *me*."

She shakes her head and starts to turn, but I stop her before she can walk away.

"It doesn't have to be like this. We can help each other. Cornelia can help you. She's generous and—"

"Don't you see what I'm trying to tell you, Maren?! I don't want to be your friend. I don't want to share a shitty apartment and split the rent and force you into some dead-end job, knowing I'm holding you back. You have what I want—what we all fuckin' want…a way out."

"What are you talking about?"

She glares at me out of the corner of her eye. "No offense, but for someone so smart, you can be a real idiot sometimes. It's an insult that you can't see what's right in front of you, the differences between us. I'm going to wake up in fifty years and be in the same place I've been my whole life: job I hate, shitty boyfriend, couple kids. And that's fine, but you're sitting on a gold mine—and I'm not talking about your job with these rich snobs. I'm talking about that talent you've had your whole life."

"You don't know that."

"I don't? Nancy and Bob begged you to apply to college. They knew you would've gotten in anywhere you applied. Tuition and shit would have been taken care of, but you didn't do it."

"Yeah well, it worked out, didn't it? I got charged with a felony that spring thanks to you. My scholarships would have been revoked immediately."

"Yeah, you're right, and you didn't give a damn. You didn't even get mad at me. It's like you just laid down and accepted it like it was exactly what you deserved."

I don't speak, scared I'll say the wrong thing.

"Do me a favor, will you?" she says, finally looking me straight in the eyes. "Move on."

"I don't know how."

She smiles and shakes her head, pushing back from the railing.

"You've always known."

By the time I get back to Rosethorn that night, the house is dark and quiet. It's late, sometime past midnight. Ariana caught the last bus back to Providence, and I went with her to the station. We stood at the ticket booth and I cried, but she didn't seem sad at all. My hands wrapped around her, squeezing her against me, and she didn't pull back, but she didn't hug me tight either.

When I let her go, she stepped back and held up her bus ticket, studied me for a long beat, and then turned and pulled open the door to go inside the terminal. Maybe I could've gone in to wait with her, but I didn't.

I hopped back in the car and let Frank drive me home. We didn't say a word.

I head up the stairs now, wondering if Cornelia and Nicholas are back from the gala yet. I didn't talk to either one of them as Ariana and I were leaving the event, but I caught Nicholas' eye and waved, so maybe he realized I was on my way out. Maybe not. I don't have the energy to care at the moment.

I walk into my bedroom and turn on my bedside lamp. Our gala dresses lie on top of my comforter, a twisted mess of red and blue. We stripped them off to change back into normal clothes before we went to catch her bus. I don't have the will to move the dresses yet, and even though this day has been one of the longest of my life, I'm not quite ready for bed. I swap my clothes for silky sleep shorts and a matching tank top, then I take the folded throw blanket from the corner of my bed, wrap it around my shoulders, and head back downstairs quietly, toward the blue drawing room.

It's secluded enough from the bedrooms upstairs and downstairs that I shouldn't wake anyone with my playing. I close the doors behind me as quietly as possible and turn on the floor lamp closest to the piano. Its light barely stretches to the keys, but it's enough.

I tug on the bench, pulling it out from underneath the piano, and sit down, feeling comforted by its familiarity. There's sheet music propped up on the stand, but I don't need it for the song I've had in my head since I dropped Ariana at the bus station.

The melody is soft and slow, heartbreaking in its simple sad sound.

My fingers play gently, and I mess up on one of the notes, so I start again, playing the song through again, then again.

It's like I'm hoping if I play it enough, I'll leave my sorrow there on the keys. Tears blur my vision every now and then, but I never cry.

The door of the drawing room opens, but I don't bother looking over my shoulder as I continue to play. I recognize his footsteps after he closes the door and his height as he steps into my periphery. He hovers at a distance, listening to me playing. I finish the song again and start anew, scared to stop.

"You must be in quite a dark mood," he murmurs.

"Why do you say that?"

"That song you're playing. What's it called?"

"'The Departure'."

He steps closer, coming up behind the piano bench and tugging my blanket down far enough that he can cup his hand on the back of my bare neck.

"I hope you're not intending I read into that. You aren't leaving us, are you?"

My heart sinks at the thought.

"Eventually. I've probably outstayed my welcome. You of all people would agree."

His hand flinches. "You have it wrong."

A flicker of a smile spreads across my lips before I shake my head and continue playing. "Be careful or I might mistake your sleepy mood for something else."

"Like what?"

"Like actual kindness."

"I've been kind to you, haven't I?" he asks, starting to skim his hand up and down my neck, beneath my hair. I tilt my head to the side to give him easier access. "In recent weeks."

"Hmm, I'm not sure what word best describes your behavior lately. Kindness might not be it."

"It's not in my nature to open up to many people," he admits, his fingers sliding up higher into my hair.

"I've seen that firsthand. You've been a puzzle I can't solve...an egg I can't crack."

"Have you tried?"

I laugh under my breath. "Desperately, and yet I can't seem to give up—can't give *you* up. You've changed me."

"And how do you think you've changed me?"

"*Me?*"

"Yes, can't you see?" he asks, bending to pull the blanket off my shoulders completely so it pools around my hips on the bench. "Haven't you managed to discover the truth? I live by your breath."

His mouth touches my neck and my fingers still on the piano. The song cuts off abruptly, leaving us in silence. His lips move confidently down to my shoulder then his fingers trace along the strap of my tank top, shifting it millimeter by millimeter until it falls down my arm. The material pools, barely covering my chest, and my eyes squeeze shut as I let him continue. His hand brushes my arm, moving to cup my breast through the silky fabric, then he tugs it down farther and teasingly exposes another few inches of my skin. My head tips back and I lean into him, giving him every advantage as he continues working the material lower, baring my skin to the quiet room.

I'm uncovered from the waist up while I still sit on the piano bench with him standing behind me. His hands grasp and tease my breasts and I tremble, keeping my eyes closed. He bends low and tips my chin up so he can kiss me, but it's brief and my eyes flick open in annoyance when he pulls away. He looks down at me with dark eyes, drinking me in with a drugged gaze. His emotions are so carefully tucked away, if not for his eyes, I wouldn't think he was affected by me at all.

His hand skims lower as our eyes stay locked, and I reach to grab his forearm in consent. He plays with my breasts again, teasing them until I don't think I can bear another second of his touch. Only then does he move lower. He slides his hand under the bunched material of my shirt and then, slowly, beneath the waistband of my shorts. I keep my grip on his forearm, pushing him down farther as I part my legs. When he slides his fingers underneath my panties, my stomach squeezes tight.

His touch stays suspended there for a moment. He doesn't move at first, but then my legs part even more and his fingers brush gently at the center of my thighs. I shudder. He stands over me, perfectly composed as he repeats the gesture, prolonging the agony as he touches me there, drawing a moan from my lips as he swirls his middle finger again and again just in the spot where I need him most.

His eyes are on mine and I want to look away, but his other hand hooks under my chin and he keeps me there, staring up at him.

His thumb brushes my mouth and my lips part at the precise moment he slides the middle finger of his other hand inside me. My back arches as he presses in deeper, then he draws back out and in again, parting me and seducing me so that I spread my thighs farther, inviting him to feel every inch of me.

His adds a second finger and I draw his other thumb into my mouth. *This won't do*, I think, digging my nails into his arm. I feel close to peeling apart, like every cell inside me might riot in a million different directions. Then his fingers start to swirl again, and I shatter there on the piano bench, rising to meet his fingers as I cry out.

I'm barely done, barely able to catch my breath when he spins me around on the bench and tugs my shorts and panties down my legs. The silk rips and he doesn't go easy. He yanks the material off and tosses it behind him before positioning himself on his knees between my thighs.

His tongue is on me immediately, lapping me up, so that I lose balance and lean back, catching myself on the piano and eliciting a loud, shrill sound from the instrument.

I curse under my breath, but Nicholas doesn't stop for even a moment. He presses my thighs apart until the outsides of my knees skim the piano bench, and then he devours me hungrily. I have no choice but to be on the receiving end of pleasure so purely wonderful it's a hair's breadth away from being painful. My hips rock up and my toes curl on impulse.

His fingers join his tongue and I grip his hair, not caring one bit if I'm hurting him, maybe *wanting* to hurt him just a little.

He finds a sweet spot, swirling his tongue around and around as my thighs try to squeeze tight. He doesn't let me close my legs. He keeps me parted and exposed, utterly useless.

I come again so quickly I can't catch hold of the feeling before it completely consumes me. It's earth-shattering and somehow better than the first, and I'm telling him that, telling him everything—how wonderful he is, how much I want him—and then I'm on top of him, pushing him back onto my blanket that covers the carpet below us so I can straddle his hips and yank ineffectively on his clothes. He's still wearing his tuxedo and there are so many layers between us. I'm nearly naked, but he's still buttoned-up.

"Maren," he protests as I try to go for his bow tie. "Don't bother. *Fuck*."

He reaches down for his pants, for the zipper there, and then I feel his length slick and smooth underneath me, so damn hard as I reach down to touch it. I pump him in my hand, though there's no need; he's rock hard. Truthfully, I just like the way he feels, like imagining how he'll feel once he's inside me. There's a condom in his wallet, he swears, and when he finds it, I send up a silent thank you to anyone listening.

I give him a moment to tear it open and roll it on and then I'm there again, straddling him so I can grind against his length, wetting him so that when I lift my hips and hold him at the right angle, he starts to slide into me beautifully. I pause for a moment, letting him stretch me, before I continue to take more of him inside me. It's been a while since I had sex, and my body isn't used to accommodating someone his size. I bite my lip against the twinge of pain, but then Nicholas' hand is between my thighs, rubbing soft circles where I need him, and just like that, my muscles relax and he presses all the way in.

For a moment, I sit on top of him, unmoving, like a queen appreciating everything I've fought hard to conquer: a tuxedo-clad Nicholas splayed out underneath me, bending to my will. I smile deviously and he grips my hips punishingly, lifting his hips so that I rock on top of him and lose my balance. I have to drop my hands to his chest to keep from falling over, my one fleeting moment of control gone in the blink of an eye. I might be the one on top, but Nicholas calls the shots, holding my hips steady as he starts pumping in and out of me, slowly at first, drawing out and then moving back in at a rhythm that will drive us both mad. As soon as the complaint hits my lips, he picks up the pace, thrusting harder and faster until I relax completely and let him have his way.

I fall against his chest eventually, pressing kisses along his jaw, letting him feel the weight of me on top of him as his hands move from my waist to the backs of my thighs. He pumps deeper into me and I hear his breath picking up, and it feeds my own pleasure, the idea of him losing himself so completely inside of me, the idea of him rushing toward the same wonderful end I've already felt twice tonight. I don't deserve to feel it a third time, but Nicholas seems to be holding off until I give it to him, and that knowledge is all it takes to get me there again. He takes my earlobe between his teeth and I clench around him as my body shakes and he growls in my ear, coming apart underneath me as a shudder racks his chest. Half-bitten curses ring out of him and I'm spent completely by the time he finally slows and then stops.

We don't move a muscle as our chests rise and fall.

"Maren," he whispers.

"Hmm."

His hand comes up to brush my hair away from my face, but I can't work up the will to open my eyes. He laughs and sits up. He's still inside me and I don't mind one bit, but we can't stay fused forever. He lifts me up and off him and sets me down on the blanket so he can wrap it around me. I rest my chin on my hands as I hear him bustling around the room. When I finally pry my sleepy eyes open, he stands above me, not so different from the way he looked when he first walked in. Sure, his hair is mussed from my hands and his bow tie hangs askew, but other than that, he could be on his way to another black-tie function.

"What are you thinking about?" he asks as he loops his arms around me and stands with my weight in his arms.

"I'm not thinking. I'm dreaming," I say, resting my head against his chest.

NICHOLAS

I carry Maren up to my bedroom so we can rinse off and climb into bed. She's wearing one of my t-shirts and lying on one of my pillows, already half-asleep when I reach out to tug her toward me. She's tired and compliant, so when I drape my arm around her waist, she curls into me more.

I don't sleep very much that night, too aware of her in my bed: every sound she makes, every time her body moves, the barest touch of her skin against mine. I consider waking her up twice with a kiss, but I force myself to close my eyes and try to nod off. Sometime near dawn, I give in to the urge to have her again. I skate my hand up underneath her shirt and feel her smooth skin until she starts to stir. She moans when my hand cups her breast, and it sounds drugged and needy. I reach for a condom in my bedside table and am inside her before she blinks her eyes open and looks up at me in the dark room.

"Nicholas," she whispers as I spread her legs and push in deeper.

I kiss her, pouring myself into her as my hips roll and thrust.

It's over before I want it to be, a slice of heaven that dissolves before my eyes.

We sleep again after that, and when I wake up, Maren's not in my bed.

She's downstairs with my grandmother by the time I shower and join them for breakfast. I have no idea where her head is at, and I feel like I'm walking on eggshells as I fill my plate and sit down across the table from her.

She glances up and smiles at me, an expression filled with all the memories of last night and no regrets.

I smile right back.

My grandmother is reading the paper, telling us about an upcoming art festival, but Maren and I are having our own private conversation.

She must have showered before she came down this morning. Her long hair is still damp, with natural waves forming as it dries. Her face is makeup-free, so there's nothing competing with her green eyes. Her lips are a soft pink, and I'm staring at them as she brings her bagel to her mouth for another bite.

"Nicholas, don't you think you'd like to attend?"

I have no idea.

"You haven't been listening, have you? I swear you're on another planet this morning."

Maybe I am.

She whips her paper back open in front of her and Maren shakes her head at me, trying to get me to behave, but I can't. I'm a fool for her.

The V-neck of her dress cuts low down her chest, revealing a little red mark on the swell of her right breast. She follows my gaze there and frowns menacingly, reaching down to tug the fabric higher to cover it.

I left that mark on her with my teeth.

Her blush tells me she remembers the moment too.

"What do you two have planned for today? I assume by the googly eyes that you've got something up your sleeve?"

"I want to take Maren sailing."

Maren's brows arch. "Oh? I seem to remember you thinking I'd be dead weight on a sailboat."

I smirk. "We've both said a lot of things we regret in this dining room."

Cornelia hums. "Maren, you really should take him up on it while he's feeling generous. I know you'll love it."

Maren shrugs then and pushes back from the table. "All right. I guess it can't hurt."

It can hurt though.

Me—physically.

Maren throws on shorts and a white button-down before we leave the house, but as soon as we're out on the water, she unbuttons her shirt so she can get some sun. Her red bikini distracts me from every task I set my mind to. I retie lines twice. I ease the sails when I'm supposed to trim them. I accidentally defer to a give-way vessel so that we're both confused about who's supposed to have the right of way. They're all rookie mistakes that have me feeling like a fool, but Maren doesn't notice.

She's grinning as the wind whips her hair, sitting close to me so she can hear my instructions.

We don't make it very far out onto the water, just to the opposite side of Rose Island. The conditions are calm so that when I drop anchor, there's no real threat of the wind picking up. I tell Maren to keep a lookout for any vessels while I go down into the cabin to get us some water.

When I make it back to the top, she's standing at the bow with her hands on her hips, taking her job very seriously.

"See anything?" I ask, handing her a bottle of water.

She smiles. "Nothing. It's dead out here."

"Yeah, not much wind. Most everyone is probably packing it in."

"We'll stay out here for a bit, won't we? I'd like to jump in the water."

"You can. It's safe. There's not much boat traffic."

I confirm the engine is off and hand her a life jacket after she strips out of her shirt and shorts.

"I can swim." She laughs, not putting it on at first.

I take it back from her and turn her around so I can put it on for her, tightening it around her chest until it's snug.

"I have no doubt, but you haven't experienced open water like this before and it's better to be safe than sorry. There's the current and swell to contend with."

"All right, all right. Now step back so I can jump in and impress you."

I laugh and watch her go, staying up on the boat while she dives into the water and surfaces a moment later, grinning in the sunlight.

"Did I look like I knew what I was doing?"

"Absolutely."

"Aren't you going to get in too?"

I shake my head. "There always has to be one person on the boat."

"You take your job very seriously," she says, lying on her back and bobbing in the sea.

If only she knew how many times Rhett and I have screwed up in the past. Forgetting to let down the ladder, forgetting to toss down a PFD on a line so we could use it to get to the boat if we were too tired to swim all the way back—and that's just mistakes on *our* end. Now that we have bare poles and no canvases up, we're at the mercy of other boats. I've seen a few crazy assholes in my time, and I won't take any chances with Maren.

When she's ready to come back onto the boat, she swims over to the ladder and starts to climb. I reach down to help her up and over then unhook her life jacket to toss it back near the storage bench.

"Feel better?" I ask as she wrings the water out of her hair.

"*Much*. You should jump in and cool off. I promise I won't screw anything up while you're off the boat."

I shake my head. "Too much could go wrong."

"All right fine, then here," she says, stepping toward me and throwing her arms around my neck. "I'll just cool you off this way."

I smile and bend down to kiss her as water soaks through my shirt. It was meant to be a quick kiss, but she doesn't let me pull away, and I don't need any encouragement to keep her pressed against me. The sun beats down, warming us from overhead as my hands skate down her back and cup her ass.

We're a flame, instantly reignited.

I have half a mind to drag her down to the cabin, but there's no one around and I like being up here with her. She doesn't protest as I deepen the kiss. In fact, her hands find the hem of my shirt so she can start working it up and over my chest.

I help her out, yanking it off and tossing it behind me.

She laughs and steps back, tipping her head to look at me.

"Think anyone will see us out here?" she asks with a playful glint in her eyes.

I shrug. "Maybe."

She reaches back to tug on the bikini string tied around her back. "So then we should stop?"

I watch, mesmerized, as the string comes loose. "Probably."

Water drips down her bare stomach, pooling in her navel then continuing down into her bikini bottom. I stand with my hands propped on my hips, my body coiled like a tight spring.

"So then why aren't you stopping me?" she asks, reaching up to untie the string around her neck.

Her bikini falls away and she stands topless on my boat, the sea and sky behind her.

I'm frozen by the sight of her, my chest heavy with longing.

She's wearing such a devious smile, and I know she can see the effect she's having on me. It's obvious how much I want her. Anything—I'd do anything to feel her underneath me again, and that power is going to her head. She loops her fingers around the sides of her bikini bottoms.

I take a step toward her and she takes a step back, tsking under her breath.

"I thought we were going to stop," she says, brow raised.

"Yeah? Then what are you doing?"

She smiles cheekily. "Drying off. My suit is wet…"

In an instant, I'm on her, kissing the rebellious streak right out of her. We collide on my boat, laughing and teasing and kissing until her lips are swollen and red. I lay her down on the deck and it's not soft, but she doesn't complain. I don't think she can form a thought now that my fingers are inside her bikini bottoms.

I prop myself up beside her, taking her in as I tease and play with her.

Her back arches off the deck and her eyes pinch closed, but I don't pick up my rhythm. It's payback for what she just did to me. Slow circles over her most sensitive skin. She begs me to continue, taking her bottom lip in her mouth when I refuse to bend down to kiss her. She rocks her hips up to meet my fingers and I finally give in to the urge to sink into her slowly. My middle finger fills her up and she uses it to get herself off.

I don't think I blink, don't think I *breathe* for that distended moment in time. Her cries fill the air, over the sound of the waves lapping against the boat and the seagulls calling overhead.

My name whispers past her lips and then my willpower gives out. I tug down my trunks and pry her legs apart, dragging my length up and down her wetness before I plunge inside of her to the hilt. Deep, then somehow deeper still. Her hands come up to cradle my face and I look down to see her staring up at me, eyes so crystal green they match the water surrounding us.

We don't say a word as I rock into her, don't dare break the spell surrounding us.

I don't have a condom handy and it's impossible to stave off. I thrust harder, hissing with the need to come, especially as she does, tightening around me, shaking with pleasure. I hold perfectly still for a moment, trying to overcome the will to empty myself inside of her just like this, consequences be damned. Then she realizes my dilemma and pushes me off her, coming up onto her knees so she can take me in her hand and then her mouth, finishing me off so quickly it's not even satisfying so much as guttural. Needy. Angry. More. *More*, I think, wanting her again. *Now*, I think as I stare down at her, cupping her cheek, proclaiming my love for her in my head and wondering if I really mean it or if it's just this moment. The sea and sky and her…a combination I could spend my whole life trying to recreate, knowing I'd never succeed.

The weekend is over in the blink of an eye. Saturday evening spills into Sunday morning and then the afternoon sun dips toward the horizon, beckoning me back to the city, back to the grind I usually love but don't want to even think about right now.

I'd play hooky if there weren't people depending on me. I think of everything waiting for me back in my office, and then I look at Maren as she walks me out to my car.

"Are you sure you didn't forget anything? Toothbrush? Hairbrush? Toilet brush?"

I laugh and tug her toward me so she tips off balance. I catch her and walk with her in front of me so that our feet have to match or we'll trip each other up.

"This weekend was really fun."

"Yeah, it was great. I learned so much about sailing," she teases.

"Same time next week?" I ask, bending down to kiss her neck.

"Nicholas," she warns, her voice taking on a serious edge. "C'mon."

"What?"

"Don't do that."

"Kiss you?"

"No." She steps out of my arms. "Don't ruin the moment with promises like that."

I frown, completely caught off guard. "What are you talking about?"

She shakes her head and looks down to the ground. "Never mind. You're leaving. I don't want to get into it."

"Right." I move around her and pop my trunk so I can toss my bag into it before slamming it shut. "I gotta go. Traffic's going to be killer."

She crosses her arms over her chest and tips back on her heels.

"Drive safe."

"Yup," I say, opening my door with an angry tug.

She's already on her way back toward the house when I think to ask for a kiss or a hug goodbye. It's obvious she doesn't want one, so I slide into the front seat, start my engine, and pull away.

I'm not even halfway down Bellevue Avenue when I regret leaving. Half of me wants to flip on my blinker and pull a U-turn, but the other half knows I have to get back to the city even if I don't want to. I spend the entire hellish drive picking apart our words, wondering what she could have possibly meant. I regret not staying and forcing her to talk, or at least ensuring that she was still happy with everything we did over the weekend.

I know we haven't discussed the future, but that's because she shuts me down every time I try to bring it up. It was little stuff, me mentioning a restaurant I'd like to take her to, a cove I think she'd love to see when we go back out on the sailboat. She'd hum or nod, but there was never much excitement. I didn't think much of it until now, until I wonder if Maren might not be feeling the same way I am.

Back in the city, I flip the lights on in my apartment and make myself a late dinner. I set my phone on the counter and scroll through a few texts from friends before I give in and call the number for Rosethorn.

Patricia answers.

"Hey, it's Nicholas. Could you get Maren for me?"

"Oh, she's already gone up for the night. She was complaining about a headache. Should I see if she's still awake?"

"No. It's okay. Don't worry about it. Would you just make sure she has my cell number if she needs to reach me?"

"Of course, and I'll tell her you called."

It doesn't do any good. Maren doesn't call me back on Monday or Tuesday. I feel like an idiot worrying about her incessantly. Part of me wonders if it slipped Patricia's mind to tell her I called. Maybe she never gave Maren my number so then Maren couldn't call me. Then I remind myself that if Maren wanted to speak to me, she could easily ask anyone in the house for my number.

My associates think I'm on edge about an upcoming appeal hearing.

I don't correct them. I work late, only bothering to leave my office when my eyes begin to ache from reading. On Wednesday, I start looking into the process of clearing Maren's criminal record. She's innocent, but proving that isn't necessarily the path of least resistance.

She can't try to expunge the felony because it hasn't been ten years since the end of her sentence. I'll have to settle for asking for a mistrial and starting over, or I could seek a writ, but I won't know which option is best until I see the court records. With some luck, I'll be able to find an error from scouring through the clerk's and court reporter's transcripts of Maren's case. I have an associate call down to the courthouse in her old district while I get back to work.

On Thursday, I still haven't heard from Maren, so I cave and call my grandmother.

I don't usually call during the week, especially not during work hours, so she's surprised to hear from me.

"Oh dear, what's wrong? Are you in the hospital?"

"No."

"Are you ill?"

"No, I'm working. Is Maren there?"

"She's out in the garden, reading."

"How does she seem?"

She hums in thought. "Oh, perfectly happy. She just got back from playing tennis with Tori and she has a few piano lessons with the students from St. Michael's this afternoon. Do you want me to go get her for you?"

"No."

"Do you want me to tell her you asked after her?"

"No."

"Well, all right. Are you sure everything's okay?"

"Positive. I gotta go."

On Friday, I cut out of work earlier than usual and arrive in Newport by five PM. Rosethorn is bustling with activity when I stroll into the kitchen. Chef's rolling dough. Patricia's polishing silver. My grandmother is sitting with an interior designer in the yellow drawing room, flipping through fabric samples.

"—water damaged. I tried to have them cleaned, but it was no use. I'd like to replicate them, but I know that will be hard. The original fabric is over two hundred years old." I walk into the room and draw her attention. "Nicholas! I wasn't expecting you until after dinner."

"I knocked off work a little early," I say as I walk toward her to give her a kiss on the cheek and then introduce myself to her designer.

"Did you? How rare. It doesn't have anything to do with Maren, does it? Because you'll be sad to find that she isn't here."

My gut clenches. "She's gone?"

My tone surprises her. "Not *gone*, dear—not yet at least. She's just out with Tori and Mary Anne. I think she said they were going to get drinks somewhere."

"She didn't mention where?"

"Frank drove her, so I'm sure he knows."

27
MAREN

Lobster rolls are heaven on earth. No—lobster rolls with fries and a cold beer are heaven on earth. I'll never be able to repay Tori for introducing me to The Mooring and its outdoor patio.

"Cheers," Tori says, clinking her beer with mine and Mary Anne's.

I take a sip just as the sea breeze blows up off the water beside us and whips my hair around. I set my glass down and throw my hair into a high ponytail so I can concentrate on what's most important: this food.

I reach for my roll again, anxious for another bite. "I can't believe I've been here all summer and haven't had one of these lobster rolls yet."

"Well to be fair," Mary Anne says after she's done chewing, "you have a private chef. It's not like you need to go out to eat like the rest of us plebs."

"He's not mine! He works at Rosethorn, and I'll only get to enjoy his food for a few more weeks."

Tori frowns. "What do you mean?"

"When I leave, I'll have to adjust to the real world again. Soup from a can, macaroni from a box—that sort of thing."

She shakes her head as if she still doesn't get it. "But why would you leave Rosethorn?"

I shrug and reach for another fry. "Because it's always been a temporary position, a seasonal thing. I doubt Cornelia will need me once the summer ends and everyone shutters for winter."

Mary Anne nods. "Winters here are pretty bleak. A lot of the shops and restaurants shut down and reopen in the spring."

"Does Nicholas know your plans?" Tori asks, glancing behind me.

"Why do you ask?"

"Oh…well, he's headed in our direction, and it looks like he has a bone to pick with you."

I freeze with my fry dipped in ketchup then turn to glance over my shoulder.

Sure enough, there's Nicholas strolling across the patio, drawing stares. He's ridiculously handsome today in jeans and a blue and white striped shirt rolled to his elbows. His dark hair and piercing eyes match perfectly with the black leather watch on his wrist.

I don't process his presence until he's at our table, bending down to kiss my cheek.

"Maren," he says, greeting me before he goes around the table and does the same to Tori and Mary Anne.

"Nicky! What are you doing here?" Tori asks excitedly.

"Hunting down Maren, apparently," he says, catching my eye.

My cheeks burn and I look down at my food like it's the most interesting thing I've ever seen.

"Stay, will you?" Tori asks. "We have room and our food only just arrived. We have more than enough to share with you."

"Speak for yourself," Mary Anne teases, staking claim to her lobster roll.

"You can have some of mine," I offer, pushing my plate toward him as he takes the last chair at our square table, between me and Mary Anne.

"Thanks, but I'll just order."

He waves down our waiter and asks for Georges Bank scallops and a Grey Sail IPA.

When the waiter's gone, Nicholas leans back in his chair, cool as a cucumber. I peer over at him, and his entire demeanor throws me off balance. Is he mad at me? If not, why am I so nervous?

"So you said you were here to hunt down Maren. Now that you've got her, what do you plan to do with her?" Tori teases.

He narrows his eyes on me. "I'm not sure yet."

They laugh, but I settle on a forced smile.

"What do you guys think I should do?" he continues, gaze still on me. "I kept waiting for her to call me this week, but she never did. Now, here I am, showing up uninvited. A guy can only pursue a woman so long before he starts to feel silly."

"It's not as if you called me either!" I protest, trying to stop them from jumping to his side. "Well, okay...*once*."

"I left a message too," he adds.

"Sounds like a classic case of one person being more into it than the other," Tori responds, as confident as a judge presiding over a hearing. "What's it going to be, Maren? Are you going to put Nicky out of his misery?"

I laugh as if the notion is completely preposterous. "Believe me, if anyone's breaking hearts in this scenario, it's not me."

He flinches in surprise. "What do you mean by that?"

I turn to Tori, looking for backup. "In all the years you've known Nicholas, how often has he been the one to break up with a girl?"

"Umm, let's see…with Viv, you broke up with her, right?" She looks to Nicholas for confirmation, but he doesn't offer any. "And then with Lauren, yeah, you did it…and—"

"All right." He holds up his hands. "I fail to see why anecdotes about my previous relationships should have any bearing on what's going on with Maren."

Mary Anne nods. "I'm actually on his side on this. It'd be one thing if he cheated on every girlfriend in the past—" She pauses. "Wait, you haven't, have you?"

"No."

"So yeah, just because he's been the one to end the relationships doesn't make him a bad guy or a bad boyfriend."

Boyfriend.

"Does anyone need another drink?" I ask, taking a lengthy swig of mine.

Tori must recognize my desperation because she carries the conversation off toward a new exhibit at her gallery. I sit silently, trying not to notice the way Nicholas keeps peering over at me, the way his leg inches toward mine under the table.

This week has been important for me, our forced distance bringing a few things into sharp clarity.

Nicholas is a force to be reckoned with, and I didn't fall for him as much as get swept up in him. It's why he's so tempting, even now. I wish I could have answered his calls this week. I wish I could have holed myself up in my room and talked to him on the phone, letting his sexy voice wash over me like a tidal wave.

I couldn't though. I had other things to think about, a future to plan.

When we leave dinner, I ask Tori to borrow her phone so I can call Frank and have him pick me up. I know Nicholas will protest, and he does, but I'm trying to prove a point. He doesn't have to take me home just because of what happened last weekend. It's not expected.

He takes my hand as he leads me to his car.

"You're fighting this."

"For good reason. For one, you're too good to be true."

"I'm just flesh and blood, the same as you."

"It doesn't feel that way sometimes."

"You're nervous I'll hurt you?"

Hurt? No. *Obliterate*.

I'm nervous that after he's done with me, there'll be nothing left.

"Maybe."

"Well, it's too late. You can't be nervous," he teases, taking my hips in his hands so he can back me up against the door of his car, pinning me there. "I can't let you go now."

"Even if it's for the best?"

His lips drop to my neck. "Not even then."

I spend my night with Nicholas in his bed, forgetting everything I thought was important all week. Nothing else matters when we're flesh to flesh, mouth to mouth. I dream about him and wake to find him there, over me, pressing inside me. I arch up and beg him for more, and he obliges.

It's so overwhelming that I don't realize until Monday morning, when he's gone again, that all of those niggling thoughts are still there in the back of my mind. They didn't go away just because I forgot about them over the weekend.

I know some of my issues lie in Ariana's parting words. She issued me a wakeup call, and I feel like I owe it to myself to heed it. I have my whole life in front of me and it's one big blur, a mess of tangled roads I can't seem to decipher. I'm sick of living paycheck to paycheck, jumping from one job to the next. I'm sick of pretending everything is okay. It's not, and it hasn't been for a long time.

Rosethorn has been a Band-Aid, not a permanent solution to my problems.

The knowledge of that fogs my mind while I'm with Cornelia for tea on Tuesday.

I'm more quiet than usual and she notices, asking me if there's something troubling me.

For a moment, I think I might brush away her concern, but then I drop my untouched tea cake back on my plate and look up at her with a question.

"When you first hired me, did you have any idea how long you'd need me to stay here?"

She smiles. "Not a clue, my dear. That's the beauty of this position. It's open-ended. You can stay through the winter and into next year, or you can use Rosethorn as a stepping stone."

"Would you prefer it one way or the other?"

"Oh yes—I'd like you to stay here forever."

I smile, knowing she's only teasing. Her words from Paris flit back into my mind. I know she wants me to find my own path in life.

She sets her tea down and studies me for a moment.

"Do you know why I first hired you, child?"

I shrug. "I've come to terms with the fact that you likely felt bad for me and wanted to give me a helping hand. You knew I was going nowhere at Holly Home."

She chuckles. "I wish I were as selfless as that. I'm afraid it was much more for my own sake than it ever was for yours." She turns to glance out the window, and I watch her narrow-eyed profile as she continues, "In the last year or so, on occasion, I've found myself taking account of my life and wondering how exactly I went so wrong. I've compared myself to the glorious woman I dreamed of being and discovered I was greatly disappointed."

I frown, wanting to jump in and contradict her. She's the most amazing person I know, truly, but she tips her head down and drags her finger around the rim of her teacup, holding my words captive.

"So many years spent in the same routine and habits. Be careful there, Maren—too much time spent doing what one ought to do leaves little room for anything worthwhile. Anyway, I took my discontent as a challenge. I didn't construct anything so cliché as a bucket list, and I'll resent it if you think so. It's just that

I've decided to become a bit unorthodox in my old age, more readily accepting of adventure. I was scared by the dwindling emptiness waiting before me. No." Her back stiffens as she sits up straighter. "There'll be no quiet slip into my elder years. 'Do not go gentle into that good night.'—a verse by Thomas I'm sure you've heard. I took it to heart. I hired a girl I knew nothing about simply because she delighted me." Her face turns back to me and her blue eyes pierce mine. "You've been a gift. Always, a gift. You see that, don't you?"

I meet her honesty with some of my own. "I'm leaving, Cornelia."

She doesn't look the least bit surprised. "When?"

"This week, I think."

"So soon?"

"It's on purpose. I'm worried if I linger here much longer, I'll never want to leave. You've given me something I've never had before…"

She stands from her seat and rounds the coffee table so she can sit down beside me, takes my hands in hers, and places them on her lap. Her thumbs brush gently back and forth across my knuckles.

"Well then, we can't be sad. We've both accomplished something great this summer, haven't we?"

Two days later, I pull my worn duffle bag out of my closet—the one from my old life—and I fill it with the least expensive clothes I can find. I run my hand along the designer dresses, lamenting the fact that I have to leave them behind. The fancy heels tempt me too, but I reach for practical shoes instead and leave the rest behind.

Chef prepares a dinner with five courses, all my favorite dishes from the last few months. Cornelia and I share two bottles of wine, laughing about memories from the summer as Louis snores at our feet.

The next day, I cash one of the paychecks and use it to buy a cell phone, a bus ticket, and a train ticket. The rest of the money will help me once I get to where I'm going. All the other checks go into a shoebox.

My bus to Providence leaves at four PM on Friday, and when I carry my things outside and down the stairs to Frank's waiting car, I find every member of Rosethorn's staff arguing nearby.

Upon closer inspection, they aren't arguing, they're playing a game—rock paper scissors—which seems absolutely insane until I realize they're trying to figure out who will get to escort me to the bus station.

"Paper covers rock!" Rita says, sliding past Bruce to take her rightful place in the back seat of the Range Rover.

Cornelia's already up front in the passenger seat with Louis on her lap. When he sees me, he starts to bark animatedly and draws everyone's attention in my direction.

"You guys don't have to do this," I say with a shake of my head. "I'll be back in a few weeks. I promised Cornelia I'd come for Labor Day at the latest. And who knows, maybe I'll get where I'm going, take one look at the scary world, and hightail it right back here."

"Nonsense," Cornelia says, tutting in disagreement. "The world is your oyster."

"She's right," Chef says, stepping close to pat my shoulder before making room for Rita.

She straightens my shirt then brushes some of my hair behind my ear. Tears build up in her eyes, and I hug her tight before saying farewell to everyone else.

The ride to the bus station is a short one, and I refuse to let anyone linger in the terminal with me. We'll only sit there crying like fools when there's no reason for it. This isn't goodbye!

I accomplish a Herculean feat in managing not to shed a single tear until I'm sitting on the bus alone as it pulls away from the station. As promised, none of them came inside with me, but there they sit, in the Range Rover, trailing beside the bus and honking to get my attention.

I wave back, laughing and drying my tears with the back of my hand.

They follow me all the way out of Newport, and then Frank pulls off to turn back home.

Once they're gone, I sit in my seat facing my future with the shoebox on my lap as I try to convince myself I'm doing the right thing.

28

MAREN

Other than the day I spent in the city with Cornelia before we flew to Paris, I've never been to Manhattan, which I realize is slightly absurd considering I've lived so close to it my entire life. A city this size takes some getting used to, and I feel like it'll dwarf me if I let it.

My hotel is at 65th and Columbus, and my walk there from Grand Central takes forty minutes with my duffle in tow. The city streets are packed and hot, and I'm sweating bullets by the time I make it into the hotel lobby and give the receptionist my name.

This place is nothing fancy. I specifically hoped it wouldn't be considering I don't have much money to spare. My room is small, the smallest one they offer, and it turns out if you specifically ask for the "cheapest" room in the place, they're really going to give it to you. I'm down in the basement, right next to where the employees go on break. I can hear their TV blaring through the walls as I set my bag down on the full bed and then sit down beside it.

I actually don't mind the noise.

I've never felt so alone in my entire life, and that's saying something. I suppose it stems from the fact that I've always lived in places where I shared a room, especially in the foster homes and at the group home. At Rosethorn, I had my own room, but the house was always filled with so much life, I didn't seem to care.

I bounce on the bed, feeling the springs, though I have no idea why I do it. Maybe it's just from seeing other people do it on TV. I unzip my duffle and start to unpack, but then I stop, unsure of how long I'll actually be here. A night? A week? Hopefully it won't be any longer than that.

On the nightstand, by the bed, I see a notepad and a pen. I use them to jot down my new cell phone number and then I rip the paper off the pad and drop it in the shoebox. I close the lid, stuff it under my arm, and head back out into the city.

The sun's down now, but the city's still bustling. I have a short walk across the street before I arrive at my destination. It's incredibly close, which isn't a coincidence. It's the reason I picked my hotel in the first place. I sit on the concrete steps that face Alice Tully Hall and patiently watch people filing in and out of the building. It's not immediately clear whether they're all students or not, but some of them are my age, walking together and chatting. There's a group of girls in tight leggings and workout gear. One of them has ballet slippers hanging down around her neck, and a few guys pass behind them with guitar cases slung over their shoulders. They walk into the glass atrium of the building, and I find myself wishing I could go in after them.

"Are you an incoming freshman too?" a voice asks beside me.

I jerk my attention to my left to see a girl with black hair and almond-shaped brown eyes smiling my way.

"I just figured," she continues. "You're staring all moony-eyed. I wondered if you were starting in the fall too."

My throat tightens. "Oh, no. I'm just…"

"Sitting. Hey, I get it. Why do you think I'm here?" she quips.

"Are you about to start here?"

She grins. "Yes. In the drama department."

"You want to act?"

"No. I've been accepted into their playwriting program."

"Wow. That's really cool."

"What about you? What are you going to apply for?"

I rear back and shake my head. "I'm not applying for anything."

She tips her head as a smile stretches farther across her face. "So, you just sit outside of Juilliard at night for fun?"

Well, when she puts it like that…

"I play the piano. That's what I'd like to pursue."

"So then just apply for a Bachelor of Music. I think those guys take some music theory and history classes, but it's primarily focused on applied training." Then she laughs, probably at the way I'm looking at her. "Sorry. It's been my dream to come here for a long time, and I've looked into just about every program they have. If I hadn't gotten into their playwrighting program, I would have applied for something else, literally *anything*, though playwriting is what I really want to do."

"It's not all that easy to apply and get in," I say, looking down at the shoebox.

"No. Of course it's not. They accept like *no one* here. I had to apply three times. My parents wanted me to stay home and go to Michigan State, but here I am, in New York City, finally *doing* it. Well, not quite doing it—classes don't start for a few weeks. I'm just here working for a little bit, saving some money up, and...*sitting*."

She chuckles, and I can't help but smile.

A guy comes out of the building with a backpack slung over one shoulder. He calls out for her and the girl stands and waves to him, looking down at me before she moves to join him. "Hey, good luck with everything."

I nod. "Yeah, you too. Congrats, by the way."

She smiles then trots down the stairs toward her friend. He throws an arm around her shoulders and they turn down the street then disappear.

I continue to sit there as people come and go around me, staring at the school, dreaming about what it would be like to attend and then trying to convince myself it doesn't just have to be a dream. It's why I'm here, I remind myself. Well, one of two reasons.

I stand up and pull a little piece of paper out of my pocket. I look at the address Cornelia jotted down for me this morning.

Nicholas' apartment.

He doesn't know I'm in the city and I have no idea how he'll feel when I just show up unannounced on his doorstep, but well...it's called a leap of faith for a reason.

It'd be quicker to take the subway from here, but I don't trust myself to get on a train and successfully arrive at my destination, so instead, I walk through Central Park, over to the Upper East Side. I get turned around once, but eventually, I find my way.

I check my phone: it's nearly nine PM. I know Nicholas works a lot when he's in the city, but surely he's home by now, right?

I pass his apartment building the first time I walk by it because I didn't think to check the address on the awning. I was looking down at the curb.

"Miss? Can I help you?" his doorman asks.

He's a short man wearing a black suit trimmed with gold, and I think he's taking pity on me.

I show him the address on the paper written in Cornelia's neat handwriting. I knew the place would be fancy, given Rosethorn, and yet I'm still surprised when he nods and tells me I've found the right building.

"Oh, okay...then I think I need to go in there," I say, pointing to the door.

He smiles and throws his hands out like, *Who wouldn't?*

"Unfortunately, I'm only allowed to admit residents and guests of residents."

"Oh, well, technically I'm a guest."

"Of who?"

"Mr. Hunt," I say, suddenly trying to sound very serious and formal, as if that will matter.

"All right, let me call Mr. Hunt and confirm that. I don't mean to be rude, but our residents expect a certain level of security from us. You seem nice, it's just rules are rules."

"No, I understand."

I watch as he goes into the vestibule that separates the lobby of the apartment complex from the street. He picks up a small black phone and dials, holding his finger up to me so I know to wait.

A few moments later, he shakes his head and drops the phone back on the receiver.

"Sorry, ma'am. Mr. Hunt wasn't home. Do you want me to tell him you stopped by or…?" His eyes fall on the shoebox.

Right.

"Would it be okay if I left this here for him? Will you make sure he gets it?"

"Sure thing. Will he know who it's from, or do you want to leave a name?"

"He'll know. Thank you, Mr.…."

"Barry." He grins. "You can just call me Barry."

From there, I head back to my hotel.

It's an hour later when the phone in my room rings. It's so loud and unexpected that I jump out of my skin, only realizing after the third piercing trill that I'm actually expected to answer it.

"Oh, hello. Hi!"

"Ms. Mitchell, you have a guest waiting for you in the lobby. He says his name is Nicholas Hunt."

"Really?! Okay! I'll be right there!"

I hang up and look down. I was in the middle of eating a gourmet vending machine dinner consisting of Nutty Buddy bars and potato chips. Crumbs are strewn across my pajama shirt. The fingers of my left hand are a winning combination of melted chocolate and salty chip dust. I leap off my bed and head into the bathroom, washing my hands and glancing up in the mirror. The reflection staring back at me is good, not great. I brush my teeth quickly and throw my hair into a ponytail.

Back in the room, I run around, trying to quickly replace my pajamas with a pair of jeans and a white shirt. In my rush, I thunk my shin against the edge of the bedframe and hiss as I try to soothe the pain.

I have no idea how much time lapses between the phone call and the moment the elevator dings before I step out into the lobby, but Nicholas isn't there when I arrive.

There's a big family with matching *FIRST TIME IN NEW YORK CITY* t-shirts filling the small space.

"Asher! Jacob! Mason! STOP RUNNING AROUND!" the dad yells before turning back to face the front desk clerk. "Sorry. Say that again, will you?"

"DAD! Are we eating dinner? I'm sooooo hungry," a little girl moans, tugging on his shirt.

"Leave your dad alone, he's trying to talk to the nice man here about our hotel room," their mom says, yanking the child away.

She throws a fit. The volume level inside the lobby reaches a piercing crescendo, and the clerk looks to me with one eye comically twitching in pain in response to the noise.

"Went outside," he says, nodding toward the door. "Just a second ago."

I throw him an appreciative smile and sidle past the family. I push the door open and step out onto the city sidewalk, exchanging the sound of the family for the sounds of the city streets. Cars and people rush past me, a bar across the street plays a basketball game for patrons on their patio, and a team must score because everyone shoots up to their feet and starts to cheer.

It takes a moment to orient myself and then I look to my right, finding there's no Nicholas.

"Maren," he says, and I turn over my left shoulder to see him leaning against the brick wall, a few feet away from the hotel's front entrance.

It hasn't even been a full week since I last saw him, but I take him in slowly all the same, appreciating the way electricity zings through my body as he pushes off the wall and starts to walk toward me. Tall, confident, sure of himself, Nicholas holds my note in his hand, the one with my new phone number on it.

"What are you doing here?" he asks with an amused smile.

I rock back on my heels and try to affect a very casual tone. "Oh, actually, I think I live here now."

His brows rise in shock. Then quickly, his eyes dart to the hotel as if he thinks I mean I live here, at this very address.

I smile and tilt my head. "Well not *here*, exactly. New York City." I wave my arm to encompass the street around me, enveloping everything in my reach. "I'm not quite sure where I'll end up, but I have a plan."

"Can I hear about it?"

He nods his head down the sidewalk and takes half a step back. It's an invitation to walk beside him, and I don't hesitate.

Together, we turn onto 65th Street, and he asks me if I'm hungry. I say I'm starved. He unfurls a wolfish grin and tells me he knows just the place. Twenty minutes later, we're standing outside his building. Barry graciously holds the door open for us.

"You're back! And you found her!"

He grins, genuinely excited as if we're all old friends.

"Yes, thank you, Barry," Nicholas says as he presses his hand to my lower back and guides me into the lobby. We ride the elevator up to the eleventh floor and when we exit, I'm surprised to find there's no hallway leading to different apartments. We're in a foyer that leads directly to his front door.

"Does your apartment take up the whole floor?"

"Yes. The whole building is set up that way," he says, as if it's not his fault he has a massive apartment in New York City. I can't help but laugh as he unlocks his door and guides me inside.

My chest tightens as I take it in. It's everything I expected, and yet still, somehow, *more*. It seems to go on forever in every direction. Dining room, living room, kitchen, hallways leading to God knows where— perhaps China?

"How many bedrooms do you have here?"

"Five."

"Jesus."

"It's been in our family forever," he says, trying to make it seem more reasonable.

"But everything looks so new," I argue, tipping my head back to look up at the decadent chandelier hanging overhead.

"I had it renovated a few years ago."

I turn in a circle, watching the twinkling light bounce off the walls.

"I'd give you a tour, but it'll have to wait. I want to talk about the box you left me."

I look back down as he walks into the living room. My shoebox sits on the coffee table there, unopened.

"Did you look inside?" I ask.

"Yes. That's how I found you."

I frown in confusion.

"The hotel's name was on the stationery you used," he explains as he sets the note on the table beside the box.

I nod, only now realizing that.

"Why didn't you cash any of these?" he asks, pointing toward the box before he turns to look back at me.

I've seen Nicholas in a million different ways. With the wind whipping his hair on his sailboat. Seated across from me at a formal dinner as we battle it out. Among friends and acquaintances.

Never have I seen him with his guard down like this. He stands with his heart on his sleeve, waiting for my answer, and I walk toward him, hoping to put his mind at ease. My first instinct is to touch him somehow—take his hand, wrap my arms around his waist—but it doesn't seem appropriate given the topic at hand. For a moment, at least, this is about business.

"Well, first of all, it didn't seem right. Cornelia liked to say I was her employee, but you and I both know what I did at Rosethorn hardly counted as work."

"I disagree. You helped her a great deal."

"Well, even if that is the case, she more than paid for my *labor* with other things. Room and board, for one. All those clothes and gifts. That trip to Paris." I shrug. "It just didn't feel right to take her money on top of all that."

"So then why did you bring them here? Why leave them for me?"

"Well…now is where I'm about to contradict myself. I need your help with something."

"Anything," he says, not missing a beat.

I bite back a smile and shake my head. "It's something related to your work, and I know you're already so busy. I don't want to take advantage. So, I thought maybe I could pay for your services."

"With these checks?" he asks, pointing down to them.

"They're all I've got."

"You don't have to pay me a thing."

"I'd like to," I argue, picking up the box and pushing it toward him. "It seems fair, and like I said, I don't want to take advantage of you."

"Does this have to do with clearing your record?"

I look away, embarrassed. "Yes. I need to get the felony removed somehow. It's part of my plan."

He smiles. "Your plan, which you still haven't told me about."

"That's on purpose. I distracted you with questions about living in New York on the way here so you wouldn't interrogate me about it. I'm still not convinced I should tell you. It's a little far-fetched, and I wouldn't blame you if you thought it was insane."

"I'd still like to hear it."

"Okay. Well first, sit down."

He sits then pats the cushion beside him. I don't hesitate before joining him on the couch, leaving a little distance between us. He laughs and reaches out so he can drag me closer to him. We're hip to hip, and the tension between us is palpable.

"Tell me," he says, bending to kiss my cheek.

His cologne consumes me, and before I can stop myself, I lean into him and kiss him on the mouth, a proper greeting we haven't shared yet. It's supposed to be a simple peck, but nothing's ever simple with

Nicholas. He kisses me back, harder, and my hands are on the collar of his shirt, fisting the material so he can't pull away. He leans me back, hovering over me as the kiss deepens.

Plans fly out the window. There is no plan that doesn't involve his mouth on me, his hands tugging up the bottom of my shirt and then unbuttoning my jeans. There is no future beyond his lips kissing a trail down my stomach, his breath falling on my panties.

Has it only been days since we were last together?

It could have been a lifetime. I've forgotten how wonderful it feels to have his weight pin me down, how out of control I feel when he takes charge, how much I like it.

"Tell me your plan," he teases, hooking his finger around the edges of my underwear and brushing them down my legs. I'm bared for him for a long, agonizing moment before he puts me out of my misery and leans down to kiss me there.

"*Nicholas*," I say breathlessly, arching up off the couch.

"Tell me," he says, swirling his tongue. "My love."

I lace my hands through his hair and words fall out of my mouth, no sentences, not even real language of any kind. I murmur pleas for him to continue, whimpers as pleasure starts to build inside me.

He gets me so close, and then he backs off, coming up off the couch to stare down at me. I wonder what he sees in me, but I don't have to wonder if he likes it. His hooded eyes and dreamy expression convince me that I'm everything he's ever wanted. His words confirm it as he bends down to unzip his pants.

We come apart together on that couch, him rolling his hips and thrusting into me, my nails scraping down his back. It feels endless, like we might never return to life as we know it. This is our new normal. This couch encompasses our entire world.

"Maren," he whispers against my cheek as we lie there together, after.

"Hmm."

"Tell me your plan."

I keep my eyes closed, all the better for concealing how nervous I am to give breath to the dream living inside me. "First promise me you won't laugh."

"I won't laugh," he says, brushing a few strands of hair off my face.

At that, I begin to talk, telling him what I envision for my future. I talk until my voice is hoarse and we've moved from the couch to the shower to his bed.

Nicholas doesn't laugh once, and when I'm done talking, he assures me we'll start first thing in the morning, once we've rested.

He goes to sleep first, his arm a band of weight across my stomach. I stay up, staring out at the city lights filtering in through his windows, too excited and hopeful, feeling for the first time in my life that things will work out exactly as they should, that the future isn't so scary and unknown.

It can be an adventure, if I let it.

EPILOGUE

MAREN

"'The Newport Symphony Orchestra Youth Program is celebrating its fifth year in residence with a free summer concert series. Families are encouraged to bring a picnic dinner and make their way to the gardens of Rosethorn at seven PM, every other Thursday from May through September, starting this week.'"

Edward pauses and looks up at us to see if we want him to continue.

"Go on," Cornelia says with a nod.

He starts to skim through the article. "There are more details about where to park and all that. And then—oh, listen! 'The symphony youth program is a collaboration between the Rhode Island Music League and the Newport Preservation Society, but it owes its continued success to its founder, Mrs. Maren Hunt. A graduate of Juilliard and a proponent of youth music programs, Mrs. Hunt works tirelessly to bring awareness and funding to arts programs across the state, and some could say she puts her money where her mouth is.'"

"Oh, I do hate that phrase. It sounds so crude when they put it like that," Cornelia argues.

Edward ignores her and reads on. "'The Cromwell Foundation—the charity organization overseen by her husband, Mr. Nicholas Hunt—is the symphony's largest benefactor. Over the years, the foundation has contributed...'" He pauses and scrunches his nose. "This is getting boring."

"Edward," I chide. "Keep reading!"

His eyes alight on something lower down in the article. "Oh! *Cory!* Listen! They talk about us. 'Their two sons, Edward (9) and Cory (7), are both participating musicians in the symphony and will take part in the concert series this summer.'"

"Mom! They mentioned us in the article!" Cory shouts, as if I'm not sitting across from him at the table, listening to Edward myself.

Cornelia covers her ears and throws him a reproachful glare. "Cory, shout like that again and I'll have you removed from this table."

His cheeks redden and he goes back to cutting into his pancakes. "Well, I think it's pretty cool," he murmurs under his breath.

"They didn't include our picture or anything," Edward argues, pushing his glasses up the bridge of his nose. "It's not like we'll be famous."

"Fame isn't all it's cracked up to be," Cornelia says with a haughty tip of her chin. "Better that you two continue to keep your noses to the grindstone. Study hard in school—that's all that matters."

Both boys know better than to argue with their great-grandmother, so they just nod along with her guidance.

Footsteps draw my attention to the door of the dining room just as Nicholas walks in with Louis in his arms. I smile at him as he comes around the table to drop a kiss to my hair before he hands the dog over to Cornelia, whose arms are outstretched. Then he starts to load his plate up with breakfast food at the buffet behind me.

"Is that the article?" Nicholas asks.

"It is."

"They mention you in it, Dad," Edward says.

"Why on earth would I be in there?"

"They discuss the Cromwell Foundation," Cornelia replies, picking up the paper and handing it to him as he takes the seat beside her and across from me.

The boys fidget in their chairs, so much like their father even though they share no biological relation with him. Still, it's been so interesting to see how much they take after him. I swear they absorb everything he does, copying his every move. They share his attitude and work ethic and, most importantly, his confident approach to life. They love to be out on the water with him. They'd much rather be sailing than sitting down for music lessons, but they humor me, especially Edward. He has such a good ear for it.

"Can I go now? I'm done eating," Cory asks, already starting to push back from the table.

"So am I!" Edward hurries to add.

"Take your plates down to the kitchen first. Don't leave them for Patricia," Nicholas says, reaching over to ruffle Cory's hair before the boy leaps out of his chair. "We'll be heading out to the club as soon as I'm finished here," Nicholas adds as they start to gather their breakfast dishes. "Don't make me come hunt you both down."

"Can I cast the main sail today?!" Cory asks excitedly.

"You got to do it last time!" Edward argues.

Cornelia levels them both with a glare that has them laughing and rushing to run out of the room as if they're worried she'll actually follow through on her threat to really reprimand them. She never has. She has too much of a soft spot for those two.

"Are you going sailing with us?" Nicholas asks me.

"I can't. Tori's coming over in a little bit so we can go over the plans for Mary Anne's surprise party."

"And what about this evening? Are you going to find time to pencil me in then?"

"I suppose."

He's teasing, so I tease him right back. He knows we have plans; it's our tenth wedding anniversary today. Ten years since I walked out into Rosethorn's rose garden and down the aisle toward a tuxedo-clad Nicholas, unable to catch my breath at the sight of him standing there with the ocean at his back. Ten years of ups and downs and fights we never saw coming, hardships we were forced to weather. The early years—when I was still at Juilliard and he was trying to maintain business as usual at the Innocence Group—put such a strain on our relationship. We'd go weeks at a time barely seeing each other, like two ships passing in the night. We adjusted. Fought. Relented. Compromised. He hired more staff and a partner. I eventually graduated. Looking back, I wouldn't trade those years for the world. Strength grew out of that time, resilience in ourselves and our love. An unshakable bond.

These ten years have been filled with bouts of suffering and periods of joy. I'll never forget the day we officially adopted Edward and the day we brought his brother Cory home as well, though Nicholas wasn't on board for that initially. I think it's natural for people to want biological children of their own, but I never saw it as an either-or scenario. I wanted to adopt *and* try to conceive naturally.

Our boys joined our family—they're ours, *officially*—but pregnancies proved more difficult. We've tried and failed. All we have to show for it is a dozen empty prenatal pill bottles, a mountain's worth of negative pregnancy tests, and years' worth of painful disappointments.

I wonder if all that is behind us now. I can't help but hope.

Nicholas doesn't know I took a pregnancy test last night.

Even though I know it's futile, I still keep a few on hand just in case.

My period never came two months ago, but I didn't get excited. I didn't even let it faze me. But then it didn't come again last month or this month either, and so I finally allowed myself to take a test last night.

Two pink lines crisscrossed before my eyes and I started laughing so hysterically I couldn't stop. My laughter turned into tears. I took another test and it proved as positive as the first one, which means I'm somewhere around twelve or thirteen weeks along—pregnant after so many years of trying—and Nicholas doesn't know.

He won't find out until tonight.

"What do you two have planned for the evening?" Cornelia asks.

Nicholas winks at me. "I don't want to spoil the surprise."

Cornelia and I lock eyes, and she shrugs. "Sorry, I tried."

I laugh and shake my head. "It's fine. I knew he wouldn't let it slip anyway."

She stands and reaches to take the newspaper from the table so she can finish reading it out in the garden, where I'll join her once Nicholas leaves to go sailing with the boys. I love spending our summers here at Rosethorn. I love soaking up every precious moment I have with Cornelia, and I find myself secretly hoping the baby growing inside me is a little girl we can name after her. I want it so badly I can barely manage a breath.

"Are you okay?" Nicholas asks, drawing my attention.

"Fine."

"You're teary-eyed."

"Oh, it's nothing. Allergies."

He doesn't quite believe me, and his expression proves it.

"You're not telling me something."

I huff out a laugh. I mean, honestly, I've kept a secret from him for less than twenty-four hours and already I'm crumbling?!

I shoot to my feet as Patricia comes into the room to start clearing breakfast. "It's nothing."

Nicholas' brows shoot up. "*Nothing?*"

"Yes. Now, if you'll excuse me—"

I take off running toward the stairs, knowing full well he'll get up and chase after me. I make it up and around the second-floor landing and halfway down the hall toward our room before he finally catches me.

"Don't!" I squeal, losing myself to a fit of laughter as he hauls me up and off my feet.

"Tell me what you're hiding."

"Not until tonight."

"I'll find out."

I mime my fingers turning a lock over my lips.

He smirks deviously. "There are ways I could convince you."

Then he drops a kiss to my lips and continues on like that all the way to our room. I'm putty in his hands, now more than ever.

I know the boys are waiting. They're likely already down at the front door with all their sailing gear, but for a moment, it's only Nicholas and me in our room as he shuts the door and locks it behind us.

"Maren," he murmurs, kissing a trail down the side of my neck. "We don't keep secrets."

"You're the one who won't tell me what we're doing tonight," I protest teasingly.

"I'd tell you if I thought you actually wanted to know," he insists.

I laugh as he tosses me back on the bed and comes down to press his weight against me, holding me captive.

"Well, can't you see that I might want to surprise you too?"

"I'm not a patient man. If you have a gift for me, I want it now."

He takes each of my hands in his and pins them onto the bed, then he sits up to look down at me. I have no doubt I look like a mess with my hair spilling out around me and no makeup on yet.

He stares down at me as adoringly as ever.

I try to break out of his hold but he tightens his grip, his wedding band biting into my wrist almost painfully.

"Nicholas," I say, catching his attention and drawing it back up to my face.

Our eyes lock and I'm reminded of that boy in the portrait. I wonder if our son or daughter will have raven hair as dark as his. A tear slips down my cheek, and Nicholas' expression turns troubled. He loosens his grip slightly, making to move off of me.

"I'm pregnant."

It's such a startling revelation, words I never thought I'd be able to say aloud. I've said the word plenty of times—*she's* pregnant and *she's* pregnant and *she's* pregnant—but never *I'm* pregnant. Never us. Not until now.

Nicholas doesn't move a single muscle. I think I've royally shocked him.

"Say something."

He shakes his head subtly, back and forth. "Tell me again."

I smile and sniff back my own tears. "I'm pregnant."

In an instant, he rolls up and off me, turning us so that we lie side by side facing each other. He lifts my shirt and looks down at my navel as if expecting a huge bump.

"He's in there."

Nicholas' eyes snap up to mine. "He?"

"Oh, I don't know. He, she—I'm not sure. Just ten minutes ago, I wanted a girl so badly so we could name her Cornelia, but a boy would be so wonderful too. We already know what to expect with boys, and we haven't done such a horrible job with Cory and Edward, have we?"

He wipes a tear off my cheek and smiles. "I don't care one bit. Either way, I'll be happy."

His hand drags along my stomach and I shiver instinctively.

"Should I cancel sailing? Hang here? Should we go to the doctor?"

"No, no. Take the boys. They'll be so sad if you cancel. I'll call and schedule an appointment for this week."

It takes some convincing before he lets me get up. He wants to see the test, so I pull it out of my makeup drawer and show him and there are more tears, an embarrassing amount, but well…we've waited so long for this moment. A bit of emotion is warranted, I suppose.

After he leaves for the club with the boys and I compose myself as best as possible, I carry a cup of tea out into the garden and walk toward the bench where Cornelia sits looking out at the ocean.

I don't say a word as I take the seat beside her. She and I are good at silence. Neither one of us gets nearly enough of it with the boys running around the house.

I sip my tea and watch the waves crashing against the shore.

There's a cloudless blue sky overhead, perfect for sailing. I already know they will have a good day out on the water.

I take another sip of tea and then Cornelia's hand reaches out to touch mine.

I know she's reading my mood. I know she's been aware of how jittery I've felt all morning. I let her hand rest on mine for a moment, calming me, and then I take it and lift it up so I can flatten it against my fledgling bump. It's a silent confession, and when her breath hitches, I know she realizes what I'm trying to share with her.

She turns toward me, and her eyebrows tug together over watery blue eyes.

I smile and nod, giving her all the answer she needs.

"How?" she whispers.

I shake my head and shrug. "A miracle?"

She nods in sincere agreement then turns her attention back toward the ocean, dabbing tears from the corners of her eyes. She keeps her hand on mine, calming my shaky nerves.

I've always been grateful to Cornelia for the ways in which she changed my life, but never more acutely than in this moment as we sit in silence watching the waves come and go, together as a family, once and for all.

Find other R.S. Grey Books on Amazon!

Doctor Dearest
His Royal Highness
Coldhearted Boss
Make Me Bad
Hotshot Doc
Not So Nice Guy
Arrogant Devil
The Beau & the Belle
The Fortunate Ones
The Foxe & the Hound
Anything You Can Do
A Place in the Sun
The Summer Games: Out of Bounds
The Summer Games: Settling the Score
The Allure of Dean Harper
The Allure of Julian Lefray
The Design
The Duet
Scoring Wilder
Chasing Spring
With This Heart
Behind His Lens